Chrissie watched helplessly as sheep disappeared in every direction.

She whistled to her collies, but she would have needed half a dozen dogs to keep the terrified sheep together.

"Max!" cried the man. "Max! Bad dog. Come here."

The big dog ignored him, but he managed to grab hold of its collar. For a moment, they struggled, and then the man staggered forward. If the situation hadn't been so desperate, Chrissie would have laughed as he sprawled to the ground.

She whistled to Tess and Fly, and they raced over. The sheep had calmed somewhat, but at best she'd be spending the rest of the afternoon gathering them. At worst...well...she didn't want to think about that just yet.

"Good dogs. Stay." The man was on his feet now, his leather shoes much the worse for wear and his suit pants ripped at the knees.

"You," she said in a cold, flat voice. "You should get back to the city...and take your idiot dog with you. I'd have been well within my rights to shoot it, you know."

He held her gaze with his piercing eyes. "But you haven't got a gun."

"Then I'll start carrying one."

Dear Reader,

This is the fourth and last book in my Creatures Great and Small series. I do hope you enjoy it. Any thoughts, comments or questions you may have about *Shadow on the Fells* or any of the other books in the series would be very welcome. I really do appreciate feedback from my readers, for without you I would have no reason to write.

You can contact me at
info@holmescalesridingcentre.co.uk
or through Facebook.

All very best wishes and happy reading,

Eleanor

HEARTWARMING

Shadow on the Fells

—

Eleanor Jones

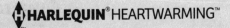
HARLEQUIN® HEARTWARMING™

Recycling programs for this product may not exist in your area.

ISBN-13: 978-0-373-36809-9

Shadow on the Fells

Copyright © 2016 by Eleanor Grace Jones

This edition published by arrangement with Harlequin Books S.A.

For questions and comments about the quality of this book, please contact us at CustomerService@Harlequin.com.

® and TM are trademarks of Harlequin Enterprises Limited or its corporate affiliates. Trademarks indicated with ® are registered in the United States Patent and Trademark Office, the Canadian Intellectual Property Office and in other countries.

Printed in U.S.A.

www.Harlequin.com

Eleanor Jones was brought up on a farm in the north of England and learned to love animals and the countryside from an early age. She has ridden all her life, and after marrying her husband at just eighteen years old and having two wonderful children, they set up a riding center together. This is still thriving over thirty years later, doing hacks, treks and lessons for all ages and experiences. Her daughter competes at the national level, and she is now a partner in the business and brings her adorable three-year-old son to work with her every day. Eleanor's son is also married with two children, and they live nearby. Eleanor has been writing for what feels like her whole life. Her early handwritten novels still grace a dusty shelf in the back of a cupboard somewhere, but she was first published over fifteen years ago, when she wrote teenage pony mysteries.

Books by Eleanor Jones

Harlequin Heartwarming

The Little Dale Remedy
A Place Called Home
The Country Vet
Footprints in the Sand

Harlequin Everlasting Love

A Heartbeat Away

I would like to dedicate this book to my grandchildren, Dan, Emma and little Ollie

CHAPTER ONE

CHRISSIE STRODE OUT across the rough, damp earth, well-worn wooden crook in hand, reveling in the signs of spring. Green shoots broke through the parched brown of tufty winter grass, bringing new life to the fell; the sound of birdsong, different now, bright with hope and promise, filled her ears with nature's own sweet music as they sang to the end of the cold, hard winter. And it had been hard this year, up here on the fell. She'd lost a dozen sheep to the snow and ice, only finding their sad, frozen bodies after the thaw.

Closing her fingers more firmly around the knotted wood, taking comfort from its familiarity, just as her father must have when he walked the fells with the help of the same curved crook, she stopped to take stock.

Today wasn't about death; that chapter was closed, until next year at least. Today she was embracing new life, for lambing time was imminent and she needed to gather the ewes and take them to lower ground. There was a time when four or five shepherds, each with at least two dogs, would meet to gather up their sheep, bringing them down all together, as a team, but right now it was just her sheep on this part of the fell.

With a low whistle to her dogs, Tess and Fly, Chrissie gazed up into the wide gray sky that never failed to soothe her soul. She watched the tumultuous clouds slide away, revealing the clearest, palest blue that seemed to stretch into eternity. For twenty-eight years she'd gazed up into that same sky, here in Little Dale, following the traditions set by her parents and their parents before them, caring for the sheep way up in the bleak and beautiful Lakeland fells. It was a tough, harsh and lonely life, but one she wouldn't swap for anything.

The border collies, one black-and-white and the other a distinctive blue merle, sank to the ground, heads on paws and keen eyes alert for their mistress's every gesture, waiting patiently as she looked back down the steep slope toward the huddle of buildings that nestled in the crook of the land.

High Bracken, the place where she had lived alone with her dogs for almost seven years since her parents were killed in a car crash. It had happened on the first holiday they had taken for as long as she could remember. She had been only nineteen then, and already dedicated to the land and the sheep, so it had seemed the most natural thing in the world to carry on the traditions she had been learning for her entire life.

After the accident, her mother's sister, Hilda, had arrived to help her niece organize both the funeral and her future. She'd been horrified when Chrissie revealed that she intended to live in her family home all alone and carry on working with the sheep; Hilda's pleas for Chrissie to pursue a more "suitable" career had been a waste of time then—and still were—but Aunt Hilda kept turning up unannounced every few months to stay a while and nag Chrissie to change her job.

Her aunt had left Little Dale that very morning, in fact, which was why Chrissie was so late. If she hadn't had to run her aunt to the station then she'd have had all the sheep safely down the fell and nearer to the farm by now.

Hilda had left, of course, with yet another well-meaning lecture.

"It's not natural for a young woman to live like this," she'd grumbled over breakfast. "You'll never meet a husband nor have any children if you don't shape up. You need to stretch your horizons, get out more...do something more feminine."

"But I'm always busy and I do get out," Chrissie had retorted. "I'm involved with Little Dale's young farmers group, I'm on a couple of committees, I meet lots of people through my dog training and I even competed in some sheepdog trials this year."

"Exactly," her aunt had snorted. "That's what I mean—it's all about sheep farming and dogs and the land. Most of the farmers around here are already married and the single ones aren't worth having. You'll never meet anyone in Little Dale."

Chrissie's insistence that she didn't need a husband and was perfectly happy on her own fell on deaf ears, but she'd been moved by the brief hug her aunt had given her at the station before heading back home to her comfortable cottage by the sea. Hilda had seemed satisfied that she'd at least tried to do the responsible thing for her poor dead sister. And Chrissie had to admit that High Bracken always felt empty after Hilda had gone.

A smile warmed Chrissie's heart as she thought about Hilda. It was comforting to know that she still had at least one relative who cared, even if her aunt did try and persuade her to give up the way of life she loved.

Then again, perhaps Hilda was right. Perhaps Chrissie was becoming a bit reclusive. There was a time when she'd dated a bit and gone to the movies with friends, but that had gradually slipped away as everyone she knew got married and settled down. Maybe she should make a bit more effort to be sociable before she ended up being pigeonholed as a batty old lady.

She'd go down to the pub in the village tonight, she decided, to have a meal and catch up with her friends; at least it would be something. It was hard to be social, though, when everyday life took such effort. There was always so much to do with the sheep and the dogs that there never seemed to be enough hours in the day.

Just yesterday she'd taken on yet another young dog to train—stupid, really, when lambing time was nearly here, but she needed the money. Although she loved the farm, it was barely paying its way. Remembering the nervous young black-and-tan Welsh collie, Floss, who had arrived last night, Chrissie put her half-hearted idea of socializing on hold. She needed to spend time with the new arrival and begin the process of bonding. Her dogs were trained through love and trust, not fear and force, which was so often the way.

She shook Aunt Hilda's words out of her mind. Chrissie didn't usually have such thoughts; she had everything she wanted right here. Yet she couldn't help but notice that the landscape she loved so much was changing. And she didn't welcome change.

As she headed even higher up the fell, Chrissie spotted movement at Craig Side, the small farm that was her nearest neighbor. There were two four-by-fours in the yard, she noted, as well as a large truck with something on the back. Tiny figures moved around it.

That was a surprise; the place had been empty and up for sale for almost a year, ever since James and Doreen Allen retired, sold Chrissie most of their sheep and moved down South to live with their son and his wife. When Andy Montgomery, Chrissie's vet, had stopped by last week, he'd told her that it had finally been sold and there was a rumor that the new owner might be converting the farm into holiday rentals. But Chrissie hadn't expected anything to happen so soon.

Yet another farm, then, lost forever. In Chrissie's opinion, there were far too many farms going the same way, turning their backs on tradition and transforming the fells into a playground for tourists. But what else to do when they could no longer make a living? James and Doreen had lived and worked there with the sheep for decades, but when their son had opted for an easier life there was no way they could afford to keep the farm.

Still, her sense of unease grew. Tourists messed with the way of things, coming up here to upset the sheep with their stupid dogs and lack of knowledge of the land and its traditions…and now it seemed they were about to infiltrate her personal space. She had always assumed that way up here they were far too isolated to have to worry about holiday rentals in the vicinity. Apparently, she'd been wrong. Though hikers crossed her land occasionally, it was nothing compared to the chaos people could create if they had accommodation right up on the fells.

Of course, that barn roof had almost caved in, she told herself, clinging to a tentacle of hope. Perhaps they were just fixing the place up.

With a heavy sigh, she turned her mind to the job at hand, heading on up the steep, rugged slope with the dogs at her side. Totally focused and eager to get to work, they sniffed the wind, tails wagging in anticipation.

The black-and-white-faced fell sheep moved closer together as they noticed the distant approach of the woman and dogs. Hefted here by their mothers and their mothers before them from time immemorial, it was ingrained into their makeup that this part of the fell was their space, their land. They knew every inch of land here, and totally aware of the invisible boundaries of their territory, they rarely moved away from it. If forced to leave, the fell sheep would overcome almost any obstacle to return to their "place," taking down drystone walls as they clambered over them in their quest to come home.

Chrissie knew the sheep well, each face familiar to her. They were hardy, tough and wild, easily scared but fiercely protective of their lambs. She respected that, and so did the dogs.

Not wanting to panic the animals, Chrissie stopped for a moment, letting them settle before beginning the outrun—the wide sweep around the flock. Then she raised her hand for Tess's attention. "Come bye," she called. "Come bye." She gave Tess the signal to run wide of the flock, clockwise. Fly trembled for action, waiting for her cue as her partner ran, low and silent, urging the sheep to move closer together.

"Away…away out," Chrissie called to Fly, and the eager dog ran wide of the flock counterclockwise. The dogs disappeared, eaten up by the vast space of the fell, and then gradually they came back into view behind a dozen or so outlying sheep who were trotting quickly, heads up and eyes wide with apprehension as the collies herded them toward the flock.

"Easy," yelled Chrissie. "Slow down."

A long, low blast on her whistle and both dogs dropped to the ground, allowing the sheep time to huddle together before they began the task of moving the flock steadily down the hillside.

Both Tess and Fly were used to the procedure, barely needing a command from Chrissie as they worked together, reading the reactions of the sheep and going wide or moving closer as the white mass trickled down the steep slopes, jumping over craggy outcrops and negotiating sharp drops and ravines.

They were almost home when it happened, in sight of the open gate that led to the lower, fenced-in land where the ewes would stay for the lambing.

For a fleeting second Chrissie thought it was a crazy sheep racing toward the flock. Then with a sinking heart, she realized that it was a big, cream-colored dog, almost as fluffy as the sheep. That was where the likeness ended, though. The dog was big and fast; it looked fierce as it raced madly toward them, intent on trouble. Its pink tongue waved from the side of its mouth and its ridiculous ears flapped against its head. Tess and Fly stopped in their tracks, looking anxiously at their mistress.

"Lie down," she shouted, and they dropped to the ground as one, whining their objection to the unwanted intruder and the interruption of their routine.

The sheep began to panic. They were accustomed to the quiet way the border collies worked and respected their boundaries. This was something different. Huddling close together, they started to run back up the fell, but they were too late; the big dog leaped into their midst, barking loudly and scattering them as they fled for the safety of the higher slopes.

Chrissie screamed at the dog. "Get away! Get out of here!" But the wind took her voice as the dog wreaked havoc with the flock before chasing after one small ewe that had split off from the rest.

Chrissie saw them heading for where the rough grass gave way to rocky scree just above an outcrop. She started to run, but she was too far away…

It was just as the ewe disappeared over the ledge that Chrissie saw the man.

CHAPTER TWO

PARKING UP IN FRONT of the gray stone farm-house he now called home, Will Devlin grabbed his briefcase from the passenger seat and climbed out of his newly acquired Range Rover. The satisfaction he felt as he took in his surroundings was shaken as a heavy banging floated over from the barn. So the men he'd hired must be here to fix the roof, he realized, and suddenly he wished he'd left it a bit longer before getting the builders in.

He'd only just moved into the farmhouse a few days ago and found himself enjoying the isolation of the place so much that he hated the idea of it being infiltrated by hammering and loud voices and music. This morning, when he went to the bank in town, all he'd been able to think about was getting back to the peace and silence of his new home.

Strange, really, when just six months ago he'd reveled in the busy buzz of the city.

When a tall, gray-haired man approached, his hand extended, Will took it briefly.

"Jim Wentworth," said the man. "I'll be supervising the work here. You must be Mr. Devlin. All we can do at the moment, of course, is redo the roof before it falls in, but I have the plans with me, and I wondered if you wanted to look them over before we put them before the local council. Roger Simmons, your architect, asked me to bring them along. He says he'll drop by later today to see if you have any comments."

Will's response was immediate. The whole idea of workmen buzzing and banging about the place depressed him. "I can't right now," he said, turning abruptly away. "Maybe later."

Will hurried into the house, breathing in the silence as he closed the old oak door behind him. But that only made him feel stifled. He'd go for a walk up the fell, he decided. That should clear his head.

The farmhouse backed onto a small garden, fragrant with wildflowers, and beyond that was the vast space of the open fell. *Well out of sight of the builders,* thought Will thankfully as he headed out through the back door, not bothering to get changed. He stopped for a moment to take in the scenery that never failed to move him, breathing in the cool, fresh air and willing nature's yawning silence and the sweet scents of spring to refresh his zest for life.

Why had he left it this long to return to the Lake District hills? He had come here on holiday just once, with his parents when he was small, but its beauty and isolation had lingered in the back of his mind all this time, reemerging when his life became too much for him to bear. Yesterday had been his birthday—thirty-five years—but he felt as if he'd lived forever. And he had, if you counted all the drama he'd been involved with in the past ten years.

Calling for Max, the big daft labradoodle he'd bought on a whim when he decided to move here, he went through the rickety garden gate. The dog bounded ecstatically around him as he headed up toward the open fell, enjoying the clear air and drinking up the silence. Already he had hope that the beauty and tranquility of this place might

heal his hardened soul and gradually erad-
icate all the cruelty and brutality that had
consumed his life.

At twenty-five, a young and ambitious
lawyer, he'd been honored to be offered a
job with Marcus Finch. After he won his
first big case, his reputation had spread. At
first he had basked in the glory, pleased to be
termed a hotshot defense lawyer who could
get anyone acquitted if he put his mind to it.
Playing with words like a cat with a mouse
had been his forte.

Eventually, though, his mind had become
clouded by the violence and inhumanity of
the cases he was being asked to take on:
murder, extortion and meaningless deprav-
ity. It had all come to a head when he was
in the middle of a particularly gruesome and
high-profile case. Will had looked at the man
he was being paid a fortune to defend and
realized with sudden clarity just how badly
his ambitions had been compromised. He
had come into law to defend the innocent
and ended up doing the exact opposite; his
client didn't deserve to walk free. And with
that thought, he had just walked away, out

into the fresh, clear beauty of the autumn afternoon.

He'd never gone back, despite the threats and pleas of his superiors. "At least finish this case," Roy Wallis, the senior partner, had begged him, but Will had turned a deaf ear. He was done. Done with listening to lies and defending those who didn't deserve it. Done with the darker side of mankind. And that was when he had remembered the holiday all those years ago and realized that the silence of the Lakeland hills might still the buzzing in his head.

The private doctor he'd been persuaded to see had diagnosed a breakdown caused by mental exhaustion, but Will had known that wasn't true. He was just sickened by humanity; that was the truth of it. When he'd handed in his notice at Marcus Finch, Roy had pleaded with him to reconsider, offering paid leave, but Will had been adamant. He needed more than just time to breathe; he needed a whole new life. And so he'd come back here to Little Dale, and found to his relief that it had hardly changed since he was a boy.

He'd been drawn to the window of the real

estate office as he strolled along the street on that first day here, reliving his childhood memories. The picture had seemed to jump right out at him and he'd stopped to read the advertisement. Craig Side, a whitewashed farmhouse with gray stone outbuildings set way up the fell, with fifty acres of land and rights to graze the fell for as far as a man could see. Isolated, totally peaceful and everything he wanted.

Will Devlin wasn't usually one to act on a whim. He thought things through, planned his every move…but not this time. He'd booked a viewing that very afternoon and made an offer right away, his head brimming with plans. The barn and outbuildings would make ideal holiday rentals. Money was no problem for now, but it wouldn't last forever and if he never went back to law then he'd need some kind of income. And he wasn't going back to law. Ever.

Within six weeks he had finalized the purchase and hired an architect to start drawing up plans. Only when he moved into the farmhouse had he realized he might have jumped into things too quickly. He should have waited awhile, taken time to appreciate the peace and solitude before putting his business plans into action.

Excited by the prospect of a walk, Max leaped up at his master in his usual unruly manner, appearing to smile as his pink tongue lolled from the side of his mouth, exposing sharp white fangs. The dog's attitude was what had drawn Will to him in the first place. Max loved everyone and everything, albeit a little too enthusiastically at times.

"Come on, boy," Will said, increasing his pace. He regretted not changing into more suitable footwear; the dampness on the vegetation was beginning to soak through his smart leather shoes. No matter, he decided. He wasn't going back now, and there was no one here to notice, anyway. He'd just throw the shoes away if they got too badly damaged.

For the next fifteen minutes, Will climbed the steep slope, hearing only the heavy sound of his breathing. He stopped for a moment to rest his aching legs, leaning forward with his hands on his knees.

"Max," he called. "Here, boy…come here." The big dog raced up to him, collapsing onto a patch of rough grass. Will smiled, pleased that, for once, the dog had done his bidding. "Why, you're no fitter than me, boy," he teased.

He could see the low huddle of buildings at Craig Side way below him now, surrounded by the bright green of the home fields. Farther down, at the base of the valley, the lake sparkled in the spring sunshine as if ten thousand diamonds had been scattered on its surface.

Cool air filled his nostrils and he took a gulp of it, savoring the silence even as he realized that it wasn't silent at all, not really. In the city there was always sound, sound that you no longer noticed after a while, the busy, constant hum of traffic, the honking of a hundred angry horns, the buzz of human voices. And here there was sound in the silence, too, different kinds of sounds: the scream of a buzzard, the song of the wind as it whispered and wailed, and the bleating of the rough fell sheep that wandered the steep slopes in their constant quest for food.

He could see a flock of them on the hillside, trickling downward with two dogs to guide them. He stopped to watch, intrigued by the way the dogs worked as a team, dropping to the ground and then creeping forward again before rushing to turn the flock if they headed in the wrong direction. It was all overseen by the shepherd, who gave low whistles and shouted commands in a loud, clear voice that carried across the distance in the thin air.

Calling to Max, who was now intent on digging beneath a rock, Will headed closer, watching the sheep and dogs, and ignoring the dull ache in his calves and the discomfort of his damp feet. He realized, suddenly, that the shepherd was a woman, a tall, straight-backed woman who strode confidently across the rough and rocky ground, a long crook in her hand. She wore blue skinny jeans and sturdy brown boots, and a thick blond braid hung almost to her waist. There was something about her that moved him. He supposed it was the timelessness of the way she strode the earth, commanding the dogs with confidence and certainty just as her ancestors must have done before her.

Ahead, the ground fell away, dipping steeply. As he headed down the slope, Will lost sight of the woman with her dogs and sheep. With a lurch of disappointment, he turned back to call Max again, surprised by his own eagerness to watch her work the dogs some more. Come to think of it, he hadn't felt much eagerness or excitement about anything of late, not even buying and then moving into Craig Side; that had just felt like a necessity. The communication between the woman and her collies was something else, though, something he had never experienced before. Strangely, it humbled him.

Another yell at Max, and the dog finally gave up his frantic digging and raced to catch up, so excited by the unfamiliar scents and sounds that, all reason lost, he bounded right past Will and down the slope, leaping over the stream in the bottom of the shallow ravine.

"Max! Come here!" he called, his voice echoing. The big dog paused and looked back at him, wagging his plumed tail as if about to obey...until a high-pitched whistle sounded and the sheep let out several bleats. Then, totally ignoring his master's urgent commands, Max took off up the slope on the other side and disappeared from view.

Will's heart sank when he heard the woman's angry cries. He started to run, ignoring the burning in his lungs and the ache in his calves.

"Stupid dog," he groaned, unable to hear anything but the rasping of his own breath as he headed for the patch of clear sky at the top of the steep incline.

She was standing farther up the hillside, bright blue eyes blazing against her lightly tanned skin, two bright spots of angry color in her cheeks. "Get out of it!" she yelled, madly waving her crook. "Get away!"

Following her gaze, Will saw Max leaping toward the sheep, oblivious to everything else, barking with excitement as they started to scatter. The woman gave a long, low whistle and her two sheepdogs sank to the ground in total obedience, staring up at her with adoration. Will felt like a fool, totally out of his depth and unsure of what to do. He wasn't used to feeling inadequate—angry, perhaps, and sickened by life, but in control...always in control.

"Max, come here," he tried to yell, but the words couldn't seem to get past his throat.

Taking a gulp of air, he tried again as the sheep began to flee in a dozen directions. "Max, here! Now!"

CHAPTER THREE

BEFORE THE CRAZY dog appeared, Chrissie had been feeling good, gazing fondly down on High Bracken, glad to be almost home with the gathering done for another year.

An unexpected rush of nostalgia had brought tears to her eyes as she remembered all the times she'd herded the sheep with her dad. He used to point out things of interest as they traversed the huge expanse of steep fellside: a dog fox observing their progress, a peregrine falcon swooping down to grab a smaller bird in its lethal talons and then dropping to the ground to boldly pluck its catch.

This was a place where only the strong survived, and she had to be strong, too— that was what her father had always taught her, and she still tried so hard to follow his advice.

An outlying sheep took her attention then,

bringing her train of thought back to the job at hand; it was moving farther away from the flock, intent on escape. She whistled sharply to Fly. The dog caught her eye, eager to follow her command.

"Come way out," she called with a sweep of her arm, and the small blue-gray and black dog was on it, calmly persuading the reluctant ewe to return to the flock with the patience and expertise that had made him a champion at the sheepdog trials last year.

It was as she'd turned her attention back to the main flock that the fluffy, cream-colored creature had burst into view, leaping up over the edge of the shallow ravine and racing toward them. For a fleeting second she'd thought it was a wayward sheep…and now she saw how wrong she'd been.

"No! Get away!" Chrissie screamed again, waving her crook madly as the big crazy dog continued to leap and bound amid her animals. One sheep had already disappeared from view, but she had to get things under control with the flock before she could check on it.

Tess and Fly sped at the dangerous usurper, but Chrissie stopped them with a low whistle;

the last thing she wanted was for her dogs to go haywire, too. That would really freak the sheep out. But it made no difference. The collies raced around the scattering sheep, trying to keep them contained, but the sheeps' survival instincts had kicked in and they fled in panic, their pregnant bellies swaying.

The fluffy cream dog, on the other hand, was in his element, running this way and that, barking madly. She yelled at it, screaming into the wind to no avail.

That was when she saw the man.

A hot flood of anger consumed her as he hurried over, a tall, dark-haired stranger dressed in city clothes. He was obviously responsible for this disaster. His face was bright red from climbing the hill and his breath came in loud gasps.

"Get your dog away from my sheep!" Chrissie yelled. *"Now."*

With a brief glance in her direction, the man carried on in a shambling run toward the flock, spooking them almost as much as his dog. Chrissie watched helplessly as sheep disappeared in every direction. She whistled madly to her collies, but she would have needed half a dozen dogs to keep the terrified creatures together.

"Max!" cried the man. "*Max!* Bad dog. Come here."

The dog ignored him, but as it ran by he managed to grab hold of its collar. For a moment, they struggled. The dog bucked against his confinement and the man staggered forward. If they hadn't been in such a desperate situation, Chrissie would have laughed as he sprawled to the ground, still holding on to the broad leather collar.

But despondency instantly replaced the momentary flicker of humor. She whistled to Tess and Fly to come back, and they raced over immediately, dropping down in front of her, pink tongues hanging from the sides of their mouths and their bright eyes eager for their mistress's next command. With the cream-colored dog in the man's grasp, the sheep had calmed somewhat, but at best she would be spending the rest of the afternoon gathering the ones that had scattered. At worst…well, she didn't want to think about that just yet.

"Good dogs. Stay," she told her collies, turning to stare angrily at the man who had caused such chaos. He was on his feet now, looking awkward, his shiny leather shoes much the worse for wear and his stupid suit pants ripped at the knees.

"You," she said in a cold, flat voice, eyeing him up and down with disdain. "You should get back to the city where you belong and take your idiot dog with you. If any of these sheep are harmed then you'll be hearing from my lawyer. I'd have been well within my rights to shoot it, you know."

At that, the man's demeanor changed and he stood tall, holding her gaze with piercing, pale eyes. "But you haven't got a gun," he pointed out in a clear, cultured voice.

Undeterred, Chrissie tossed her head, blue eyes sparkling as they boldly met his. "Then I will start carrying one," she said. "For the next time that wild, untrained dog of yours terrifies my sheep. And if I lose any lambs from this, you will be paying for them, too."

FOR A MOMENT, Will was speechless. A crazy urge to laugh made his lips twitch as it occurred to him what his colleagues would think if they could see him now. Will Devlin, stuck for words for what felt like the first time in his life, his opponent a simple country shepherdess with no apparent culture but a very fierce temper.

When he made the decision to move to the country, he'd imagined it would be quiet and relaxing, a peaceful place with room to breathe. He definitely hadn't expected to get told off like a schoolboy on his first outing.

Two bright spots of color burned in the woman's cheeks as she noticed his smile. "You may think this is funny," she said, refusing to be daunted by his efforts at trying to appear imposing. "But the sheep are now way too spooked to get down the fell today. I'll have to wait until they've settled down again, and that's at least a whole day wasted. Anyway…" She lifted her chin, pushing back the stray wisps of blond hair that had escaped from her braid to curl around her cheek. "What makes you think you have the right to look down on me when you are walking the fells dressed like that?"

"But I don't look down on you…" Will objected. "At least—"

"Oh, yes, you do," she cut in. "I can see it in your face. You think I'm just a simple country bumpkin. Well, let me tell you now,

Mr. Whoever-you-are—you may be some kind of hotshot in the city but it counts for nothing here."

Will glanced at his ruined leather shoes and torn, mud-splattered trousers, feeling suddenly ridiculous. "I…I was in a rush," he muttered, still hanging on to Max's collar. "And it's Mr. Devlin, by the way. Will. Of course I'll pay for any problems I've caused. I do have the right to walk these fells, though, whatever I'm wearing. You can't stop me."

"What rights?" snorted the shepherdess. "Being a tourist doesn't give you the right to ruin my day and injure my sheep."

Determined to stand his ground, Will tried his well-practiced courtroom stare again. She just stared back, flicking her heavy braid back over her shoulder.

"I have grazing rights," he said.

"Grazing rights don't come with holiday cottages, you know," she retorted, turning away with her dogs at her heels. "Anyway, I have enough to do without standing around talking to you. You'd better just hope that the sheep are all okay and go buy yourself a lead for that crazy dog. My name is Chrissie Marsh and I live at High Bracken, just down the fell from here. In case you end up owing me for lost sheep."

He watched her walk over to the ledge where the ewe had disappeared. She was tall and almost stately, walking the hills with proud strides and her crook in her hand. Her dogs followed, totally obedient, while Max strained and pulled at him, eager to run off. For the first time in his adult life, Will Devlin felt out of his depth.

In another way, though, he felt somehow free, as if all the layers of artificiality that had been such a big part of his life for so long had been torn away. Another urge to laugh hit him as he took in his situation: his totally unsuitable clothes and his silly dog. A hotshot from the city, she'd called him, and she hadn't been too far off with that. Well, he was certainly no hotshot now. Out here in the wilds of the Lake District a silver tongue and a steely gaze counted for nothing.

AWARE THAT WILL DEVLIN was watching her as she headed toward the place where the ewe had disappeared, Chrissie held her head high, determined not to let him sense her discomfort. There was no way she was letting him see that he'd bugged her. She wasn't used to folks like him; he didn't belong up here, with his posh voice and fancy clothes. This was her place, her land and her way of life.

Resisting the impulse to look back and see if he was still there, she peered over the ledge. To her dismay, the little ewe was on her back, trapped in a crevice upside down with her black legs in the air. Panic hit like a sledgehammer; there was no way Chrissie could get it out unaided.

She didn't want to ask the man to help, but there was no other way. In desperation, she turned to see him heading off down the hillside, hobbling slightly and still hanging grimly to the dog's collar.

"Excuse me," she called. "Please…I need help here."

WILL STOPPED WHEN he heard the woman's cry. She was standing in the spot where the sheep had disappeared over the ledge. He gritted his teeth; he could really do without this. Her braid had come loose, and her long fair hair was streaming around her shoulders. She caught it up impatiently.

"Please," she repeated, her desperate voice carrying across the distance. "It's the least you can do."

With a heavy sigh he retraced his steps. His knee smarted and throbbed, and his calf muscles ached relentlessly. Max pulled at him and he gave his collar a yank. "And what am I supposed to do with the dog while I help you with whatever it is you want?"

In response, Chrissie pulled a long piece of orange baler twine from her pocket. "First lesson," she said. "Always carry some of this with you—you never know when it might come in handy. My sheep is stuck down here and I need you to help me get it out."

Shaking his head, Will tied the twine to Max's collar and fastened the end around a stubby, windblown bush before peering over the drop. She was right; he was duty bound to help her, even though the thought of wrangling a sheep was definitely not at the top of his to-do list.

Chrissie climbed down next to the sheep and began hauling at it.

"We need to call for help," he suggested.

"You *are* the help," she snapped. "What I need is for you to get down here and undo some of the damage you and your stupid dog have caused."

Reluctantly, Will did as he was told, scrambling awkwardly down the rocky outcrop to grab hold of the oily wool on the ewe's back. It was thicker than he expected, and kind of sticky.

"Just pull," she said.

They tugged with all their strength, shoulder to shoulder, and suddenly the ewe came free. She leaped up, knocking them both over before heading off across the fell to find her companions. Will lay winded for a second with Chrissie sprawled over him. She wriggled to free herself, pushing against his chest, her face a fiery red.

"Well, at least the sheep seems okay," he remarked, lips twitching.

"She'll probably lose her lambs, though," she remarked coldly, sitting up and struggling onto her feet. He stayed on the ground, contemplating.

"You are very pessimistic," he said. "It's not a good trait, you know. Positive thinking can move mountains."

Chrissie brushed herself down. "You need more than positive thinking to survive up here. I'm telling you the ewe will probably lamb too soon—and you'll have to pay for it. Plus probably others that I haven't even found yet."

Will sat up. "Ah, but how are you going to catch all these ailing and injured sheep that you haven't even found yet? And if you can't find them, how will you prove their problems were mine and Max's doing?"

"Well I can't, can I? Not right now, at least. But I'll be keeping a closer eye on the ones that got loose because of you. Tomorrow I have to do the gather all over again, and they will come in with the rest of the flock...as long as there isn't a tourist with a crazy dog around."

Clambering to his feet, Will gave a short, sharp salute. "Well, you don't need to worry on that score...*ma'am*. Max will definitely be locked away tomorrow, and as I'm not a tourist, there will probably be none of those around to bother you, either."

Chrissie bristled, obviously displeased with his mocking tone. Without another word, she whistled for her collies and the dogs leaped up at once, happy to be doing something. Max yipped after them as they moved off down the steep slope.

Now Will was the one to bristle. He *did* have rights to this land. He didn't have to suffer her disrespect. She was fifty yards away from him, but he called out anyway, his voice cutting easily through the clear, thin air.

"For your information, I'm a property owner. I live here, too. For now, at least."

Chrissie stopped in surprise, looking back to where he still stood on the rocky outcrop, hanging on to his dog as it leaped against the restraint of the orange baler twine. Her curiosity was so obvious that it made him feel a bit better about the way she seemed determined to make him feel out of place and unwelcome here. Who was she to judge him, anyway? He had as much right on this fell as she did. If she thought he was going to fill her in on the details of the property he had bought, she was about to be disappointed.

For a moment she just stared at him, an unspoken question in her eyes. He returned her gaze with a half smile on his lips, refusing to be drawn in, and eventually, with a curt nod, Chrissie turned abruptly away.

CHAPTER FOUR

WILL STEPPED THROUGH the back door of the shabby white farmhouse at Craig Side with a heavy sigh of relief and, to his surprise, a sense of homecoming. The walk up the fell with Max had been meant to clear his head, invigorate his senses and push back the dark thoughts that the builders' presence had brought on. Great idea that had been; his clothes and shoes were ruined, his whole body felt battered and bruised, and he ached all over.

"It's all your fault, Max," he complained to the muddy dog, who had sprawled in front of the stove the second they got in.

Max half raised his head in response, thumping his bedraggled tail on the floor.

"And you need a bath," added Will, wishing the farmhouse boasted a shower. The thought of standing under a hot shower was so appealing, and a bath just wasn't the same.

His upmarket bachelor apartment in Manchester had a power shower, so the pressure was always good, and the first thing he did when he came home from work in the evening was to strip off his clothes and stand underneath it for at least fifteen minutes, allowing the force of the scalding-hot water to wash away the trials of the day.

Perhaps he should get a shower fitted here right away. He had big plans for the place eventually, but it would be some time before they were put into action and he didn't think he could stand only having a bath to wash in for the next year or so. The holiday rentals were his first priority, of course… which reminded him about the builder wanting him to look at the plans his architect had drawn up.

Just as the thought came into his head, the banging that had made him go out in the first place started up again. So the builders were still here. He groaned. *Well, might as well get it over with.*

Will stepped outside again and waved at Jim, calling him over.

"Hi, Jim, come in," he said brightly, opening the door wider. The tall gray-haired man he'd met earlier stepped inside, looking around intently.

"So, I guess you'll be wanting to do this place up next, when the holiday cottages are done," he remarked. "Will you be living here, then?"

Will nodded. "That's the plan. I could probably do with putting in a shower right away, though."

Jim took in his muddy shins and tattered clothes and seemed to be suppressing a smirk. "There's no water pressure, that's the problem. Having your own supply is great, but it can be a bit unpredictable. I'll get the plumber to have a look, if you like."

"Great," said Will, part of him wishing he'd never said anything in the first place, as much as he craved a shower right now. He already regretted starting on his building plans so soon.

After the gruesome child-murder trial that had been the final straw for him, he had put in his offer on Craig Side and filled his mind and imagination with ideas of what to do with it right away, anything to drown out the details of that case. He'd even had Roger Simmons, his architect, check out the property to brainstorm before the deal was properly finalized.

Now that he was actually living here, though, Will realized he didn't want to share it with anyone…not even the workmen. What he needed to recover from his breakdown was peace and quiet, not the stress and tumult of a huge project. But what was done was done, and he had to deal with it.

Jim laid the plans out on the kitchen table. "Have a good walk?" he asked.

Will thought about his clash with the woman on the fell. "I wouldn't exactly put it like that," he replied with frown. "In fact, you may have noticed that I look as if I have been dragged through a rather thick thorn hedge backward."

Jim raised his wild, gray eyebrows. "Well, I did wonder…"

"I upset some sheep on the fell," Will explained. "Or, at least, Max did…"

Jim glanced at the mud-splattered labradoodle, unable to contain a smile. "And I'll hazard a guess that, as she is your nearest neighbor, the sheep were rough fells and they belonged to Chrissie Marsh."

Will shrugged. "I wouldn't have a clue

what the sheep were, but the shepherdess— can you call them that these days or are they all just shepherds?—was definitely Chrissie Marsh."

Jim grinned slowly. "If you've upset her sheep then I wouldn't like to be in your shoes."

"It will take more than a disgruntled sheepherder to upset me." Will thought of all the hardened criminals he'd mingled with in the past ten years. "Unless she has a violent husband…"

"Oh, no," Jim said. "Chrissie is a loner. She loves her sheep and her dogs, and she doesn't suffer fools gladly. She's never been married." He went back to the plans. "Now, what about this entrance hall? Roger wondered if you wanted a central entrance—you know, like a foyer, and then have apartments inside the barn rather than build individual cottages in the farmyard."

Will shook his head, cupping his chin between thumb and forefinger thoughtfully. "No, I'm beginning to think that perhaps they need to be…authentic. You know, traditional, just like they were in the past."

"What…no showers or microwaves? Electricity?"

"It's just a thought. Roughing it is all the rage these days. City dwellers love the idea of going back to nature and experiencing how things used to be."

Jim rolled up the plans, securing them with an elastic band. "It sounds as if you need to have a meeting with Roger, then. He wanted you to look these over because he was hoping to get them ready for next month's planning meeting, but it seems like it's going to take a bit longer than that. I'll drop these off at his house on my way home and tell him to give you a call."

Will nodded. "Thanks. My first thoughts were to have apartments, but to be honest since coming here I've been realizing how strong the traditions are. I mean, take Chrissie, for instance. I reckon shepherds just like her have been walking these fells with their dogs in the same way for hundreds of years."

"Thousands, more likely," Jim remarked. "Maybe you have something there, then, but I am no architect—or expert on what folks want, for that matter. You need to talk to people who know about stuff like that.

Anyway, I'll see what I can do about your shower. Oh, and I'm afraid the roof trusses in the barn are rotten, six of them, at least. It would be a big mistake not to replace them."

"Just order what you need," Will said. Suddenly, he felt stifled. He had come here to relax, not open himself up to a whole new set of problems like rotten roof trusses and planning applications. Perhaps he should just tell the architect to put everything on hold for a while…but then again, he still had to survive, and his savings weren't going to last forever.

He saw Jim off then turned to the woodstove. "Come on, Max," he said. "Let's go and get you cleaned up."

It was much later, as he sat in the garden watching the sun slowly disappear, that Chrissie's face slid into his mind.

She had been so angry with him, standing stalwart with her dogs at her feet, blue eyes blazing. And then she'd surprised him by revealing a different side to her nature, when they had hauled at the trapped sheep together, side by side, their fingers locked into its oily wool. Her sheer determination had freed it. There was no doubt in Will's mind about that.

Yet her face had been a picture when she'd ended up sprawled on top of him, bright red with embarrassment. Funny, really, when she came across so tough and strong-minded. Perhaps some of that self-assurance was an act.

Who was he to judge her if it was? He had acted a part every day in his job, putting on a front for his clients, judges, juries... the whole world, if he was honest with himself. Maybe that was what most people did. Maybe, underneath, everyone was vulnerable. Some just hid it better than others.

The relief Chrissie had shown when the tough little ewe eventually ran off up the hill with a series of stiff-legged jumps had been no act—he was sure of that. Her face had crumpled with emotion...until she'd turned to look at him. And the way she'd just walked off with her dogs down the steep hillside, her head held high... He had never met any woman like her.

Anyway, he had certainly learned his lesson. If he saw her again—especially if he was walking Max—then he'd know to steer well clear.

CHRISSIE WAS CONSUMED with anger as she headed homeward with Tess and Fly at her heels. Will Devlin, whoever he was, had ruined her day. Not just because he'd let his dog terrify the sheep, but because he'd made her feel like a fool when they'd pulled the ewe out of the crevice and she'd fallen on him. No one ever made Chrissie Marsh look foolish.

Her whole day had been wasted and it was all his fault. What kind of idiot let a dog like that loose on the fell, anyway, especially at lambing time? Well, if there was any damage then he would be paying for it; she hadn't been joking about that.

The ewe that had fallen was quite likely to lamb too early after all that stress. It was hard enough for the lambs to survive up here as it was; premature labor would mean Chrissie would have to keep mother and lamb—hopefully not lambs—on the lowlands for longer. Well, at least lambing time was imminent so they couldn't be very premature, but shock could have unpredictable effects, even resulting in lambs being stillborn.

And she hadn't yet ruled out the possibility of finding more damaged sheep. Anything could have happened to them when they ran away from the dog. In normal circumstances, fell sheep were sure-footed and knew their territory far too well to get into difficulties, but today had been something else—something she really could have done without.

Homeowner or not, Will Devlin and his fancy clothes had no place up in these hills. He must have bought a holiday cottage somewhere around here. In the village, probably.

It was Tess who noticed it first. She stopped, head up to sniff the air, whining into the relentless wind that bent the stunted trees and bushes toward the ground. Chrissie followed her gaze with a prickle of apprehension. "What is it, girl?

The black-and-white collie raced off toward a rocky outcrop, closely followed by Fly. Chrissie headed off after them, using her crook to stop her from slipping on the sharp scree. Her heart fell when she peered over the ominous drop. A white shape lay on the rocks far below.

On a normal day the ewe could have easily traversed the dangerous surface. Today, though, in an obvious panic and separated from the flock, she must have lost her footing on the patch of unstable scree and slipped over the edge…falling to her doom.

Although she was used to the harsh ways of nature, where death often seemed to loom around every corner, losing one of her flock so needlessly—so wastefully—filled Chrissie with rage at the man who had unwittingly caused it. He was so *ignorant*. She could only hope that this sheep's death had been quick and painless. And it *was* dead, she was sure of it. The ewe's legs were twisted into peculiar shapes and it stared up at her through vacant eyes.

A rush of tears overwhelmed her, cutting through the anger. What if it was still holding on—and suffering? She had to be sure.

Telling the dogs to "lie" and "stay," Chrissie carefully negotiated the rocky ledge and found a place near one end where it sloped off more gradually, allowing her to climb down and inch across to where the sheep was lying. Its body was still warm and soft to the touch, but its eyes were glazing over and it gazed right past her, into eternity.

"Poor lamb," she murmured, stroking the rough hair on the ewe's black-and-white face, recognizing its distinctive markings at once. This would have been the sheep's first lambing and now it would never happen, all because of a misfit from the city and his stupid dog. Tourists like him should be banned from everywhere but the villages that depended on them for their livelihood.

With a sharp whistle to Tess and Fly, Chrissie headed homeward. There was nothing else to do here.

THE YARD AT High Bracken was quiet. As quiet as the poor dead sheep, thought Chrissie with a knot in her stomach. Despondency flooded her veins. She certainly hadn't expected the gather to end like this. Tess and Fly looked eagerly up at her, whining softly.

"Okay," she said. "It wasn't your fault. Come on, I'll give you a feed."

As she made for the barn, a frantic barking broke the tranquility, reminding her about the new dog, Floss. She opened the small door set into one of the two big barn doors and stepped inside, breathing in the sweet fragrance of hay. Here on the fells they still made small bales of traditional meadow hay—and always would do, as far as she was concerned. Sheep did best on meadow hay, and small bales were easy to handle.

"Hey, girl," she called softly as the nervous young dog wriggled and squirmed on the end of her chain. Chrissie intended to bring her into the kitchen tonight, where the other dogs slept, but for now she was safest tied in the barn. She leaned down to rub the pup's ears before unclipping her chain. The little black, white and tan Welsh collie raced around her.

Chrissie laughed, her unsuccessful day temporarily forgotten as Floss rolled over onto her back. "I hope you're going to settle down a bit, or I'll never be able to train you," she said, scratching Floss's tummy. She liked to spend time with new trainees, get them to trust her before proper training sessions began.

Tess and Fly flopped down in the hay, noses on their paws as they waited patiently, watching their mistress's every move. "You were young once," she told them. When she stood, Floss leaped up at her and she lowered her palm in a signal to sit.

"Down," she said firmly. The little dog

wagged her plumed tail and when she repeated the command, Floss did as she was bid.

"Well someone has certainly taught you something." Chrissie reached into the feed bin for the bag of dog food. Tess and Fly jumped up and stood by their bowls, while Floss held back submissively.

The shadows were lengthening by the time Chrissie finished feeding the dogs and turned to her other animals.

With Floss on a long piece of twine, she fed and locked away the chickens and the Indian Runner ducks that she used in the sheepdogs' early training. It was too early yet to test out Floss's natural herding instincts, so she kept the young dog close and gave the command to sit on a regular basis.

The two shorthorn cows she kept for her own milk lowed hungrily, and she fed them before milking them in the old traditional way, enjoying the warm feel of their teats and the rhythmic sound of the milk squirting into a stainless steel bucket.

People around here thought she was as mad as a box of frogs to bother milking twice a day. "You could buy your milk from the shop," Andy, her vet, had reminded her for the thousandth time just the other day. "It would be a darn sight cheaper and a lot less hassle." Her response had been just to smile and shrug. The truth was she enjoyed it. The age-old task helped her relax.

And after her bad experience with the city dweller and his dog, she definitely needed to relax.

Remembering the poor, broken sheep, a flood of emotion overtook her. If Will Devlin thought he was getting away scot-free, then he could think again. Nothing could bring back the ewe or her unborn lamb, but he could pay for it. That was the *least* he could do.

Tomorrow, she decided, she'd get an early start and make the gather again. Once the flock was safely down on the lower pasture adjacent to the farm, she'd try to find out where the man was from. She stood, lifting the pail of milk and covering it with a cloth. In fact, she would write out a proper invoice as soon as she went inside. Perhaps she should take it with her in the morning, in case she saw him on the fell again, though surely he had learned his lesson there. Someone in the village must know where he was staying.

No matter what, she was determined to find him and make him pay.

CHAPTER FIVE

WILL DEVLIN ROLLED OVER in bed, breaking into a sweat as he woke in the darkness, horrible images flooding his mind. He sat up, flinging back his blankets. Would he never get a good night's sleep again?

There was something heavy on his legs, pinning them down, and he made out Max's pale shape in a beam of silvery moonlight. The big dog raised his head and flopped around, spread-eagling himself happily.

If anyone had told Will a year ago that he would be living alone in the country and sharing his bed with a dog, he'd have said it was impossible…and yet now here he was. Max slid off his legs and jumped onto the floor, instantly full of life. He was used to his master's nighttime ramblings; sometimes they even went out for a walk in the darkness.

Tonight, though, Will felt too maudlin for

a walk. Pulling on his dressing gown, he ran downstairs with Max at his heels, poured himself a stiff whisky and sat down beside the stove in the kitchen.

Had he been right to come here? Or was life in the Lake District just a crazy notion that he'd tire of soon? Remembering his disaster the previous day with the woman and her sheep, he realized he had an awful lot to learn if he was going to stay around here.

Max sat on his haunches, watching Will's every move, his tail waving.

"Perhaps I should get you some proper training, Max," Will said thoughtfully. "Assuming you're even trainable…"

Max just looked at him, his brown eyes glowing with trust and happiness. That might have been what had drawn him to the pup in the first place, thought Will—the joyous innocence in his eyes. Innocence had kind of faded from Will's life of late.

On the other hand, it had been Max's innocence that caused the chaos on the fell today. Though Will doubted Chrissie would call the big dog "innocent" after what she thought he'd done to her sheep.

Taking another sip of his whisky, he pictured the straight-backed woman with her long blond braid. *Chrissie.* She didn't really look like a Chrissie—more a Lorna or an Alice. A smile curled up inside him, warming the cold, hard place in his heart…

He shook his head. What did her name matter? In fact, the last woman he'd dated had been called Summer, and there wasn't much about her that reminded him of the season—unless you counted how short-lived the relationship was. The shepherdess was no Summer, either. *More of a Winter,* he thought with a smirk. Remembering her honey-colored skin, though, he changed his mind to Autumn, with its golden tints and beautiful browns.

Summer had soon stopped getting in touch when he'd told her he'd given up his job and was moving to the country. He'd been put off at first, but now he was glad; he needed to be alone, for the time being, and he couldn't see a future with her anyway.

Sighing, he dropped his empty glass into the sink and headed back up the narrow staircase. Tomorrow, he guessed, the architect would be on the phone. Will was so exhausted that it crossed his mind to put the whole project on hold, completely rethink the decisions he'd made recently.

He stood at the bedroom window, staring out at the formidable dark mass of the fell etched against the pale moonlit sky. This place held his future, he was sure of it. Fading dreams tumbled back into his consciousness, taking form again, meaning something. No, he couldn't stop now. He needed this. Maybe he would have to rethink some of his plans so they would fit in with the environment here, but he wasn't going to give up on the one thing that had carried him through these past dark weeks. Somehow he was going to make this work...no matter what the locals thought.

THE MORNING DAWNED bright and sunny, one of those early spring days when the whole world felt as if it was filled with promise. *Is* filled with promise, he corrected himself, feeling a resurgence of last night's positive thinking. He glanced at the clock as he flung open the small window and leaned out to gulp in the sweet, clean air. There was a fog down in the valley, obliterating the rest of the view. Thick and white, it made the fells seem even more majestic as they loomed toward the clear blue sky.

"We are kings in our castle, Max," Will said. "And when we are here, no one can touch us."

Max just wagged his tail and twirled in a circle, impatient to go outside. Will smiled, feeling more lighthearted than he had in a long while. "Well, I'm a king... You're probably more a court jester."

He needed to get his head straight before meeting with his architect, so Will grabbed a piece of buttered toast and headed for the back door, remembering to take Max's long leash from the hook. "No sheepherding for you today, young man," he said, clipping the leash onto the dog's collar.

The fog was lifting now, evaporating into nothingness to reveal the silver, sparkling lake and gray stone buildings way, way down in the valley. Will went through the gate that led onto the fell, noticing the patches of fresh white snowdrops coming up at the edges of the garden. They must have been there yesterday, announcing the arrival of spring, but he'd missed them. Funny how every day he seemed to see a new thing. It felt as if he'd just removed a blindfold that he'd been wearing for years, and now nature's beauty was being revealed to him little by little.

Max pulled on the leash as they headed up the steep slope behind the house. He had decided not to go the same way as yesterday, just in case Chrissie—or Autumn, as he'd started thinking of her—was bringing the sheep down again. Today he wore sturdy boots, blue Wrangler jeans and a thick cream-colored sweater. Today, he was prepared; if he did come across her, she could keep her smiles to herself. He was dressed right and his dog was under control.

Will climbed for twenty minutes or so, not following a path but just aiming for the sky-line and avoiding loose rocks and boulders.

He heard the high-pitched, ear-splitting sound from what felt like miles away, a piercing whistle that filled the clear air. Max stopped, whining in excitement, and Will took a firm hold of his leash. "Not today, boy," he ordered, squinting into the distance.

No sign of her, thank God. The fellside was so vast that surely he couldn't come across her by accident again. He continued on, his breath burning in his chest as the air got thinner.

CHRISSIE WAS PLEASED with herself. She'd been up before dawn to let Floss out, feed the animals and milk her two cows before grabbing her crook and calling to Tess and Fly. Perhaps today they could actually get the job done.

The heavy mist in the bottom of the valley made everything seem eerie and strange; Chrissie was used to mornings like this, but they never failed to move her soul. Taking a deep breath, she set out with long, easy strides, turning her face toward the pale early morning sun that cast its spell on the world.

By eight she was almost there, on the smoothest slope where the sheep liked to graze. To her relief she saw them at once, heads down and nibbling the sparse foliage. They looked up as one when she came into view, startled but not yet spooked by the woman and her dogs.

Today, she would have to take special care. Fell sheep were feral, they'd been badly frightened yesterday and their instinct to survive was strong. They moved closer together, herding up to face danger as a group, and she slowed her steps, motioning to Fly to go wide of the flock.

The sharp blue-and-white collie lowered herself to the ground, slinking around the back of the sheep that were starting to move down the slope. Tess waited, nose on paws, keen eyes and ears alert for her command.

Her moment came when a small ewe moved out from the flock. With one low whistle from Chrissie, Tess was straight on the sheep's tail. Before she got close enough to truly spook it, Tess hung back, gently persuading the sheep to close in with the others. Chrissie felt a warm rush of pride at the way her dogs worked, hardly needing a command from her, and her confidence grew. Perhaps she'd actually manage to get these sheep down today.

For the next twenty minutes, they trotted almost amicably, content to be coaxed down the steep slope by the two easygoing dogs. And then the little ewe decided to make a break for freedom again and Chrissie let out a piercing whistle to warn Tess. Within minutes, the sheepdog had regained control and the flock streamed obediently toward the gate into the low pasture.

The sky was darkening, and Chrissie was relieved that they had almost reached the fields. Gray clouds descended, casting out the sun and obliterating the patches of clear blue. A slow, steady drizzle of rain enveloped the fell. Glad of the waxed-canvas jacket she wore, Chrissie pulled up her hood and kept on moving.

Rain was almost an everyday occurrence in the North of England and she gave it as little thought as the sheep, whose thick, oily fleeces glistened with raindrops. Still, poor visibility and high winds were risks up here and she was happy she hadn't faced any more complications with the gather today.

The man appeared suddenly, as he had yesterday, and Chrissie suppressed a curse. At least today he had his crazy dog under control, she noted, and he was better dressed for the territory…except that maybe he should have thought to wear a coat.

She waved, signaling for him to stay back. He hesitated. His dark hair had curled in the rain and his sweater looked heavy and damp. He still hadn't gotten it right, then, she thought, trying not to smile. What did he think he was doing hanging around these fells? She felt in her pocket for the bill; at least now she could give it to him.

"Meet me at the bottom," she called, and he stopped in surprise. She pointed to the open gate that led to the fields by the farm. "Down there."

He frowned, puzzled, but he began moving in that direction, hanging determinedly on to the leash as his dog strained against him, desperate for another bit of fun.

With a collie at either side running to and fro, and Chrissie behind the flock waving her crook, the sheep streamed through the gate. She pushed it shut with satisfaction, almost forgetting about Will. His deep voice behind her made her jump. "Why did you ask me to follow you down here…? Is it just so that you can give me another ticking off?"

"Ticking off?" she repeated, unable to stop her wide smile. "What kind of person says that? Reading the riot act, going mad, even telling off. *Ticking* off sounds, well, kind of private school, I guess. Posh. Come to think of it, you do sound a bit posh."

Will nodded briefly. "And you sound very Northern. Anyway, why did you ask me to follow you? I know, don't tell me—it was my good looks you couldn't resist."

A flicker of heat in Chrissie's cheeks revealed her embarrassment; she wasn't used to eloquent men out-talking her. In fact, talking to anyone was not her forte. She pulled a slip of paper from her pocket. "You owe me this…for the ewe."

He frowned, his silvery blue eyes darkening. "But it ran off…we both saw it. I helped you, and it was fine."

"Not that one."

"There was another?"

She looked anywhere but into his piercing gaze. "One fell down a cliff face…it's dead and so is its lamb."

He stepped forward and took hold of her arm, but she pulled it away. "I'm so sorry."

Chrissie met his eyes for a second, lifting her chin. "Sheep die up here. It happens. But you have to pay for this one."

Will studied the crumpled piece of paper in his hand. "That much?"

"That much," she repeated decisively.

He stared at her a moment longer then

sighed. "I presume this is where you live," he said. "High Bracken, you called it? I'll bring you a check. You do take checks, I suppose?"

Chrissie glared at him. "Yes, can you believe it? I actually have a bank, in fact." Suddenly she smiled again, a tiny smile that just turned up the corners of her mouth. "I even have the internet…and I can work it."

It was his turn to appear uncomfortable. "I didn't mean…"

"Yes, you did," she said. "You think I'm some kind of country bumpkin with no brains. Well, I am a country girl and I'm proud of it, but I do have brains. It was either sheep farming or training to be a vet, and I chose sheep farming. I've never regretted it. I'll be around the farm tomorrow if you want to drop the check off. The vet's coming."

She turned away with her dogs at her heels, but spun back to face him a second later. "Oh, and you certainly look a bit more in keeping with your surroundings today, but a coat is always a good idea around here."

She strode off without another word. There was something so arrogant about the man, with his high-handed manner and his posh accent, and yet, standing there in his wet sweater, he also seemed kind of vulnerable. Bottom line: he was just another tourist and the sooner he headed back to his city life, the better.

She remembered what he'd said about owning property, but it had to be a just vacation home. Men like Will Devlin didn't live around here; they just arrived with their families and interfered with the way of things before scuttling back to the city.

Did he have a family? she wondered. Did she really care? The answer that jumped into her head was not the one she wanted. For some bizarre reason, she was interested in the man who kept appearing on the fell as if from nowhere. Perhaps he was a ghost, she mused sardonically as she made her way down to the farm. *Well, I'll find out tomorrow*, she thought. *Because ghosts can't write checks.*

WHEN CHRISSIE REACHED High Bracken, the sheep safely enclosed in the low meadows, she made straight for the new arrival, Floss. The nervous little dog was excited to see her, and Chrissie played with her for a few minutes before leading her to the house.

The way Floss stayed close behind her told her that perhaps she would be one of the easier ones to train. That belief was strengthened when Chrissie stopped to gaze across the valley toward Craig Side and Floss sat obediently down beside her.

There were workmen in the yard again, she noted, tiny figures in the distance. Perhaps they were just repairing the roof. Andy had been pretty sure about the holiday rentals, though.

She imagined clusters of bright-coated tourists wandering across her land, letting their pet dogs chase the sheep and leaving gates open. They seemed to think they owned the Lake District just because it was a national park.

She'd go to the council offices in Kendal this week, she decided, to find out what was going on. One thing was for sure: if there was a planning application going in, then she'd be fighting it. She'd write a letter of protest and get signatures, and she could have a meeting with the local council to state her objections.

With a fresh boost of determination she pulled herself away from the view of Craig

Side. What *were* her objections, though? *I don't like having tourists too close to my farm?* The shops, hotels and holiday cottages around here—her neighbors—depended on tourists. But encouraging them to stay as far up the fell as Craig Side could cause all sorts of problems—as she'd witnessed firsthand with Will Devlin's crazy dog. She could form her objection around that: tourists needed to be based closer to town, or in other nearby villages.

Smiling, she remembered that when tourists used to come tramping through Billy Parker's yard at High Ridge, he would turn the garden hose on them. True, that was probably taking it a bit too far, but the thought still amused her. She'd been half in love with Billy when she was sixteen, and his impetuous behavior had drawn her to him even then. He was happily married now with two young children, but they had always remained friends...

"Come on, girl," she said to Floss, heading back toward the house. She was eager for a late lunch and a cup of tea. "One thing is for sure. Whoever has bought Craig Side is in for a fight if they're hoping to bring tourists all the way up here."

CHAPTER SIX

As WILL MADE his way home with Max still straining on the leash, he felt a flicker of irritation at the way Chrissie made him feel so small.

Even when he'd walked away from his career he had felt principled, never awkward or uncomfortable. He'd become totally sickened by the way the law worked, the way that clever words could help guilty men and women walk free when the whole world knew they didn't deserve to. And the worst part was that very often they were his words. That was what had truly finished him. He wasn't proud of what he'd done as a lawyer, and he'd made the right decision by walking away.

Chrissie's face slid into his mind, a strong face that didn't need makeup to enhance it. There was something about her whole demeanor that drew him in, something starkly beautiful about the proud way she held her head and the spark in her blue eyes.

He had come to the fells for peace and quiet, a chance to take stock and sort out the good from the bad, but already he was inviting chaos into his life at every turn. What he needed to do, he decided, was avoid Chrissie at all costs. He didn't want any more antagonism in his life, and sparks seemed to fly whenever they met, sparks that emphasized his confusion.

He realized that Autumn was too warm and mellow a name for the fierce, independent shepherdess. Winter, he decided, smiling at the thought.

Back at Craig Side there were men up on the roof. He could see them clearly from the fell, little ants busily working. He'd come here for solitude, but solitude seemed to be evading him—even when he sought it out on the wild slopes. Part of it was his own fault, of course; he had called the workmen in and he had let Max chase the stupid sheep. Still, he needed to talk to Jim and Roger Simmons soon. Though, right now, getting out of his soggy sweater and warming up were his first priorities.

Will had just managed to pull the demon sweater over his head and stuff it in the laundry basket when he heard a knock on the kitchen door. He ignored it, hoping that whoever it was would think he'd gone out. No such luck.

"Sorry to intrude, but we really do need you to look at these plans again." Jim Wentworth poked his gray head around the corner just as Will ducked out of sight. "But if you're busy…"

"No, it's fine," Will said awkwardly, emerging from the laundry room. "I got a bit wet, that's all."

"I saw you coming down the fell." Jim smiled. "You did look a bit sodden. To be honest, it's always a good idea—"

"To wear a coat when you live around here," Will finished for him. "Autumn—I mean, Chrissie Marsh—said just the same thing."

Jim raised his bushy eyebrows. "You've seen her again already, then?"

"Only by accident. You'd think you could never accidentally bump into someone way up here, but I've managed to do it twice."

"With better results than yesterday, I hope."

Will laughed. "Well, Max didn't chase her sheep, but she presented me with a bill for one that fell down a cliff yesterday...and she let me know I was wearing the wrong clothes yet again."

"As I said, Chrissie doesn't suffer fools gladly."

"So you think I'm a fool, now?"

When Jim looked at him in dismay, Will placed a reassuring hand on his arm. "Don't worry. I know that's not what you meant. Tell you what—give me half an hour to get changed and we'll go and meet Roger together."

Jim nodded. "He said he was working at home all day. I'll give him a ring so he knows to expect us."

As he ran up the stairs to get changed, Will realized just how much more lighthearted he felt already, and all because his sense of purpose was filtering back. He could feel it, the drive inside him that made life worthwhile. Chrissie Marsh might have made him feel out of place and out of his comfort zone, but he wasn't one to give in easily. At least that was one good thing to come out of being a lawyer.

It was a culture shock, that was all. For years he'd been revered and admired; no one messed with Will Devlin unless they wanted a lawsuit on their hands, a lawsuit that they would definitely lose. He just had to adjust to the principles of life here. They were different than in the city, more basic and more honest. *Better...?* he asked himself. The answer came at once. *Yes.* Well, at least he definitely hoped so. All he had to do was keep well away from the shepherdess and he'd be fine. After he gave her a check, of course; he'd go there first thing tomorrow and get it done with.

His cell phone buzzed as he ran down the stairs. Roy Wallis? What the heck did he want? Ice seeped through his veins, weighing down his heart once more. Would they never let go of him? Putting the phone to his ear, he pulled on his professionalism like an invisible skin. "Roy! How are you? To what do I owe this honor?"

"Fine, and how are you?" replied the head of Marcus Finch and lawyer extraordinaire. "Feeling better, I hope."

"Getting my head straight, if that's what you mean," Will said cautiously.

"I won't mince words. I have a case for you, an important case."

"Well, give it to someone else because I am no longer a part of Marcus Finch."

"Look, Will…" Roy hesitated, piquing Will's interest. Roy Wallis never showed his unease.

"Look at what?"

"Ezra McBride has insisted that you handle it, and I think you know what that means."

Will stayed silent, digesting the information. His palms were sweaty. "I guess it means a heap of money for the company."

"It also means the loss of a very good client…not to mention the repercussions if he gets convicted." Roy's frustration sneaked through his usual steely tone. "Our reputation is at stake here, Will. You can't deal with these people lightly."

"Then perhaps the company should change the people it represents," Will suggested coldly. "Don't tell me…what is it this time? Murder, perhaps? Extortion? Bribery? Or maybe he just wants to cover up an even worse misdeed, like—"

"No!" Roy was quick to stop his tirade. "You know I can't mention the details. We need you back, Will. You have responsibilities."

"My only responsibilities are here," Will said. "Get some other mug to do your dirty work. I'm too busy."

He ended the call and had to pause at the bottom of the staircase, trying to still his shaking body. He thought he'd finally got his point across to Marcus Finch, but it seemed they just wouldn't let him go. It disgusted him, the way they valued winning—and getting paid for it—over the greater good.

You were like that, too, he reminded himself. Getting this or that murderer off when everyone knew they'd done it, and worse, knew that they'd do it all over again…and again…and again as long as they had people like Will to protect them from the law. Well, not anymore.

"You okay?" asked Jim when Will walked into the kitchen. He was waiting by the back door, looking awkward.

"I'm fine…let's just get this over with."

"We can leave it for today, if you like."

"I have nothing else to do." Will's voice was cold and cutting.

"You're a bit pale, that's all."

Will took a breath. He wasn't in court now and never would be again. "Sorry, I really am as keen as you are to get these plans sorted. I just had a difficult telephone conversation, that's all."

"Perhaps you should leave your phone behind, then," suggested Jim.

The idea alone left Will reeling. "But what if…"

"What if nothing. If someone wants to speak to you badly enough, they'll get hold of you later."

Feeling anxiety and freedom all rolled into one, Will dropped his phone on the table in triumph and reached for his jacket.

"Come on, then," he said. "Let's go."

WILL HAD ONLY spoken to Roger Simmons on the phone up until now, and the architect proved to be totally different than he'd expected. Average height with a middle-aged paunch, graying hair and kind blue eyes, he was the epitome of grandfatherhood.

Will had hired him for his reputation, and in his world that meant expensive suits and lean bodies achieved through hours in the gym—men and women who were trying to make a statement to the world. This man's statement, it seemed, was in his work, not his appearance. He was what he was, and Will could tell it by the firm, honest grip of his handshake.

"Now," Roger said, ushering him to a seat at the table and laying out some large sheets of paper. "Jim here tells me we have crossed wires regarding this development."

Will leaned forward, poring over the precisely drawn plans. "Since I first spoke to you, I guess I've had a change of heart. Instead of the rather grand communal idea, I thought that maybe we should keep it more traditional."

"He wants to give visitors the opportunity to live as people used to do," Jim added. "Cut out a lot of the amenities."

"And you think it will work?" Roger asked, frowning.

Will shrugged. "Well, it seems to be fashionable in places like London and Manchester nowadays. You know, to get away from the pressures of business and modern living, return to your roots and see how things used to be. It will have to be cleverly done, of course, to make the visitors feel that they're stepping back in time without it being *too* uncomfortable. I thought we could get quite a few cottages in there and make it like a real community, so that they can socialize if they want but have their own space, as well."

Roger tapped his pencil against his chin. "Mmm…that will take some working out. And do you intend to live on-site, too?"

Will hesitated. "I had intended to, but…"

"Well then, why don't we put the farmhouse plans aside for now and focus on the outbuildings first? You may end up wanting to move somewhere more private."

"That makes sense," Will said. "I'm enjoying the solitude at Craig Side and I don't want to lose that. I'll look forward to seeing your ideas."

Roger nodded, smiling. "I really think I understand where you're coming from now. I'll have some plans for you very soon."

Will stood and shook Roger's hand. The architect had a firm grip.

"You do realize you'll get some opposition from the locals?"

Will frowned. "But why? The new plans are going to be very traditional. Why would anyone object?"

"You obviously don't know much about the folks around here," Jim remarked. "They don't like tourists wandering about, upsetting the sheep, leaving gates open and messing up the land."

"Well, there aren't that many people around here to object, anyway," Will said. He might not be a defense lawyer anymore, but that didn't mean he had to give up his skills of persuasion. "We can overcome anything they have to say, I'm sure. In my experience, there is always a way."

Roger appeared doubtful. "It's not quite as easy as that," he said. "And I wouldn't underestimate our local council, but we'll just have to do our best with that. Anyway, I'll be in touch in the next couple days and we'll take it from there."

Roger left, and Will walked Jim to his car.

"Do you think we'll have objections from the locals?" he asked the builder.

"Probably," Jim said. "People around here object to everything."

Back at Craig Side, Will ate a late lunch beside the stove. For the first time in what felt like ages, he felt a flicker of enthusiasm for the future, followed almost immediately by regret that he might have to leave this place he had become so attached to. The builders' presence was irritating enough, but it was temporary; what would a property constantly full of tourists do to him?

It was kind of weird that he—who not so long ago thrived on the hubbub of city life—now felt threatened by the idea of sharing his space with just a few tourists.

Closing his eyes, he listened to the silence. It was total and welcome, calming his troubled mind. Later, he supposed, picking up the crumpled invoice from where he had thrown it earlier, he would have to go up to High Bracken and drop off a check. And this time, after the trip he'd made to the men's outfitters in town, at least he would be dressed right. Hopefully he could act right, too; no one had made him feel as awkward as Chrissie Marsh since he'd become a lawyer.

CHAPTER SEVEN

FLOSS GAZED UP at Chrissie, eyes alight with interest, and she gave the little collie the command to sit and stay.

"Clever girl," Chrissie said as Floss obeyed. "Perhaps we should do the duck test."

When she went around the back of the house to the small, walled paddock just beyond the barn, Floss followed, padding quietly along behind her like a dog twice her age. She was eager to learn and keen to please, Chrissie noted—all the attributes of a promising sheepdog. The duck test would show how much natural ability she had. Collies were bred with an inherent instinct to herd, but it came easier to some than to others.

The Runner ducks were already out, moving around the paddock like a group of slope-backed soldiers with their heads held high. When they saw Chrissie and the dog, they huddled closer together, moving as one with the weird gait that gave them their name.

"Time to earn your keep, boys," Chrissie called, firmly holding the baler twine that was attached to Floss's collar. The pup whined with excitement, and Chrissie pulled sharply on the twine. "Lie down, Floss."

Floss faltered, agitated by the strange creatures and impatient to run to them.

"Lie down," Chrissie repeated, lowering her arm with her palm outstretched.

When Floss sank down obediently, still quivering, Chrissie smiled. "Good girl." She stroked the backs of the dog's ears.

After fifteen minutes of making Floss lie and wait, watching the strange little group of drakes and generally beginning to get used to them, Chrissie took the plunge and turned the dog loose to see what she would do.

"Lie down," she called, and Floss did so immediately, eyes bright as she glanced across at her trainer before turning her attention back to the flock of Runner ducks.

"Come by," Chrissie ordered and the dog reacted at once, skirting the flock slowly and cautiously and soon moving them around the paddock with an inherent skill.

"Good girl!" Chrissie let out a sharp, two-tone whistle and patted her knee. "Come here."

Floss ran toward her, and when she reached Chrissie she rolled onto her back to get her tummy scratched. Chrissie laughed, sinking down onto her knees to do just that.

"Good, good girl," she cried. "Your owner has certainly made a good start with you."

The Runner ducks, well used to the routine of being herded around by young sheepdogs, began quacking in alarm. *That's odd*, thought Chrissie, and she looked up to see them running to the corner of the paddock. Suddenly, she became aware of a figure peering over the wall.

"What are you doing?" Will asked, and her heart sank. She really didn't have time for his stupid questions right now.

WILL SET OFF up the steep slope behind Craig Side with Max, as always now on a long leash. He had considered leaving the unruly labradoodle at home, but responsibility won out. He may have chosen the wrong dog for sheep country, but he was stuck with him now…and very fond of him.

Not having owned a dog before, Will had never really appreciated their innocent and unquestioning company. He needed that right now; it gave him comfort to know that there was always someone to listen to his woes without judgment, someone who was always there to welcome him home with no ulterior motives.

Besides, if Will didn't take Max for a walk, who knew what kind of havoc he'd wreak in the house or the yard? At least Will could keep an eye on him this way, and maybe exercise would mellow him out.

Will walked in silence, listening to the world around him as he and the big dog climbed up the slope. For Max, every rabbit hole was exciting, every fluttering bird and moving creature something to chase.

"No!" Will shouted when Max pulled at his leash, trying to race off after yet another litter of baby rabbits. When the tiny creatures ran in panic toward their burrow, Will felt a strange and slightly alien lump form in his chest. The tiny rabbits were so scared and vulnerable. How were they going to survive until adulthood?

You, Will Devlin, he told himself, *are getting soft.*

High Bracken was not very far across the fell from Craig Side, but it took almost half an hour for Will to negotiate the harsh terrain. Max didn't help, pulling and barking, but eventually they reached the meadow near the farm where she'd handed him the bill for the dead sheep. He could see the flock she'd brought down from the fell to lamb; they seemed calmer now, but they tensed up immediately when they saw Max. Will made a detour along the wall, not wanting to spook them again.

The gray stone house came into view beyond the barn, tucked into the hillside. Would she be in there? Or maybe he'd better check in the barn or the outbuildings—she had mentioned the vet coming.

Deciding he'd try the barn first, Will strode toward it, but he saw her before he even got there. That is, he heard her somewhere near the small paddock that ran alongside the looming structure. He heard another sound, too—a strange one. Did she keep ducks?

Taking a firm hold of Max's collar and

silently pleading with him to stay quiet, Will approached cautiously; the last thing he wanted was to cause any more problems for Chrissie.

For once, overcome by the unfamiliar sound, the labradoodle obliged and Will was able to peer over the drystone wall that surrounded the paddock.

Chrissie stood with her back to him. She was dressed, as usual, in blue jeans, a thick quilted jacket and brown boots; her thick, blond braid hung down almost to her waist.

Will knew he should get her attention to avoid startling her, but he paused, intrigued to hear her giving commands to the pretty little brown-and-white collie that seemed to be taking in her every sound and gesture. Slowly, it approached a flock of funny-looking waddling ducks then started to herd them across the grass. Chrissie gave a sharp whistle and the dog returned to her, flopping onto the ground for a belly rub.

"Good girl," she cried, and then she noticed him standing there. Her piercing gaze made him feel guilty and self-conscious. How did she manage that? Well, at least she couldn't laugh at what he was wearing; the country boots, moleskin trousers and tweed jacket had been highly recommended by the men's outfitters in Kendal.

"What are you doing?" he called, breaking the silence that stretched between them.

"What does it look like I'm doing?" she snapped.

He shrugged. "Well, I don't really know. I thought you trained dogs to herd sheep, not ducks."

The hint of a smile flitted across her face. "They have to start somewhere, and it gives the ducks a purpose."

"Shouldn't they be laying eggs and getting fat enough for dinner?"

"Not these ducks. They're a bit small to eat and they're drakes, so they don't lay eggs. Getting them to help with the dog training means I can justify keeping them."

"They could just be pets," Will suggested. "Odd pets, to be sure. What are they, anyway?"

The wind rose, freeing wisps of hair from Chrissie's braid to frame her face, softening its contours. She pushed it back impatiently, shaking her head. "There is no room for pets on a farm, and all the birds and animals here have to earn their keep. These ducks would have no purpose if they didn't help with training the young sheepdogs, and in return they are fed and cared for. What can I do for you, anyway? Or is this just a social visit?"

"No… Yes… I mean, I brought your check," he said, pulling it from his pocket.

As she raised her eyebrows, her hair escaped again. He liked that look. It made her seem softer, though he knew full well that she was as hard as nails.

"I'm surprised you had enough money left after you've forked out for that outfit," she said, looking him up and down. The smile in her eyes belied her stern expression.

Will gazed down in consternation, placing his palms on his chest. Was she just trying to wind him up?

"What's wrong with it? The store manager said it was about as country as you can get."

"And it is," she agreed, walking toward him. "If you're going to the races, that is. You'd fit right in in the owners' enclosure. Why don't you just wear something comfortable? Jeans, boots and a warm jacket is all you need to walk these fells."

They stood quite close, facing each other with the wall between them. He handed over the check and she inspected it carefully before pushing it into her pocket.

"There's nothing wrong with it. It certainly won't bounce."

"I'd come looking for you if it did," she said in a tone of voice that made him believe it.

Will turned to head back home without replying, not knowing how to react to her hostility. Three times he'd met her now, and each time had been the same. As soon as he thought she'd softened to him just a little, she had become sarcastic and biting. It was as if she was trying to make him feel like a fool.

And it had worked.

Perhaps she was trying to keep him at bay. But why? Well, she needn't have bothered. He didn't want friendship, and he didn't need a shepherd's help for his tourism venture, so what was the point?

"Come on, Max," he said, and the big dog bucked against his collar, taking Will by surprise.

The leash slipped out of his hand, and he tried to catch it but lost his footing and stumbled, struggling back to his feet to see Max racing for the gate into the paddock. He yelled, but the dog ran on, alight with excitement.

At first, the ducks ignored the dog barreling toward them...until Max leaped into their midst, scattering the tightly huddled group. They fled in all directions as he bounded this way and that, not knowing which fluttering bundle of feathers to chase next.

Will shouted at him, but it was Chrissie who managed to grab hold of the trailing leash. She handed it to Will, a bright spot of color on both cheeks and her blue eyes dark with anger.

"Get your dog off my land, now, and don't bring it back here again. And you'd better get it some training before it does even more damage. If any of these ducks are harmed—"

"I know," Will cut in with a weary sigh. "You'll be sending me a bill for the damage."

"Too right, I will," she responded. "To be honest, I think it's time you went back to the city. That's so obviously where you belong."

"Oh, right. I forgot." He didn't even try to keep the sarcasm out of his voice. How dare she use that high-handed manner with him?

"You hate all tourists and outsiders and you seem to think you have the right to decide who walks these fells—which are, if I remember correctly, common land. And I have grazing rights."

She glared at him. "So what if you do? You've just proved why I want to keep *townies* off these hills. Just like the rest of your kind, you are totally ignorant of life around here, and it's the land and the animals that suffer from your mistakes."

"My kind!" Will exploded. "Who do you think you are? I have as much right here as anyone, I've put money into this place and I intend to make it work for me whether you approve or not."

"What do you mean?" she asked. "What *place* have you put money into?"

His anger deflated. "Craig Side, of course. Surely you must have realized that I'm your nearest neighbor."

Chrissie seemed at a loss for words. She opened her mouth then closed it abruptly.

"Look…" He attempted a smile. "I really want to fit in here, and any plans I may have are in the very early stages. Life will be much easier if we try and get along…"

Chrissie spun on her heel, tossing her head back. "We'll see about that."

Will simmered with anger the whole way home. What right had Chrissie Marsh to talk to him like that? Okay, so Max had gotten loose and chased the stupid ducks, but it was an accident and the ducks were fine. At least he'd put her straight about his right to be here; he couldn't believe she hadn't already figured out where he was from. The best thing he could do from now on, he decided, was to stay away.

By the time he reached Craig Side, however, he had changed his tune a little. He would get some training for Max, he decided. He would prove to Chrissie Marsh that he could fit in here, no matter what she thought of him. And he wasn't about to let her spoil his plans, either. He needed the income. He was prepared to compromise a bit with the locals if necessary, but that was all.

CHAPTER EIGHT

WHEN CHRISSIE SAW something fluttering between the duck shed and the drystone wall, her heart sank. Surely the stupid dog hadn't done it again...not that it was the poor dog's fault. Will had chosen to buy an excitable dog, and it was his responsibility to teach it the difference between right and wrong. If he couldn't do it himself then he needed to get some help.

The little Runner duck lay quite still, long neck outstretched and eyes closed. The movement she'd seen was just its feathers fluttering in the breeze, giving the semblance of life. The dog must have nipped it, or perhaps it had died of shock.

For a sheep farmer in the Lakeland fells, death was an everyday occurrence, yet still she felt the pressure of tears against her eyelids. What had the poor little duck done to deserve this? Robbed of a natural life as a working drake with females at its disposal, it had found another use in helping her train the young sheepdogs. Along with the other unwanted drakes, it had become quite accustomed to being quietly herded around the paddock in exchange for food and a weatherproof shelter. And it should have been safe here. That's what upset her most.

Well, Will would pay, just like he had for the sheep, although this time she would ask for more than the duck's real value. Maybe then he'd make an effort with his crazy dog.

Determined to make Will pay his dues, she wrote out a bill and put it in her jacket pocket. She'd have to wait until she came across him again to give it to him. However, she soon forgot she was even carrying it because before she got a chance to hand it over, the lambing began.

Chrissie knew that lambs were imminent since all the ewes had been scanned and the dates were pretty accurate nowadays. She had been checking the flock regularly, ever since they came down into the low pasture, driving slowly around the meadows just as it got dark, watching for signs of a ewe in discomfort or maybe even prostrate on the ground with a head or a pair of black cloven hooves protruding, which might mean that the animal needed her help. Apart from routine visits that she paid a set fee for, she only called the vet in exceptional circumstances.

Most of the flock was grazing when she began her routine check. They looked up into the Land Rover's headlights, their eyes like bright torches in the twilight. An older, experienced ewe was the first one she saw with a lamb—a big, strong, healthy lamb, she was pleased to see. Nothing to worry about there.

After making sure the lamb had started to suckle, she drove on and was almost ready to go back to the yard when she spotted another ewe in the farthest corner of the field. Two tiny newborn twin lambs were standing beside it on wobbly legs. The ewe licked their backs, forming a bond as she nudged them toward her teats, which they both latched onto eagerly. Small though they were, they both appeared okay for now. She watched them for a little while and decided to let them be. The weather was dry and mild for the end of March—it was icy rain that caused problems—and they'd come to no harm out here with their mother. A pity, though, that there were two. On lower ground, farmers welcomed twins, but way up on the fells a single lamb had a better chance of survival.

FOR THE NEXT week or so, Chrissie was kept busy with the constant arrival of lambs. Night after night, she was up until the early hours, awakening at dawn to check the flock again.

She was proud of the fact that there had been no casualties so far, though one of the twins was having difficulties. It had been weak when it was born, and had already been getting cold when she found it the previous evening. She helped it suckle, making sure it had milk in its belly, and she kept it warm all night by the stove in the kitchen, but in the morning it was almost lifeless. Still, she had to try. Where there was life, there was hope.

Bundling the lamb up, Chrissie took it out into the semidarkness to the pen in the barn where its mother had bleated restlessly all night. She placed it carefully down on the hay and grabbed the fell sheep's thick, oily wool.

With a twist of her knee, she flipped the

ewe expertly onto its back. It lay helplessly against her, forelegs in the air, as she reached for the lamb. Its udder was bulging, she noted with satisfaction, and when she squeezed a teat, warm milk ran onto her hand. She tried to get the lamb to latch on, to no avail. Realizing it was too weak now to suckle, she eased its jaw open and squeezed the milk in drop by drop, lifting the little one's head and rubbing the underside of its throat to try and get it to swallow.

"Come on," she pleaded as she felt its first weak gulp.

After almost half an hour of effort, Chrissie moved the lamb out of harm's way and turned the ewe upright, letting her loose. Chrissie stood with her hands on the small of her back to ease the dull ache. The anxious mother went straight to her baby, letting out low bleating sounds as she licked its tightly curled coat. The lamb remained motionless, and Chrissie's heart tightened as she realized the milk hadn't helped enough.

"Come on, little one," she murmured, picking it up again. "Let's try a couple more hours in the warm."

Chrissie settled the lamb down in its box

next to the stove, then headed out to check on the lambing sheep, feed the animals and milk the two cows. Tess and Fly were at her heels, as always, but the young trainee, Floss, leaped around her in crazy circles, thrilled to be out in the open with her companions.

As she worked, Chrissie found herself questioning her lonely existence and wondering if maybe some of what Aunt Hilda had said was right. In all honesty, if Chrissie died tomorrow, who would there be to miss her? It was a sobering thought.

Her thoughts went, unbidden, to Will. The fact that he'd kept his ownership of Craig Side from her made her blood boil. Then again, had he really made a secret of it... or had she been ignoring what was right in front of her? The way he behaved irritated her, too, but if she was being honest with herself, their spats made her feel...alive. Apart from making small talk with the postman and the occasional villager, she had so little interaction with other people. So the passion he invoked in her, even though it was generally based on anger and frustration, was kind of fulfilling. And there was something about him that intrigued her. She'd never met a man like Will before.

At eight thirty, when all the jobs were finally done, Chrissie headed wearily back into the kitchen, satisfied with her evening's work and looking forward to a nice cup of tea and a sit-down. Her sense of well-being faded, though, as she checked on the lamb. Milk trickled from between its small black lips, and the life had faded from its eyes.

She placed her hand on its motionless rib cage and found the body cold and still. Her efforts hadn't been enough, and now she needed to find a "pet" lamb to replace it. The ewe had milk, and her mothering instinct was strong; she needed another lamb to care for right away, or her milk would dry up and she would be good for nothing. A ewe without lambs was not worth keeping.

Grabbing her phone, breakfast forgotten, Chrissie rang three local sheep farmers before finding an orphan lamb at Chris Bolton's farm on the other side of the village.

"Come on, girls," she called to her dogs, pulling on her jacket. They ran eagerly out behind her to jump into the back of her Land Rover, excited to be going somewhere.

As she drove along the main street in Little Dale, stopping for a duck to waddle across the road, Chrissie was reminded of the Runner duck killed by Will's dog. Well, she may have been distracted by the lambing, but he wasn't getting away with it. He needed to learn that here in the countryside, he was accountable for the actions of his crazy dog… and hopefully that would help him realize how irresponsible his plans for holiday rentals were.

Come to think of it, though, it was strange that she hadn't seen him in the past week. Maybe he'd decided to go back to the city after all, but she doubted it. During their last encounter, he'd sounded very determined to settle here. She would be glad if he was gone; he'd already caused enough problems for her. Yet, unbelievably, she realized she'd miss the way his silvery gray eyes sought to overpower her, the way they glinted with anger when their conversations got heated. The touching thing was that in an instant, that glint could disappear and reveal vulnerability. She couldn't deny that her heart rate doubled when she glimpsed that unexpected softness… She shook her head out of the clouds. If he was still around, she needed to see him so she could give him the bill. He wasn't getting away with not paying her back.

Approaching the village store, it occurred to Chrissie that she might as well stock up on groceries while she was here. She'd used the last of her coffee earlier that morning and coffee was something she definitely couldn't do without.

The shop door pinged as Chrissie walked in. She marveled at the abundance. Each shelf was crammed with goods ranging from fresh bread and basics to some exotic items that never seemed to leave the shelves, like dates in small wooden boxes with Arabic writing on the lids.

After filling her basket she waited to pay, idly glancing at the ads pinned to the notice board. There were border collie puppies for sale, as usual, and a tall pine wardrobe, badly photographed, but beneath that, in bright, eye-catching color, was a more professional-looking flyer.

COBBLE COTTAGES. Holiday lets still available. Walk the magnificent Lake

District fells by day and relax in front of a log fire at night.

Chrissie tensed as she studied the accompanying photo of a family: mum, dad, two kids and their springer spaniel walking together way up on the hills. What right did this company have to encourage people to put themselves at risk like that? And what chance did sheep farmers like herself have with that kind of advertising around? It made the Lake District look like a playground, and that could mean serious repercussions not just for those who were trying to farm on the fells but for the visitors themselves.

She hurriedly paid for her goods and left the shop, still fuming at the advertisement as she headed back to her Land Rover. Maybe there was a way to create guidelines for promoting holidays here. There must be someone she could approach about it.

Chrissie was still contemplating the problem as she nosed her cumbersome vehicle out into the street. That was when she saw Will walking along the side of the road, being pulled along as usual by an impatient

Max. Slowing to a stop, she rolled down her window.

"I see your dog is being just as obedient as ever," she remarked dryly.

"And it's your business because…?" he snapped.

"You could ask my dead duck about that."

Hot color flooded his cheeks. "What? You mean…"

Chrissie nodded, rummaging in her pocket. "'Fraid so. Here."

Will ripped open the brown envelope she handed him and studied her bill, narrowing his eyes. "Are you kidding?" he exclaimed. "Fifty pounds…for a duck?"

"For that duck, yes."

For a moment, he held her eyes with his and to her annoyance she felt her heart rate rise. "You do have to pay for your dog's mistakes, I'm afraid."

He nodded curtly. "I'll drop off a check… or cash, if you prefer it. It will probably be tomorrow."

"Thanks," she said. "Oh, and perhaps you'd better leave your out-of-control dog at home."

"He's just young and exuberant," objected Will. "He needs some training, that's all."

Chrissie nodded. "Well, that's true. A different breed of dog might have been a good idea, of course… Labradoodles are renowned for being a bit mad." The advertisement popped into her head again, and her irritation surged. "Maybe you'd be having an easier time if you'd taken your environment into account before buying a farm here."

"I'm sticking around for some time yet," Will remarked dryly. "And I do intend to learn about life here, you'll see." In one of his sudden mood changes, he grinned. "You never know, I may even eventually get some sheep."

Chrissie rolled her eyes in mock horror. "Poor sheep," she called, putting her foot on the gas. No matter how much he managed to annoy her, she thought, as she drove off down the village street, he always seemed to make her smile.

IT WAS DAWN when Will woke the next morning, just as the first pale rays sneaked over the dark mass of the fell. He lay for a while watching the light grow brighter as nature greeted the day. At night, there was another world, a world where the familiar became unfamiliar, where creatures padded secretly around in the darkness, living their lives without sun. He thought about the city at night, where anything could happen, loud and vibrant and dangerous, and much brighter than daytime. He used to love the city at night.

In one smooth movement, Will slid from the warmth of his bed and went to the window to peer out onto the fell. It looked so fresh and vital now that spring was here. Green shoots were everywhere, brightening the tips of the stunted trees and low, thorny bushes, finding their way through the dead brown bracken and giving it new life. That was why he had come to love it here, he realized; everything was so real and alive, ruled by natural cycles and laws. Life out here was cruel sometimes and even savage, but without the corruption that lurked in the city.

As Will pulled on his socks, Max nudged and licked him, eager to go out.

"In a minute," Will said, turning his face away from the dog's exuberant kisses. Max ran out of the room, long tail waving, and headed down the stairs with a *thump, thump, thump*. He'd better find the labradoodle a trainer soon, Will thought, before he did even more damage.

He smiled to himself. The whole situation was like a ridiculous farce, a comedy of errors. How could poor, daft, friendly Max—who wouldn't deliberately hurt a fly—have managed to cause so much trouble? First the poor sheep that fell over the cliff, and now he had contributed to the death of a Runner duck. Will dug the bill Chrissie had given him out of yesterday's pants pocket. How could she ask fifty pounds for a duck?

Well, she'd get her money, and then he'd hire the best dog trainer there was, no matter what the cost, and walk Max across the fell when Miss frosty Autumn was herding her sheep. He couldn't wait to watch her eat her words. Unfortunately, though, he had to go pay her yet again for Max's misdeeds. At least it would be over with soon.

Chrissie was still on his mind as he took Max for a quick walk up the fell. The way she'd glared at him when she ranted about her sheep—not to mention the ducks—had been fueled by her passion for her animals, and he liked that.

Yesterday, though, when she'd handed

him the new bill, her tone had been cold and hard, her blue eyes holding no reflection of the fire he'd seen in them before. Like the first time he ever saw her, way up on the fell, defending her sheep.

She had been ablaze with anger that day, but although she'd made him feel stupid and out of place, he'd felt a trickle of admiration for her passion. Their backgrounds couldn't be more different and they didn't really have much in common, aside from loving this place in their own ways. Still, there was something about her that drew him in. He didn't want to feel that way and he certainly hadn't expected to, but he couldn't control it. Perhaps he should just try and avoid her altogether. He'd give her the check, he decided, and then stay well away. He needed to stay focused on his plans, and getting into spats with someone he was never going to see eye to eye with was a waste of time and energy.

Although it was spring, the mornings were still nippy, and Will was grateful to step back into the warmth of the kitchen. He'd go over to High Bracken before the builders arrived, he decided; he couldn't face all that knocking and banging, and no doubt Jim would come looking for him as soon as they got here, or Roger Simmons would stop by with the revised plans.

He'd felt a real surge of interest in the holiday rentals when he'd talked to Roger about his ideas. The thought of people coming here to experience how things used to be gave the project a whole new, refreshing slant. The age-old way of life in the Lake District should never be forgotten, but the area needed visitors to spend their money here and this was one way to combine the two goals. All he needed to do was convince the locals, like Chrissie Marsh. Sure, he'd gotten off to an awkward start here, but surely she'd come around when he explained his intent. She might not think so, but there were some things he did understand about this place and its traditions.

First, though, he needed to take her that check.

The phone rang just as Will was pulling out of the yard. He answered without checking the caller ID, immediately wishing he'd screened it when Roy Wallis's voice came out over the Bluetooth sound system. He responded before Roy could even ask the question. "I am not doing it."

There was audible, lengthy silence. "All I want," Roy began, obviously straining to remain patient, "is for you to talk to Peter, the lawyer who has taken over from you… You know, give him a few tips on how to deal with people like the McBrides."

"Don't tell me—he's having trouble with Ezra?" Will felt immense relief that this was no longer his problem.

"Just a few words on the phone," Roy pleaded. He was not one to beg, so he must be desperate. "Or a meeting here, perhaps. You owe us that, at least."

Will's every instinct screamed at him to refuse. He couldn't afford to go down that dark road again—there were too many gruesome memories. He'd lost himself once already, and he'd barely recovered. He wasn't sure he could do it a second time.

"Please, Will. Just a few questions, that's all. Give him the lay of the land, so to speak."

Will listened to the plea in Roy's voice, remembering all the help and support his ex-boss had given him throughout his career, and in a moment of weakness he found himself agreeing to a meeting. Even as the words left his lips, something tightened inside him, something he thought he had overcome. It threatened his peace of mind. "Just twenty minutes or so, though," he added. "I'll be there before lunch."

With a heavy sigh he turned his big vehicle around and drove back to Craig Side. If he was going to do this then he needed to feel right and that meant getting changed into the clothes that made him look strong and confident. One thing was for sure: this was going to be the first and last time they'd ever persuade him to come back, even fleetingly.

As he searched in his closet for a suitably expensive suit, it occurred to him that Chrissie did not need outward apparel to give her a facade of strength. She was strong from the core, facing adversities from bad weather to her animals' deaths on a regular basis. She would never allow money and power to tempt her away from what she felt was right.

He, on the other hand, had allowed money and power to rule his world for the last ten years, the power of words and the buzz of success that followed his victories...until he'd come to realize that they weren't really victories after all, and money wasn't everything. He did feel a sense of responsibility toward Roy, however, and though he didn't regret leaving Marcus Finch, he could see now that his sudden departure had been unfair. Early in his career, his boss had believed in him, mentored him, even when things went wrong. He owed Roy, so he'd agreed to this meeting. But that didn't mean he was looking forward to it.

Glancing critically in the mirror, he saw his old self, smart and distinguished; a far cry from the man he was now...the man who always seemed to be dressed in the wrong clothes and was the laughingstock of the local shepherdess. He gritted his teeth, drawing his mouth into a thin line. He would get through today, and then he would prove to her that he really could fit in here. Because he didn't intend to go anywhere else anytime soon.

CHAPTER NINE

THE MEETING WAS just as Will expected it to be. The familiar, imposing classical board-room with oak-paneled walls, the impeccably-dressed secretaries with perfect hair and plastic smiles. They were a complete contrast to Chrissie with her natural, sun-kissed skin and practical clothes.

He was annoyed when Ezra McBride turned up at what was supposed to have been a private meeting, brash and loud with heavy gold chains that declared his wealth in vulgar fashion. He held out his broad hand, but Will declined it.

"Will...I need you on this case," Ezra insisted. "Just name your price."

"I don't have a price anymore," he responded, his tone cool and firm. "I don't work with Marcus Finch now, and I don't intend to take on any more cases...whatever they are."

Ezra's face hardened. "I don't think you understand," he said.

Refusing to feel threatened, Will stared him straight in the eye. "Oh, I understand perfectly. I think it's you who doesn't understand." He turned to Roy Wallis. "And as for you…"

His former boss had the grace to drop his gaze to the floor as Will stared at him accusingly. "I believe that I have been brought here on a false pretext."

"No…it's not what you think," Roy said. "I didn't know Ezra was going to be here."

"Look…" Ezra's voice took on a sinister tone. "If you don't do this—"

"Are you threatening me?" Will growled. "If you want to go down that route then I have an awful lot of ammunition to fire back at you."

Ezra's expression turned shifty. "You wouldn't dare."

"Try me."

The criminal turned on his heel. "You haven't heard the last of this."

When the door banged behind him, Roy let out a sigh of relief. "You see how it is? We need you to deal with clients like him."

"No." Will shook his head. "Because you don't *need* to have clients like him. What you really need is to change the way you do things around here. Just because this company has a reputation for successfully defending hardened criminals doesn't mean it has to keep on doing it."

"Then come back, Will. I do agree that we need change around here, but we also need you to help motivate that change. You're not a country kind of person anyway—*this* is what you love. The courtroom, the challenges, the success. We can have that success with different types of clients. *You* can have it. You miss it, Will. Go on, tell me you don't."

"I don't miss meeting people like Ezra, criminals who have no scruples and think they're above the law. They *are* above the law, with lawyers like I used to be to help them. Can't you see, Roy? That's why I left. I didn't have a breakdown, I just got sickened by the whole sordid business."

"Then come back and help turn things around," Roy pleaded. "Make yourself proud of being a lawyer again... Prove yourself."

Will hesitated and, noting that hesitation, Roy smiled. "You know it makes sense."

"No…" Will shook his head firmly, convincing himself as much as Roy. "It doesn't make sense. I'm done with law."

"We'll see," Roy said, shaking his hand. "At least think about it."

Driving home, Will felt a rush of elation. In the back of his mind, he'd felt guilty about just running away from a situation he didn't like, abandoning his responsibilities because he couldn't cope with what they were. But now, having been given the opportunity to face up to Ezra McBride, he felt absolved of the guilt that had lingered alongside the relief his decision had given him. He'd taken a leaf from Chrissie's book and stood his ground, going back to Marcus Finch to stand tall and have his say. The surprise was that Roy had kind of agreed with him. There was even a small part of Will that had considered Roy's offer. But the satisfaction he'd once felt from winning cases was nothing compared to the freedom he now felt, the freedom to enjoy his new life…as long as he could make a go of it. He had a new future to build in Little Dale, and he planned to succeed at all costs.

AT HIGH BRACKEN, Chrissie was struggling to bond the ewe to the orphan she'd picked up from Chris Bolton.

The sheep's refusal to take the lamb was a common enough problem, of course, but this ewe was being particularly stubborn, pushing the tiny lamb away every time it tried to feed just because the scent wasn't right. She had milk and a mothering instinct, she just needed to believe that the orphan was really hers. That was essential in order for her to have a purpose and stay here with the flock. Chrissie had penned them up together and milked the ewe a few times, feeding the lamb from a bottle to get its adoptive mother's milk through the little creature's system. That usually worked. Not this time, though. The ewe just butted the poor lamb away every time it tried to suckle.

In desperation, Chrissie went for the age-old remedy of skinning the dead lamb to make a kind of coat for its replacement. She placed the orphan back in the pen and watched closely, holding her breath as the ewe sniffed her surrogate offspring. Suddenly, she made a snuffling, bleating noise, then nibbled and licked the lamb's back, accepting its smell. When the little one took a firm hold of the ewe's teat and started to suckle, Chrissie let out a sigh of relief. She stood there a few minutes longer, just to be sure.

The sun was sinking when Chrissie finally left the lamb with its new mother. It was almost time to check the lambing sheep, but first she needed a hot drink and a sandwich.

When she heard a vehicle approaching, her heart sank. Who could it be at this time of day? She was too tired to make small talk.

When she recognized Will's four-by-four, something leaped in her chest...much to her annoyance. She clamped down on her reaction, setting her lips into a tight line. "Oh... it's you," she said, as Will pulled up beside her and rolled down his window.

"Don't look too pleased to see me," he remarked dryly, opening the door and climbing out. "I've only come to bring you some money. Do you have a pen on you, by the way? I've forgotten mine."

He waved his checkbook in her face, and Chrissie sighed. "You'd better come to the house. I'll get you one there."

She walked just ahead of him to the back

door, acutely aware of his tall frame right behind her. When she stepped into the cozy warmth of the kitchen, instead of staying on the step he followed her inside, standing too close for comfort.

"I don't know why you're so annoyed with me," he said, "when I come bearing gifts."

"Paying for your mistakes is hardly bearing gifts," Chrissie said, glancing up from the drawer where she was rummaging for a pen. "I'm in a rush, that's all. I still have the lambing sheep to check and I need food and a coffee first… I haven't stopped all day."

Will stepped past her and reached for the kettle. "Well, then, I'll make the coffee while you look for the pen. And technically it wasn't my mistake—it was Max's."

Chrissie glared at him. "Your dog's mistake *is* your mistake," she said. "You have to take total responsibility for anything your dog might do."

Ignoring her, Will spooned instant coffee into two mugs, poured in boiling water and opened the fridge. "You do take milk, I presume? Sugar?"

"I don't remember offering you anything." Putting down the milk jug he stood tall, returning her cool gaze. "Listen," he began. "I really am sorry about both the sheep and the duck, and I don't blame you for being mad at me. I know I haven't quite gotten used to this country thing yet, but I do want to try and fit in here."

For a moment, his eyes met hers, and a heavy pulse began to beat in her throat. He seemed so much taller here in her kitchen, and he was standing so close that she could feel his heat.

Despite her discomfort, Chrissie couldn't stop a smile from turning up the corners of her lips. "Well, you won't fit in around here dressed like that," she said, raising her eyebrows at his expensive suit and shiny black shoes. "Don't you ever get it right?"

"For your information, I happen to be dressed like this because I'm a lawyer. Or, at least, I was. I'm recently…retired. I've just been to the city to finish up some…stuff."

"Bit young to retire, aren't you?" Chrissie asked, reaching across to finish pouring the coffees. "What happened there?"

"You really don't want to know," Will replied, writing out the check. "But I'm not retired, because I'm about to embark on a new career…in tourism." He handed it over with a flourish. "At least you can't say I don't pay my dues."

"You do know how I feel about tourists?" Chrissie said bluntly.

Will nodded. "Since you have mentioned it before, several times, I reckon I've got a pretty good idea. But you don't need to worry—none of my plans are final yet… Who knows what will happen. Take the money, with my apologies. I really am sorry for all the trouble my ignorance has caused."

Chrissie tucked the check in her pocket and passed him a mug. Perhaps he really was sorry. "Okay," she said, smiling. "Truce. We got off to a bad start. Well, a couple of bad starts, actually, so let's just start all over again. Drink your coffee and then I must go and check the sheep."

"Thanks," he said, taking a sip. "Are you actually going to go around the field now? It's almost dark."

"That's exactly when sheep tend to lamb," Chrissie explained.

"Then I'll come and help you," he said.

He looked as surprised by his offer as she was. Well, he had seemed so earnest about fitting in a moment ago. She would show him what country life was really like. "You're hardly dressed for it, but I do believe there's a big old jacket in the cupboard. I'll go and get it for you."

"I mean, if you'd rather go on your own..." he tried.

Chrissie wasn't going to let him off the hook. "I could use the company, actually." She drained her mug. "Come on, there's no time to lose. Sometimes we can get eight or ten lambs a night."

Will seemed even more uncomfortable when she brought him the coat.

"Um...what exactly is it that we'll be doing?" he asked cautiously.

"Help the lambing sheep, like I said." She headed toward the door.

"You mean actually help the sheep give birth?" he spluttered.

Chrissie turned, wondering if it would be a mistake to bring him along, after all. "Oh, yes. And if they're having trouble or the lambs are weak we have to bring them into the barn. So are you coming or not?"

Will nodded, though he was pale, and Chrissie hid her smile as she stepped out into the twilight.

WILL FOLLOWED CHRISSIE across the yard, trying to fasten the waxed jacket she'd lent him. The arms were too short and it was tight across his chest, but at least it would keep out the wind. When she walked right past her Land Rover, he caught up to her.

"I thought that we were going to drive."

"I'm having trouble with its clutch," she explained. "I haven't had time to take it into the garage, and besides, the hillside gets quite steep. We're better with the tractor."

"Tractor," he repeated, and he could swear he saw Chrissie smile in the semidarkness.

"It has good lights and it's very reliable," she told him, climbing up into an elderly red Massey Ferguson with a trailer attached. "Do you want to sit in the cab? It's not that comfortable, but at least you'll be out of the wind."

"What is the alternative?" Will asked uncertainly.

"Well, you could just climb into the trailer."

Will responded by climbing awkwardly into the cramped cab, folding his tall frame in next to Chrissie.

"All you have to do is keep your eyes peeled for a sheep in trouble," she told him.

"It might just look uncomfortable, usually in the shelter of a wall or bush, or it could have the lamb's feet or even head out. Usually they manage to lamb by themselves, but sometimes they need a pull…and then we have to make sure that the lamb, or lambs, have suckled."

As the tractor rumbled into life, Will felt about as far out of his comfort zone as it was possible to be. All her talk about pulling lambs out and helping them suckle was making him panic. Was she just winding him up or was she serious? Surely she would call a vet if a sheep had a problem. Yes, she was just having him on. He grew calmer. If she needed him to help get a sheep into the trailer to take back to the barn to see the vet then he supposed he could manage that.

"Gate, please," Chrissie said, and Will struggled out of the cab to open it. "And don't forget to shut it behind us," she reminded him. He nodded, turning his face away from the drizzling rain that was being buffeted around by the rising wind.

As Chrissie drove slowly around the first meadow, Will saw dozens of sheep in the tractor headlights. Most were huddled together in the shelter of the drystone walls, but through the darkness he made out one figure all alone in a corner. "Over there," he called in excitement. "There's a sheep on its own over there!"

Chrissie maneuvered the cumbersome vehicle so they could see the sheep in the headlights. It was standing with its head down, and even Will could see that it wasn't happy. As they walked quietly toward it, he was horrified to see a black head protruding from beneath its tail.

"Is that a bad sign?" he murmured in Chrissie's ear.

"If the lamb's front legs are back, it could be," she said, taking hold of the wool around the ewe's throat. Will hung back, not knowing what to do.

"Give me a hand, then," she said. "You hold her against the wall, and I'll take a look."

The sheep was easier to control than he expected, almost as if she knew they were trying to help.

"She's been struggling for a while," said Chrissie, feeling inside the ewe to see how its lamb was lying. She cursed under her breath. "The forelegs are back."

Will fumbled for his phone with one hand while holding the ewe firmly against the wall with the other. "What's the vet's number?" he asked. "I'll ring him for you."

"Vet!" He was shocked to hear a smile in her voice. "If I called a vet for every problem, I'd be losing money by the day. I just have to try and push the lamb back a bit to release the legs. As long as it hasn't been like this for too long, there's a chance it will be okay."

Will watched in awe as she closed her eyes to concentrate on what she was feeling. Her face was tense with effort, wet and shiny with the rain that was battering against it.

"Shouldn't we take them back to the barn?" he suggested, but she shook her head.

"No time. We may be too late as it is."

When he saw two tiny pointed front feet appear, Will sighed with relief. With a slurping noise, the yellow lamb slid out onto the ground. Chrissie pulled it around to its mother's nose, clearing the mucous from its nostrils and rubbing its tiny chest, willing it to breathe while the ewe began licking its back and head. The tiny lamb shook itself, trying to stand within minutes of birth, wanting to suckle.

"We'd better make sure it gets a good feed," said Chrissie, deftly flipping the sheep over so that its back was against her knees. "It's so important that lambs get the colostrum."

"Colostrum?" Will repeated. It was as if Chrissie was speaking a foreign language.

"The first milk. It's full of antibodies from the mother, to help stop any infection before the lamb develops its own immune system."

Reaching for a teat, she squeezed out some milk. "You see," she said, leaning down to try and persuade the lamb to latch on to its mother. When it began to suckle voraciously, she smiled, catching Will's eye. Her joy was contagious, and he smiled back.

"So it's going to be okay?"

Chrissie nodded. "I hope so."

She stood up and released the ewe, stepping back to leave the lamb with its mother. For a few minutes, they watched them bond.

"Do you know," she said after a while, "I must have seen this well over a thousand times, but it never fails to move me."

"Well, this is the first time for me and it seems like a miracle," Will said.

"It is," she agreed. "Life's miracle."

The lamb was standing strongly on its legs, and Chrissie began to move away. "Come on... I think it'll be fine now. The rain seems to be letting up, too. We'll stop by again once we've checked the rest of the flock, and if it's still okay then I'll be back to take a look first thing in the morning."

"And that's it?" asked Will. "They'll just stay here out in the open?"

Chrissie nodded. "If it was a very wet or cold night, or if the lamb seemed weak I'd take them in, but it's a big, fine, single lamb. These fell sheep are tough, you know."

In the next half hour they found two more newborn single lambs, which were strong and healthy, and a set of sickly twins.

"We'd better take them into the warm," Chrissie said. "Just to keep an eye on them and make sure that they're getting enough milk."

"And how are we supposed to do that?" asked Will.

"I'll put the ramp on the trailer down while you keep the ewe here, and then we'll just have to persuade her to walk in. It's usually quite easy because they tend to follow their lambs."

Will's anxiety rose at the idea of seeing to the sheep on his own, but he had no other choice but to deal with it. As Chrissie disappeared into the darkness, the fell felt like the loneliest place in the world. Never had he been so out of his comfort zone. To his relief she was back in minutes.

"Right, then," she said, lifting the lambs by their back legs and letting their mother get their scent before walking up the trailer ramp. "You help guide her."

Will did as Chrissie asked. How had he managed to get himself into this situation. His shoes were wet and he had mud all over his trousers, but seeing the ewe with her newborn lambs was an honest and real experience, a lifetime away from the boardroom where he'd been just that afternoon.

"True mothering instinct," he cried as the sheep bravely followed her lambs up the ramp, her love for them much stronger than her fear for herself.

"Strongest instinct in the world," agreed Chrissie, latching the trailer shut. The contours of her face seemed softer as she looked over at the ewe and her lambs. It held warmth and caring, and he found himself wondering why she was on her own. It seemed kind of sad that someone who had so much tenderness and care to give only had animals, and not other people, to share it with.

"Come on," she said. "Let's get them home."

After a brief detour to check on the single lamb they'd helped first—who was still suckling happily—they headed back to the farm. The darkness was total, soft and black, their route picked out by the yellow lights of the elderly tractor, and it was starting to drizzle again.

He glanced at Chrissie, who was concentrating on driving, her chin jutting forward as she peered out into the night. A strand of hair had escaped and was stuck against her cheek. Will almost reached over to push it back, but quickly withdrew his hand. He felt so close to her after all they'd been through tonight, yet in truth, he hardly knew her. He sat back to take stock. He was out here in the middle of nowhere with someone he'd only recently met, soaked, cold to the core and way out of his comfort zone. And yet he felt…alive. He'd achieved a lot in his career, and before things went wrong he'd been proud of himself. But he'd never felt this type of satisfaction before. This was life-and-death stuff, real and raw. And Chrissie took it all in stride.

Chrissie parked the tractor beside the barn and cut the engine; it rumbled into silence and she climbed out.

"If you let the ramp down I'll open the doors and we'll get them into a pen," she said. "Then we can go back to the house. I guess I owe you another coffee."

It occurred to Will that she was assuming he was going to stay and help. Funnily enough, he realized that he wanted to.

The barn was barely lit by the few warm yellow lights that glowed down from its lofty ceiling. Will breathed in the unfamiliar aromas that mingled together, the sweetness of meadow hay and the strong smell of sheep, the delicious aroma of feed and something else, something he couldn't identify.

Chrissie persuaded the ewe to follow her and the lambs to a row of pens. "You close the gate as soon as they're in, and then we can make sure the lambs have suckled," she said to Will.

He did exactly that, feeling a lifetime away from his previous life in the city and the courtroom.

"You're a natural," she declared, smiling at him as he pushed the ewe in through the gate and fastened it. Their eyes met and held. She looked so tough and yet so vulnerable that for a moment Will felt like taking her in his arms and holding her tight. He took a step toward her but stopped.

"You must be tired," he said. It wasn't like him to have such impulsive notions.

Chrissie nodded. "I'm always tired at this time of year. The night and the day seem to fade into one with catnaps in between."

"Should we go and get that coffee, then?"

She laughed, her face glowing in the soft light. "Good idea. I just need to see to the or-phan and its adoptive mother. Oh, and check on all the other animals."

"What can I do?" he asked.

"Please, you've already done so much."

"I've enjoyed it," he said with a broad

smile, pushing back a lock of damp hair from his face. "In a strange kind of way."

When Chrissie motioned for him to follow her, he didn't hesitate. "I'll see to the other animals then," she said. "Perhaps you could go and make sure that the ewe is still letting her adopted lamb suckle and check that the last lot are settling in. Oh, yes, and there's an orphan to feed, too. Fortunately it's a big, strong lamb, but his mother died just this morning. I'll bring a bottle back with me."

The gratification he felt at being given his own tasks surprised him almost as much as the casual way she announced the ewe's death. "That's terrible," he said.

Chrissie shrugged. "It happens. There are always farmers looking for orphans, though, so he'll soon have a new home. Make sure that those new lambs are warmed up and that they're suckling—I won't be long."

Will watched her walk away, her strides confident and sure. Was there any situation that might faze her? he thought, with a surge of admiration.

Will was so focused on the lambs that he didn't notice Chrissie standing beside him until she cleared her throat. He looked up to see her watching him with a thoughtful frown. "So, what kind of lawyer are you, anyway?" she asked, totally out of the blue.

"I *was* a criminal lawyer…defense," he told her, wondering why they were standing in her barn, cold and wet and tired, talking about him. "But that's all in the past—another life. These two seem fine…is there anything else I can do to help? I really don't mind."

"Okay, then," she said, handing him a bottle. It warmed his hand, reminding him of just how cold he was everywhere else. "You can feed the lamb…unless you want to get going?"

"No," Will said quickly. "I'd like to. You'll have to show me how, though." She bent toward the little lamb, and he noticed her hair had come loose; it cascaded down her back and over her shoulders, shorter wisps framing her face and emphasizing her brilliant blue eyes. Her skin glowed with health, he noted, but how could she be suntanned when it was still winter?

"Have you been on holiday?" he asked on impulse, and she burst out laughing.

"A holiday—what's that? Now who's asking daft questions? Here we are, soaked and exhausted and asking each other ridiculous things. Come on, let's get the lamb fed and then I'll make you that coffee."

CHAPTER TEN

CHRISSIE FELT SELF-CONSCIOUS as she filled the kettle at the sink, deliberately taking her time. Something had changed as she and Will worked together in the barn.

In fact, there had been a kind of camaraderie between them while they fed the "pet" lamb and checked on all the other animals. Will had been determined to bottlefeed the lamb himself, and she'd laughed with him at his first awkward attempts. Once he got the hang of it, he'd seemed quite comfortable, kneeling on the floor in her dad's old jacket. Here, though, in her kitchen, cleaned up and imposing, he seemed very much the lawyer again.

She brewed a pot of coffee in silence, and when she sat down her tongue felt as if it was stuck to the roof of her mouth. Conversation evaded her, and to fill the void she busied herself pouring two mugs and handing him one. It was Will who eventually broke the silence.

"So what do you do for fun around here?" he asked with genuine interest.

An unexpected giggle fought its way out of her. "You just did it."

"What!" He put down his drink with a thud. "You mean messing around with sheep in the cold and dark...that's your idea of fun?"

She shrugged. "I suppose it's not exactly fun—more like fulfillment—but I enjoy it. Why, what's your idea of fun?"

A shadow fell across Will's face and his silver-gray eyes seemed to turn a shade darker. "To be honest, work was always my main priority. I used to get such a buzz from it that I wasn't really interested in much else."

Chrissie stared at him for a moment, softening to him as she sensed his vulnerability. "So why did you leave?" she asked quietly.

His answer came from the heart. "I suppose I woke up."

He looked at her and she held his gaze, all awkwardness forgotten, waiting for him to tell her more, knowing that he wanted to. He took a gulp of his coffee.

"I was a sharp young lawyer, keen and ruthless, and the firm I worked for, Marcus Finch, was at the top of its game. They gave me opportunities, spotted my strengths and pushed me in the direction of being a defense lawyer. It was the words I loved, the power to change lives by saying just the right things. I gained a reputation for handling difficult cases."

"What kind of cases?" she asked, intrigued.

He hesitated, gripping his mug with both hands. "At first it was things like robbery and arson."

"And you defended the criminals?"

"Yes, that's what defense lawyers do… someone has to. Later, though, as my reputation grew, I was asked to handle more hardcore cases—armed robbery…even murder. I was good at it and at first I was proud of my success. That was all I cared about for a while—winning—and I didn't question the morality of my work until later."

"So what changed?"

"I think I did. The cases got worse…worse than you can imagine. You would never believe how much corruption and brutality there is in the world. I was in the middle of a really huge case, and as I listened to the evidence I realized I didn't want to be involved anymore. I couldn't. So I walked out. I didn't want that life anymore. I was just sickened by the whole thing."

"And your bosses, what did they say?"

"It was more the clients than my bosses," he explained. "We were involved with some serious mob leaders, powerful and cruel men who'd stop at nothing. They paid a lot of money to have me defend them."

"And when you refused?"

"When I refused to finish the case, they threatened me. So Marcus Finch made a statement to say that I was ill and incapable of continuing with the current case or any new ones in the foreseeable future. They said I had a breakdown."

"And were you? Ill, I mean."

Will ran his hand through his hair, holding his fingers for a second against his scalp. "Maybe I was," he admitted. "All I knew, though, was that there was no way I could go on. And so I came here, hoping things would be a bit more normal…" He smiled suddenly. "Not that I think it is very normal around here after tonight."

"It's normal to me," said Chrissie. "And necessary and natural. What can be more normal than births and deaths and all that goes in between? Life up here may be tough, but it's real and rewarding." She caught his eye. "And there's no greed and corruption..."

Will sighed. "It definitely is a whole world away from all that," he agreed.

"So will you be staying at Craig Side for a while, do you think, or is it just an investment?"

Will hesitated, apparently surprised by the question. "I'd like to stay," he said. "For a while, at least. I like the way of life here, and when my holiday rentals are up and running, hopefully I'll have a decent income."

Something cold trickled down Chrissie's spine. After the way he'd helped her with the sheep, she'd almost forgotten the shadow that loomed between them. "Oh." Her tone was sharp. "So you do still intend to change the place into a tourist destination?"

He shrugged. "Hopefully, but you don't need to worry—they'll be tastefully done. You know, authentic, I suppose you'd call it."

"It's not the decor that's the problem though, is it?" she said. "It's the people the rentals attract, the people who wander the fells doing all kinds of damage."

"By 'them' I suppose you mean me," Will remarked dryly. His manner had changed, Chrissie noted. Hardened. Once again he was the hotshot lawyer with no trace of the man she had just been talking to. It made her uneasy, his sudden ability to change faces. Made her wonder, *Who is the real Will Devlin*? And could she trust him?

She turned away, plunging her hands into the warm, soapy water in the sink, pretending to wash the dishes.

She sensed him step up behind her, so close she could feel his breath on the back of her neck. For a moment, she froze, and then she spun to face him, suds flying everywhere, her blue eyes blazing. "Of course, you'll have to *try* and get planning permission," she said, hiding her vulnerability behind anger.

Will just smiled. "Don't worry about something that hasn't even happened yet," he said softly, taking her chin between his thumb and forefinger and tilting her face up to his. His eyes, gray now rather than silver, seemed to smolder as they held hers, and Chrissie couldn't—didn't want to— look away. Slowly, he leaned down to place his lips on hers. They were warm and soft and unexpectedly tender. Despite her reservations, Chrissie felt herself respond, her lips trembling beneath his…until common sense kicked in. This was the man whose very presence threatened her way of life.

She pulled away, hot color flooding her cheeks. "I think it's time you left," she said, stepping back.

He studied her with an amused smile. "Why? Afraid of your own response, are you?"

"Of course not," she snapped. "It was just a kiss."

He stared at her for a moment longer. "Are you sure about that?"

She shivered. He was right about her fear.

He turned and walked out the door, allowing it to bang shut behind him. Her fingers lingered where his lips had touched hers. As his vehicle roared out of the yard she felt a sudden sense of loss for the connection they'd had…the camaraderie they'd shared when he helped her with the sheep. Will Devlin was dangerous, a man of many faces, and she must never forget about his plans for Craig Side. She would fight them tooth and nail if she had to.

If he believed that he was going to get approval for rentals this far up, he was in for a fight. There was no way she was letting strangers wander around her land. She couldn't stop them from walking on the fells, but the farther away they were from High Bracken, the less likely they would be to interfere with her sheep. And if he thought that one kiss was going to change her mind then he was sadly mistaken. Tomorrow, she decided, she would go and see Tom Farrah, the local councillor, and make an objection to Will's plans.

Anyway, she told herself, she had other things to think about right now. Floss was still in the barn; she'd go get her and check on the sheep again at the same time. The sickly twins could still need some attention, and she might even have to bring them inside to warm up. There was work to do, and she couldn't afford to spend her energy worrying about a man.

WILL DROVE TOO FAST down the narrow lane from High Bracken. Was he angry at the way she'd reacted, or disappointed at how their pleasant evening had ended? And how could he even think of running around in the dark and the rain helping ewes give birth as a pleasant evening, anyway? Six months ago he would have called it hell. Tonight, though, despite his disagreement with Chrissie, he had relished the experience. It was real and honest and rewarding. Just like she'd said.

He tried to process the evening and the way it had ended. He was good at that, good at getting to the truth…or twisting it to suit himself. He shook that thought aside. All that was behind him. He really was after the truth now. Unbelievably, he had enjoyed Chrissie's company, even though he regretted revealing so much of himself to her.

When they'd had the disagreement about his plans for Craig Side, the fire in her eyes had been so appealing that he hadn't been able to resist kissing her. He'd never met a woman like her before. He prided himself on controlling his life and his emotions. Chrissie Marsh seemed to be making him lose his hold on both. She wanted to oppose his plans for Craig Side, yet he wanted to kiss her? *Had* kissed her? What was going on with him?

It wasn't until he was halfway home that he heard the whining. He gradually became aware of the soft, gentle sound and slowed his car. Was it the radio? He turned down the music, but the sound was still there... and then he felt something against his cheek, something warm and wet. Surprise made him stand on the brakes, and he braced himself as the big vehicle slithered to a halt. Something hurtled past him from the back-seat...

It was a little black-and-tan collie, and she scrambled onto the passenger seat, seemingly unharmed. She stared up at him, wagging her plumed tail.

"Now, how did you get in here?" he asked. It was the sheepdog Chrissie was training. She wriggled forward, standing on her hind legs to lick his face, and he stroked her pretty head. Well, this was awkward. He was going to have to take her back, and he dreaded having to see Chrissie again so soon, especially after the kiss.

Trouble was, he had made a kind of statement with his dramatic exit, and now he was going to have to go crawling back like an idiot. How was it that Chrissie Marsh had managed to get so far under his skin in such a short time?

THE NIGHT WAS BLACK when Chrissie stepped into the yard, and she wrapped her jacket more tightly around her to fend off the wind that was whipping down from the fell. The barn door rattled and banged as she struggled to open it; she shut it behind her with relief, glad she'd left the lights on.

"Floss," she called, surprised that the little collie wasn't barking for attention. "Hey, girl, aren't you pleased to see me?"

When she peered over into the dog's pen her heart turned cold. Where was she? She'd left Tess and Fly in the house, so Floss wasn't with them. She must have managed to jump out when they were seeing to the sheep earlier. What if she had escaped up the fell? That could be catastrophic on a night like this.

She went back into the yard. "Floss," she yelled again, but the wind ripped her voice away.

When the bright headlights appeared around the corner she ran toward them with no thought of being afraid of who it might be at this time of night. All she cared about was finding the missing dog. The vehicle door opened, and annoyingly, her heart started pounding. What to say to him?

"Have you lost something?" Will's voice was deep, almost jovial.

"Er…no," she began. "I mean…yes, I can't find Floss."

He let out a low whistle and the little black-and-tan sheepdog jumped out of the car. "Somehow she must have managed to get into my Range Rover," he said. "Gave me a shock, I must say, when she started whining."

Chrissie crouched down to make a fuss of the dog, hiding her embarrassment in Floss's soft, fluffy coat. "Thanks," she mumbled, standing up.

Will was staring at her through the darkness, his silvery gray eyes sparkling in the light filtering out from the barn. The wind seemed to have dropped as quickly as it had started.

"Right," she said, hoping he wouldn't be able to see her blush. "I guess I should say thanks, but maybe if you'd noticed her before you set off then I wouldn't have needed to worry." It was a weak attempt to regain the upper hand, and she knew it.

"Okay…" He sighed, rolling his eyes. "I get that you're annoyed about the kiss."

"Annoyed isn't even halfway there."

"I did it without thinking. Don't read so much into it."

"So, you aren't sorry?"

"Why should I be?"

"Oh, I see. I suppose in your world you're used to kissing glamorous women who swoon in gratitude. Well, I am not some glamorous woman who…who…"

He smiled. "And obviously *not* swooning in gratitude. How are the sheep, by the way?"

Confused by his change of tack, she stood up straighter and flung her braid over her shoulder. "Thanks for bringing Floss back, but I need to get on." She started to turn toward the house.

For a moment he seemed to be considering a response, but he remained silent. She strode away with the dog at her heels, her head held high.

"I'm sorry," he called, but she didn't look

back, going into the house and letting the door bang behind her.

Chrissie heaved a sigh of relief as the sound of his vehicle faded. At least he'd had the decency to apologize. Not that she cared, of course. She'd walked away from him to make a statement—a pathetic one, maybe, but it made her feel better.

The only problem was that she still had to go back outside to check the sheep. "And as for you," she said to the little collie that was staring up at her, wagging its plumed tail. "It's actually all your fault. What were you doing getting into his car in the first place?"

Floss wriggled with pleasure at the attention, and Chrissie stroked her head before calling to Tess and Fly, who were both lying prostrate by the stove. "Come on, you two, there are sheep still to check."

They jumped up at once, immediately wide awake. It never failed to impress Chrissie how dogs could go so quickly from sleep to full alert…or maybe it was just her dogs. It occurred to her just how little she knew of the world. In Will Devlin's eyes, she must seem so gauche and naive.

Did she care, though? She remembered

the way his silvery eyes seemed to be able to see right into her soul. No, of course she didn't care; hotshot lawyers had no place in her world, and she couldn't understand why she'd accepted his help, anyway. All told, his presence had probably prolonged her night rather than lightened her load.

"Come on," she called to the dogs, and they fell in behind her as she headed back out into the night.

No, hotshot lawyers had no place in her world, but this one had inserted himself into it. And his plans could put everything she loved at risk.

CHAPTER ELEVEN

THE BANGING CAME on Will's door just as he was finishing his breakfast: two thin slices of toast with low-fat spread and a cup of black coffee. The importance of being in shape had been so much a part of his other life that he found it hard to break the habit.

Heavy lunches with clients had had to be overcome by watching everything else he ate. Of course, always looking good and in control of every aspect of his life wasn't really necessary anymore. He ate when and what he wanted and saw so few people these days that he didn't feel the need to impress anyone with his appearance. And all those strenuous walks with Max on the steep fell slopes had made him fitter than he'd been in years. Old habits died hard, though, and he still liked to look at least halfway decent. He certainly hadn't impressed Chrissie Marsh, that was for sure; she must be the first person ever to stand and laugh at him for his unsuitable attire. As for all that mud and afterbirth…what had he been thinking?

The banging came again and he downed his coffee, feeling irritable as he strode to the door. Why couldn't people just leave him alone?

At the sight of Roy Wallis's tall, imposing figure he took a step back.

"Why don't you answer your phone?" asked Marcus Finch's top man, pushing past Will to go inside. "I've been trying to call you since you left the office."

"Because I chose not to bother," Will replied.

Roy stopped in the hallway, glancing around in dismay. "Why on earth do you want to live in this godforsaken spot?"

"Because it's real."

Roy stared at him with the same authority that Will himself exuded. "Don't be ridiculous. What's 'real' about living here? Reality lies in the city. What you do there really means something, changes lives. Can't you see you're just wasting away here?"

"Don't you mean what I *used* to do there? And I'm not wasting away."

"Well, you are wasting your talent. There is no better lawyer than you, Will. Marcus Finch needs you back."

"I told you, Roy. I'm done with defending the wrong guys, done with the corruption and cruelty. It's barbaric."

"No!" Roy splayed his manicured hands on the table. "Can't you see *this* is barbaric? They are a hundred years behind the times here. I could hardly even find the place."

Will just shrugged. "Then why did you try?"

"Because you don't answer your phone."

"Then don't try and call me."

Roy took a breath, making an obvious effort to tamp down his temper. "I've thought about what we discussed, and I have an offer for you."

"I don't remember *discussing* anything. I just remember you telling me what you wanted. I'm not interested in your offer."

Roy sat down heavily. "Why don't you make me a coffee while I at least explain what's on the table? Please, Will, for old time's sake if nothing else."

Will rolled his eyes and reached for the kettle. "Black, no sugar, I presume."

The two men sat in silence for a full five minutes, sipping their coffees. "Nothing you have to say will tempt me back, you know," said Will. "I've had enough."

Roy Wallis leaned forward. "But why, when you were so good?"

Will grimaced. "Yes, I was, wasn't I? And I enjoyed it at first, changing people's fates. I never thought about it as real, you see… never thought about how it affected people's lives…never thought about the cruelty and corruption. It was all just clever wordplay to me…until that last case. The fact that children were involved made it come alive and then I thought about all the other cases… murder, extortion and the rest. I made myself sick…so I had to walk away."

Roy placed a hand on Will's arm. "I get it, I really do. We all do, at the firm, and we want to make you an offer."

Will stood and poured his coffee down the sink. "There is no offer that can tempt me back to law."

"What if I said you can pick your cases and be paid twice much as you were before for each one? You can still do criminal law, but maybe only defending wrongfully accused clients. Imagine it, Will, your chance to stamp out some of the violence and corruption you have come to hate so much. You know these people, know what makes them tick. You'll be magnificent."

Will gripped the edge of the sink, his knuckles turning white. The smell of the courtroom filled his nostrils…the tension…

Roy walked across and placed a hand on his shoulder. "I won't keep you any longer. The offer is there if you want it. All we ask is that you give it some thought and think of it as undoing past wrongs. You left us in the lurch, Will. It's payback time."

For over an hour after his old boss and mentor had left, Will sat at the table, his mind in turmoil. How could he have felt such elation at winning cases when his victories were unworthy of joy? It had all been about him, his successes, his clever words, finding gaps in the evidence or loopholes in the law and seeing the amazement on people's faces as he won yet another big case. Not for the first time since he walked away, he realized he didn't really like himself much. Roy was right that it was payback time, but not the way he'd meant it.

The sound of Max whining outside broke into his thoughts. Will cringed. He'd let the dog out first thing and then, with Roy Wallis turning up, he'd forgotten all about him.

"Max," he called, hurrying to the door.

The big dog burst into the kitchen with a wide smile on his face, jumping up to plant his huge front paws against his master's chest and leaving two muddy prints.

"Now where have you been?" asked Will, pushing the exuberant dog down and reaching for a damp cloth.

"Chasing sheep that's what," Jim Wentworth replied, stepping into the kitchen without being asked. "I saw him up the fell earlier, running after a ewe with a single lamb, but when I shouted he totally ignored me. I came to tell you, but you had an important-looking visitor and I didn't like to interrupt."

Will grimaced, dabbing at the dirty marks. "Oh, he's important, all right—in his own world. Here, he is nothing." When Jim looked at him quizzically, Will shook his head. "You really don't want to know. Anyway, obviously Max came back."

"Yes, but you really are going to have to keep him under control," Jim insisted. "Or some farmer will shoot him. It's perfectly legal and none of them would think twice."

"What, not even my nearest neighbor, the formidable Chrissie Marsh?"

"Especially Chrissie… Now, she really is passionate about her sheep, and you wouldn't believe the damage a rogue dog can do. They rip and tear at the sheep, even kill them, and then trot off back home as if butter wouldn't melt to curl up in front of the fire."

"Not Max, though," Will said. "He would never actually hurt the sheep. He just thinks it's a game." Guiltily, he thought of the sheep and duck whose lives had been cut short by Max's recklessness. But those had been accidents.

"That's what all owners think, that their dogs wouldn't do that, but believe me— almost all dogs have deep-rooted instincts that can turn them into killers. It can begin with excitement, to be sure, but the hunting instinct lurks just beneath the surface. Max is no different from any other dog."

"I still can't see Chrissie shooting him, though."

Jim shook his head. "You don't really get it, do you? Up here it is all about survival.

The farmers may love their creatures, but they have to earn their keep."

"And if they don't?"

Jim shrugged. "Put it like this—they wouldn't keep a ewe if it didn't produce lambs. It wouldn't be economically viable. And if a sheepdog won't work, it has to be sold as a pet...or put down. There are exceptions, of course. An old dog, for instance, that has worked for years and earned the right to retirement, or the odd pet terrier—although even they usually kill rats to earn their keep."

"And I thought this was a tranquil place," remarked Will. "It seems I was wrong. Obviously life can be cruel and harsh around here, too."

"Never without reason or regret, though," Jim said. "And never from greed and envy... It's just about necessity and survival, like in nature."

"Then there it differs totally from the city, where greed and envy rule most people's lives."

"That's very cynical."

"I have reason to be cynical," Will said, walking across to peer out the window. "And you really do believe that Chrissie would shoot my dog?"

Jim nodded determinedly. "I know she would. You need to keep him under better control and get him some serious training."

"Then that's what I shall do," Will said. "Can't have you shot, can we, Maxy boy? But where can I find a trainer?"

Jim's smile held a hint of irony. "Chrissie is the best there is, but she only trains sheepdogs. If I were you, I'd go to the vet's and see if they can recommend anyone."

"Well, it definitely won't be Chrissie. She and I don't really see eye to eye on things."

"What things?" Jim asked curiously. "I didn't realize that you knew her. There was the incident with the sheep, of course, but I thought you'd gotten past that."

"Well, we kind of had but then there were the ducks…"

"What ducks?"

"The Indian Runner ducks—she uses them to help train the sheepdogs."

"Don't tell me that Max chased them, as well."

"Worse," Will said. "He killed one…well, not intentionally, but it did die."

Jim held back a smile. "Better not ask her, then."

"It's not just that."

Jim held up both his hands in dismay. "Go on," he said. "Tell me."

"We had a bit of an argument about my intentions for Craig Side."

"And?"

Will sighed. "I don't think she's too keen on the idea of holiday rentals."

"She'll object to the planning, then," Jim said. "Nothing more sure. Chrissie Marsh hates tourists with a vengeance. Trouble is, she can't accept the fact that the Lake District can't do without them. Think how many jobs would be lost if there were no tourists."

"I helped her with the sheep last night." Will threw in the comment as an afterthought, changing the subject. "It made me realize just how ancient and entrenched in tradition the way of life around here is. I'll bet that shepherding hasn't changed for hundreds of years. Do you know that she actually skins a ewe's dead lamb to try and get it to accept an orphan lamb in its place?"

Jim shrugged. "It's still common practice around here. I may be a builder now, but I was brought up on a farm and I worked with the sheep a lot as a boy. They have lambing crates nowadays—the ewe's heads are held so that they can quite happily eat and drink but they can't actually sniff the new lamb until the ewe's own milk has gone through the orphan's system, helping to make its smell familiar to her. You can get sprays, too, that are supposed to help with the bonding process. Most farmers revert to the old tried and tested methods, though. So you enjoyed working with the sheep, then?"

Will smiled. "Do you know, I actually did. I mean, don't get me wrong, it was cold and wet and muddy, but there was something very satisfying about it. I've never really seen anything born before…but I don't suppose I'll be helping her again after she found out about the planning permission. She wasn't happy, that's for sure."

"Doesn't sound very promising," Jim agreed. "She's a stubborn woman, Chrissie Marsh. If she gets a bee in her bonnet then it's difficult to sway her."

Will nodded. "Well she definitely has a bee in her bonnet over the holiday rentals. We got off on a bad foot, but after I helped her with the sheep I thought we were past it. Anyway, the holiday rentals are going ahead no matter how much she protests. They are my income for the future."

Jim nodded. "I don't think there's any doubt that you'll get the planning permission, especially now that you want to make them more authentic... Which reminds me, Roger Simmons wants you to look at the new plans. He said that he'd called you several times but your phone was switched off. Anyway, he gave me a copy for you—it's in the van. He said to ring for a meeting with him when you've looked at them."

"And have you seen them?" Will asked. "What did you think?"

"Yes, I've seen them...and they seem fine to me, though I'm still not sure people will want to go back in time like that. Couldn't you at least have some discreetly disguised showers?"

Will shook his head determinedly. "That would ruin the whole concept. Trust me, there are people who would love to stay somewhere like this. For city dwellers, it would be a huge adventure."

"Well, you know best, I guess," Jim said,

still not convinced. "I'll go and get them, then. Or…" He smiled impishly. "Maybe I'll just go over to High Bracken and run them past Chrissie first. See what she thinks."

Will bristled, unused to joking around. "You'll do no such thing."

ON HER HANDS and knees in the meadow above High Bracken, Chrissie was helping a ewe give birth to a very stubborn lamb. After a great deal of effort, the lamb slipped out onto the ground and she removed the mucous from its tiny black nose, rubbing its chest roughly to try and get it breathing. When it let out a bleat and began to wriggle, Chrissie stood back to let it get on its feet and allow its mother to bond with her new offspring.

In the wild, lambs needed to be up and running as soon as possible, for any number of predators could be lurking. This lamb's instincts seemed to be just as strong as her truly wild ancestors' had been. Just as well, thought Chrissie, watching the wobbly little creature starting to suckle. With dogs like Will Devlin's labradoodle on the loose, no sheep or lamb was safe.

In fact, the man was a liability, she decided

as she headed back to the farm with the dogs at her heels. She was confident enough now to leave the lamb with its mother. In a flash, she remembered how he'd helped her with the sheep the night before and how they'd talked after. For a little while they'd had a real connection, and she'd seen the man behind the lawyer with the silken tongue, the man who'd been sickened by his profession.

Of course, it hadn't lasted; when she'd turned on him over his holiday rentals he'd become defensive. And that kiss… What had that been all about? She touched her fingers to her lips, feeling them tingle at the memory. It was easy enough for him to make his fancy plans; all he cared about was the money he could make. For her, tourists running around up here would be a real hazard. There were bound to be more incidents of sheep being spooked or killed by dogs. Her flock might stray in panic and split up, mothers and their lambs could get separated… Not to mention having to worry about gates being left open, potentially dangerous litter and erosion of the land. There was just no place for tourists up here.

Chrissie was still pondering it when she walked into the kitchen at High Bracken. She'd go and do some training exercises with Floss; that should clear her head. "Come on," she called to the little black-and-tan sheepdog, who was eager for company. "You and I have work to do."

Attaching a long line to Floss's collar, Chrissie headed up to the paddock where the Runner ducks were. They waddled across the grass, heads held high, well used to the routine.

"Lie down," she told Floss, and the pup wavered for a moment, torn between running off to investigate the strange-looking ducks and being obedient. She knew full well what she was supposed to do, but life was way too exciting to lie down. Chrissie repeated the command, rewarding the young dog when she did as she was bid, and soon she was sitting, lying and staying with total disregard for the ducks.

"Come way out," called Chrissie, casting out her arm, and Floss stood, apparently confused. When Chrissie repeated the command and hand gesture, though, she headed toward the ducks, moving around them slowly with the natural instinct bred into a good sheep-dog. When Chrissie let out a low whistle and called for her to lie down again, Floss dropped to the ground immediately, enjoying the game, her keen eyes focused on her trainer.

"That'll do," Chrissie said with a pleased smile, confident that the training was going to be relatively easy. Some dogs just didn't get it, and then there were others, like Floss and Tess and Fly, who seemed to know what you wanted and actually enjoyed the work.

She walked over and gave the little dog a treat, scratching behind her ears. "Come on, girl," she said. "Let's go home."

Returning to the house, she could see way across the valley. Green shoots were pushing through the brown of winter and the wide sky was the clearest, palest blue, unlike yesterday when she'd been soaked to the skin most of the day and the sky had been a daunting shade of gray. The thought reminded her yet again of her new neighbor and she looked way over to her left and a little lower down to Craig Side. There were vehicles in the yard and tiny figures up on the roof yet again.

Her heart sank. It couldn't wait. She'd have to go see Tom Farrah today and start a petition against Will Devlin's plans. She had to do something before it was too late.

her fright knee. She leaned back, she'd have to go out from time to time and exert a little pressure, as well. Over in a glade, she tried to join some little children who were out there.

CHAPTER TWELVE

"So, HAVE YOU sorted it?"

Jim Wentworth was standing in the yard at Craig Side watching Will yelling, yet again, for Max. The big cream-colored dog totally disregarded his master's angry cries, intent on following an enticing scent, and Will fell silent, feeling like a fool.

"Sorted what?" he asked, his bad humor turning on Jim.

"Whoa…" Jim raised his hand in objection. "It's not my fault you can't control your own dog. I told you what to do."

"And I am," snapped Will, making a split-second decision. "Today."

"Glad to hear it," Jim said, letting out a low whistle. Max stopped in his tracks, peering down at the two men in the yard below him. "The thing is," he went on, as the dog returned in their direction. "I need to keep my men in work, so if you haven't obtained the necessary planning permission by the time we've finished the barn roof then I'll have to take on another job. It could be months, then, before I have the time to get started on your project. All you have to do is approve the plans Roger drew up."

Will started to answer, but Max had reached them and he leaped up at Will, almost knocking him over. "Bad dog," he cried.

"I'm not surprised you can't manage him," Jim remarked. "He's just done what you wanted and come to call, so you should be rewarding him, not telling him off."

"But I need to discipline him, don't I? Or he'll have won."

Jim scratched his head in despair. "It seems to me that you need as much training as your dog. They don't think like us, you know…don't understand things in the same way we do. He needs to be rewarded for coming back to you and then maybe he'll want to. Anyway, about these plans."

Will tentatively patted Max's broad head "I'm a bit new to this dog-owner stuff," he admitted, and Jim rolled his eyes.

"So why buy one in the first place…especially one like Max?"

Will couldn't help smiling at his own ineptitude. "A stupid impulse, I'm afraid. I was changing my life around and it seemed like a country kind of thing to do."

"A Labrador or a collie would be a country thing to do. But seriously, get the dog some training, and attend the classes if you can, too. You need to understand how he thinks. Dogs don't reason like us—they just react."

"I'm beginning to realize that," Will said. "I understand the way lawyers think and even the workings of the criminal mind, to a degree, but dogs—any animals, really— are way out of my comfort zone."

"Sounds like you've had an introduction to sheep, though," Jim said with an amused smile. "Thanks both to Max here and to Chrissie Marsh."

"I've learned that they're nervous and wild, and I've also found out that caring for them is a dirty, tough and often smelly job, if that's what you mean."

Jim raised his eyebrows. "And satisfying, too?"

Remembering how the lamb Chrissie had helped to be born had struggled to its feet and suckled almost immediately brought a tight feeling into Will's chest. "Yes," he admitted. "I suppose it is satisfying. They are so delicate and yet so tough, full of the will to survive. It's humbling, really."

"Then get down to the vet's and find out if they know of any good dog trainers so that Max here doesn't start trying to kill them again. Oh, and when you get back, maybe you could attach some importance to those plans."

"Will do," promised Will.

WILL PULLED UP outside the veterinary center later that day and climbed out of his four-by-four, leaving Max in the back. On the drive into Little Dale, his thoughts had wandered back to Roy's visit. Did he really want to go back to law to try and right some of the wrongs he'd inflicted? The idea held some appeal, but did he really want to become embroiled in all that again? Well, the only way to make sure he never needed to go back was to get his holiday rentals built and start making money.

While life in the country was harsh and

tough, at least it was totally honest. He certainly couldn't say that about his career as a lawyer.

Trying to push the confusing thoughts from his mind, he went into the clinic. The pretty young receptionist smiled at him.

"Can I help you?"

"I hope so," he responded. "I mean, I'm not here to see a vet or anything, I just wondered if you knew of any dog trainers in the area."

"I think there's an advert on the wall over there," she suggested, pointing to a notice board covered in dozens of brochures and slips of paper.

Will passed a row of waiting patients ranging from a rabbit that was sitting on a little girl's knee to a thin woman with an Afghan hound, and was intercepted by a tall fair-haired man.

"Hi," he said, holding out a large hand. Will took it, confused, and the man pumped it firmly. "I'm Andy Montgomery, a vet both here and at Cravendale Animal Sanctuary. I couldn't help hearing you ask about a dog trainer."

"Yes," Will said. "I need someone really good."

"Frankly, there is only one around here who I would confidently recommend. Chrissie Marsh from High Bracken—she's always very busy, but it might be worth trying to persuade her."

Will felt the hairs on the back of his neck stand up. Why was it that every way he turned, she seemed to be there? "But doesn't she only train sheepdogs?" he asked.

"Mainly," Andy said. "But she's done some work for us with all sorts of dogs that have come into Cravendale. She seems to have a way of communicating with even the most difficult ones. Some of them would quite probably have had to be put down if it wasn't for her. I suppose you're new in town?"

Will nodded, regaining some of his confidence. "That's right. Will Devlin. I've just bought Craig Side."

"Ah…" Andy smiled knowingly. "And now I can see why you're wary of approaching Chrissie. I heard about the dog-chasing incident."

"That's why I need to get Max trained properly," Will said.

"Well, I can't see Chrissie holding grudges. She may be mad at you, of course, but if you just apologize—and maybe beg a little—then I'm sure you'll be able to persuade her to help you out."

Will grimaced. "I'm not so sure about that."

"Go and see her," suggested Andy. "Offer her enough money so that she can't refuse. All the sheep farmers around here are strapped for cash."

"Thanks," said Will. "I might just do that."

The idea formulated and grew as Will wandered through Little Dale and then suddenly, as if she had been plucked from his thoughts, there she was. Chrissie Marsh, dressed for town without her usual shepherdess apparel. She was striding along the pavement in much the same way that she walked across the fells, but now her long blond hair cascaded around her shoulders, almost reaching her waist, its golden streaks enhanced by the rusty autumn color of her jacket. Seizing the opportunity to approach her on neutral ground, Will hurried across the street, trying to position himself so that their meeting would appear accidental.

Peering into a shop window without even seeing the contents, he kept half an eye on her approach. She stopped a couple of times to chat to people and he felt like a nervous teenager as he pretended not to notice her. Her voice in his ear took him by surprise.

"And why would you be looking in a toy shop window?" she asked. "I saw you crossing the street—are you by any chance waiting for me?"

"No, no, I...I'm shopping. For a present." His explanation sounded thin even to him.

Chrissie gave him an amused smile, raising her eyebrows, and he couldn't help but notice how the touch of makeup around her eyes made their clear blue more vivid. Like the Lake District sky, he thought, feeling stupid.

"Oh, well, in that case," she said. "Good luck with your shopping."

He tried to step in front of her as she turned away and accidentally knocked into a passerby. "Sorry," he said to the elderly lady, who was scowling at him, then he grabbed Chrissie's sleeve before she could move on. The scent of her perfume flooded his senses. "Actually," he admitted. "There is something."

"Yes?"

"It's Max."

"What about him? Has he been killing more sheep…or ducks, perhaps?"

A surge of irritation brought Will back down to earth. "That's not fair," he insisted. "Max may be a bit wild, but he doesn't have a bad bone in his body."

"Not yet," she warned. "But every sheep killer has to start somewhere."

"And that's why I want you to train him." There, it was out. "Please?"

"I'm sorry," she told him. "But I only train sheepdogs."

He stood his ground. "That's not actually true, is it? Look…I know you're angry with me because of the holiday rentals, but can't we just put that on hold for a while? I haven't even finalized the plans yet. Andy, the vet, told me that you've trained all kinds of dogs for the animal center."

"Cravendale hasn't put in a planning application for tourist accommodation," she replied in a clipped tone.

"And neither have I...yet," he told her, trying to keep his frustration at bay. "Please think about it at least. Max deserves a chance. I really don't want him to end up being shot by some farmer."

"Then you'd better keep him under control." Chrissie walked off without a backward glance. Will watched her go, fending off a rush of disappointment. *Never mind her*, he decided. He would just have to find someone else.

As Chrissie passed Will's vehicle, she paused. He'd left the window open wide enough for Max to push most of his head out, and he was whining at Chrissie, eager for attention. She let him lick her hand and said a few words in his ear.

Will waited until she gave Max a final scratch and continued on her way before he approached the Range Rover. She must actually like the daft dog, or she wouldn't have made such a fuss over him. Which meant *he* was the reason she refused to get involved.

Well, he could work on that. There had to be some way to persuade her that he wasn't all bad. Will remembered Andy's suggestion to offer her too much money to refuse. That was the approach he was going to have to take. He would just turn up at High Bracken with his checkbook, and she could name her price.

Max went crazy when Will climbed into the driver's seat, leaping around and overcome with excitement.

"Settle down," Will said, doubts forming. What if the silly labradoodle was untrainable? Perhaps he was wasting his time.

As he pulled out into the road, his phone rang. Will answered it on the Range Rover's console and Roger's voice came over the Bluetooth.

"Hi, Roger Simmons here. About these plans…"

"I'll be there in fifteen minutes," replied Will. "If you're in, of course."

"Yes, I'll be in all afternoon. I'd like to get them ready for next month's planning meeting."

When they ended the call, Will found himself thinking about Chrissie again. It would probably be better for him and Max if he held back on the planning for a while, but

Jim had told him that if they didn't move forward soon, he'd have to take on another job. Will needed to do this and it really had to be now.

He headed out of the village and up into the hills where Roger had renovated an old farmhouse into something really special, mixing the old and the new with both skill and good taste.

Maybe if Chrissie saw the tasteful authentic design he had in mind for Craig Side, she'd warm to the idea. But he knew he was kidding himself. It was the tourists who were the problem, not the houses themselves. She needed to accept that there would always be visitors to the Lake District—more and more, in fact—and that they were actually an asset to the community, bringing both money and jobs to the area.

Times were changing, and Chrissie Marsh needed to change with them. She had to learn to live in the present, not the past, and find a way to live with tourists around here. He wished he could talk to her and try to make her understand. She had such warmth behind her facade of anger and hostility. He'd seen it with the sheep and lambs… the way she cared for them. And with him, when he'd kissed her. He wanted more of that warmth. He wanted it to scald him.

Roger's car was parked on the immaculate gravel drive and Will pulled up beside it, stepping out into the serenity of the spring afternoon to hear birdsong all around him. The whole place seemed alive with excitement as another year began to flourish, heralded by the mass of purple crocuses that were spread in abundance across the lawn.

He walked around the side of the house to a large conservatory that looked out onto the vast, rugged fells, a place to sit and take in the surroundings no matter what the weather.

Roger waved at him from the front window, and by the time Will reached the back door it was already open. "About time," Roger said, hand outstretched. "Come on in. Mary already has the kettle on."

"Tea or coffee?" she called from beside a large cream AGA stove. At her feet, a toddler sat banging on a pan with a spoon, and toys were strewn all over the granite-tiled floor.

"Coffee, please," Will responded. "Seems like you've got your hands full."

Mary smiled. "First grandchild," she said,

laughing. "I know, don't tell me, I don't look old enough."

"Well, you don't," Will agreed.

"Come into my study and I'll show you these plans," Roger said, ushering him down a wide hallway into a pleasant room filled with natural light. "Here, I'll show you the computer images first to give you an idea of where I'm at, and then we can look at the proper plans."

Will focused on the screen as Roger flicked through images of small cottages made of Lakeland stone clustered together around a central area.

"You see," Roger said, his voice rising with excitement. "Because the buildings you are converting are set around the farmyard, the visitors will have a degree of privacy at the back, but at the front there's a kind of communal feel for those who prefer to socialize. There is one thing, though..."

"Go on, then," Will said apprehensively.

"I'm not sure about the properties being so basic. Perhaps you could have a shower block, or even a disguised shower in each one—it's what people expect."

"Do you know," he said. "I'm not really interested in what people expect."

Roger gulped. "Don't you think that's…"

"Pompous?" Will finished for him.

"Well, I wouldn't put it quite like that, but—"

"The thing is, Roger, I have a vision for this. I know city people—or at least the kind of city people I used to mix with. They love the idea of getting back to nature, and I believe that they will pay a small fortune for the experience of living here in the fells in the same way that our ancestors did. I don't want it to feel like pretense—I want it to be real. Open fires with old-fashioned cooking stoves, and—"

"Please don't say tin baths in front of the fire," Roger groaned.

Will stifled a smile. "That did cross my mind, but then I decided that was going a bit too far. So it will just be the most basic of bathrooms—with running water, of course, but it will be heated only by the fire."

"I suppose that's something, but I'm still not sure that people will go for the whole experience."

"That," Will said, "is for me to worry about. Now, about these plans."

Turning away from the computer, Roger spread a large sheet of paper on the table. "This is the main plan for the whole setup," he explained. "We need to sell it to the planners because they aren't too keen on turning these outlying farms into anything else. They are our heritage, pieces of our past, and we don't want to lose them."

Will nodded. "Yes, and I get that. The last thing I want to do is change Craig Side—I want to keep it traditional. Despite what Chrissie Marsh and some of the other locals may think, I really don't want life, or farming, around here to change at all. Surely, the Lake District needs the revenue tourists bring into the area in order to thrive."

"Ah, but if they are way up here, living in the past, as it were, then surely they won't be spending money in the local shops," Roger pointed out.

"They may want this experience, but they'll also still want to go into the shops to buy gifts and mementos. They'll probably want to go to the local bars and restaurants, too."

"Oh, well…it's your project." Roger pulled

off the top sheet and spread out the one beneath. "Now, this I am really pleased with," he continued. "I just need your input regarding bedrooms etcetera. It depends on how many you want to cater for... Are we thinking couples or families?"

"That is something I haven't really given much thought to," Will said.

"Well, it's probably time you did. Yuppie couples or affluent young families. You are, or at least were, a city dweller—would you have come here for a holiday?"

Will smiled with genuine humor. "No," he said. "I definitely wouldn't. The thing is, though..."

"The thing is what?"

"I know lots of people who would. Both couples and families."

"Okay." Roger began rolling up the plans. "Just let me know when you've decided. Two large bedrooms per cottage, or three average ones."

As Will drove home half an hour later, the answer suddenly came to him and he rang Roger immediately. "We'll cater for both," he told him.

"If you're sure..."

"I'm sure."

"All right." The relief in Roger's voice was plain enough for anyone to hear. "I'll get the drawings finished right away and then we can go for next month's planning meeting."

CHAPTER THIRTEEN

CHRISSIE HURRIED DOWN the main street in Little Dale, late for her appointment with Tom Farrah. She'd have been on time if it hadn't been for her run-in with Will. How did he always manage to show up at just the wrong moments? Still, it felt nice to be going out somewhere for once.

Tom had suggested they meet for lunch at The Dalesman, a popular pub in the center of the village, and as she approached the long, low whitewashed building, she thought about what Will had asked her.

At first, she'd wanted to laugh out loud at his audacity, but there was something moving about the way he pleaded for his dog, so she held back. Still, she'd had to turn him down, harden her heart against him. Why should she help Will with his dog, anyway? It had chased her sheep, killing one—albeit indirectly—and it had claimed a duck's life, too. The creature was a menace. And Will's entire reason for being here threatened her way of life. He didn't deserve her help, arrogant lawyer that he was.

Then she'd seen Max, and his delight at seeing her had made her feel guilty again. She had to make a stand over this, though. Trying to put Max's naive smile out of her head, Chrissie increased her pace. She needed to focus on the positive: today she was going to voice her objections to a member of the south Lakeland planning committee. Tom Farrah would be on her side, she was sure of it.

Chrissie stepped through the front doors of the pub, looking around for Tom. An open fire roared in the grate and horse brasses gleamed in its rosy light. Old oak floors, worn by thousands of feet over the past two hundred years, shone with polish, as did the huge oak bar. A long row of colorful beer taps denoted a dozen different real ales. The whole place had a warm, comfortable, lived-in atmosphere.

"A small glass of white wine, please," she said to the barman, reaching for her purse before realizing with a sinking heart that she'd forgotten it. Maybe she really did need to get out more.

"Allow me," said a voice from behind her, and she turned around to see Tom Farrah's smiling face. He produced a twenty pound note and ordered a half-pint of Blonde Witch ale. "I'll bring them over," he said. "You get us a table."

Chrissie chose a small round table near the window, annoyed with herself for leaving her purse at home. She had instigated the meeting, after all, and it had been good of Tom to agree to it. She'd intended to insist on paying for the meal.

Tom approached, carrying the drinks. He appeared very self-assured and professional today, with his neatly combed gray hair and his sharp navy suit. Last time she'd seen him he'd been in his farming clothes. Today he looked like a councillor, not a farmer. She squirmed in her seat, embarrassed to have to tell him she'd forgotten her purse. She, too, had made an effort to dress for the occasion, hoping to be taken seriously, but she'd let herself down.

"Thanks so much," she said as he placed the two glasses on the table. "I'm sorry to start us off on the wrong foot…" He sat, raising his eyebrows. "But is there any chance you could cover my lunch? I intended to treat you, but I've forgotten my purse. I'll pay you back right away."

Tom grinned as he handed her a menu. "Absolutely not. I mean, no, you won't pay for me back and of course I'll cover it. You did a darned good job of training Tilly for me and the least I can do is stand you a meal and, hopefully, give you some advice."

"Well, if you're sure?"

"I'm sure. Now, let's order the food and then you can tell me why you wanted to meet. The fish is very good here, by the way."

"Fish it is, then," said Chrissie, glancing briefly at the menu before putting it down. She was eager to get her point across. "The thing is—"

"Are you ready to order?" asked a bright-eyed young girl, pen poised above her pad.

Tom lingered over the menu, settling on steak pie, and Chrissie hurriedly ordered fish and chips, taking a gulp of her wine before trying again.

"The thing is," she repeated. "My neighbor at Craig Side is putting in a planning application—"

"And I presume that you want to object," Tom cut in, raising his eyebrows.

"Er…yes," Chrissie said. "I suppose that's about it."

He pressed his fingertips together, studying her thoughtfully. "You know, planning isn't always quite as simple as people think. We have strict guidelines to follow—it's not just a case of what we want personally. For instance, there are firm rules surrounding new builds, and they are only allowed in selected areas. Conversions, on the other hand, must be tastefully done to fit in with surrounding buildings. There are exceptions to this, of course, and we do have to promote tourism in the area."

"I hate tourists!" The words just burst out, making Chrissie feel like a sulky child.

"Ah," said Tom. "But would you hate tourists if they provided your livelihood?"

"Sorry. Of course I don't hate tourists, and yes, if they provided my livelihood then I guess I would like them. It's just the countryside, you see—I can't stand to sit by and watch it being altered by people who don't appreciate it...you know, dogs that create havoc and gates being left open, causing all kinds of problems for farmers. I just think that holiday rentals should have to remain down in the valleys and not be allowed to encroach on our farms."

"So can I take it that this new neighbor of yours wants to make Craig Side into some kind of holiday accommodation?" Tom asked.

Before Chrissie could answer, the food arrived, breaking up the conversation.

"So, what exactly is it that you want of me?" Tom asked abruptly.

Chrissie put down her knife and fork with a clatter. "I want to find a way to stop him."

"Unfortunately, we can't refuse planning permission just because someone doesn't like it," he told her. "You need to have valid objections as to why you feel it shouldn't be given."

"Like what?"

Tom finished his beer and shrugged, placing his glass down on the table with deliberation. "Like if it's not in keeping with the surroundings, or if there's a safety factor. All in all, we are advised to promote tourism, but the rules are fairly strict so as not to spoil the character of the area. I can't really say much, anyway, until I've seen the plans. You need to start a petition and have valid objections, then you can put it all to the committee when the plans come up for approval. Everything will be taken into account before a decision is made."

"And does the planning committee meet regularly?"

Tom finished the last bite of steak pie and placed his knife and fork neatly in the middle of his plate. "Once a month, usually—I'm off there now, as a matter of fact. I'll pay at the bar on my way out, and please give me a call if you have any more queries." He stood. "Lambing going okay?"

Taken aback by his sudden change of subject, Chrissie took her final sip of wine before replying. "Yes…thanks. The weather has been good this year—makes all the difference."

Tom nodded. "Well, as you know I've taken rather a backseat on the farm since Sam took over. It's nice to have less to do, but I still help out quite a bit. Unfortunately, we've had a lot of twins this year… Makes life harder."

"They need that extra time and attention, don't they," Chrissie agreed, "before you can let them go back onto the fell. Single lambs are so much stronger."

"Anyway," said Tom, holding out his hand. "I hope I've been of some help."

Chrissie took it with a smile. "You have, thanks. And I expect to see you winning some sheepdog trials this year, remember."

"I'm not sure about that, but we will be competing and we'll do our best. Perhaps I could bring Tilly up to High Bracken after lambing is over, to have a refresher."

"Good idea," said Chrissie. "Give me a call. I'll probably be in touch with you again, anyway, over this planning. The guy who has bought Craig Side has no idea about farming, is the trouble. He's a retired lawyer."

Tom raised his bushy white eyebrows. "So he's an older fellow, then?"

"Oh, no," Chrissie said. "He's only in his thirties, I think."

"You'll have to try and appeal to his better nature, then." Tom laughed. "Be persuasive… you could do with a man in your life, Chrissie."

"Definitely not *that* man."

He was still laughing as he raised his hand in farewell and headed out the door.

Chrissie sat for a little while longer, reflecting on what Tom had said. She couldn't deny that she was drawn to Will, but she couldn't understand why. He wasn't her kind of person at all. She would never have believed she could be attracted to a lawyer, but she'd seen another side of Will that rainy night with the sheep, a softer side. Disregarding the weather and way out of his comfort zone, he had thrown himself into the tasks she'd asked of him. Then he'd talked, opening up about his reasons for quitting his city life, and she'd been moved by his strength. Many lawyers—many people, for that matter—would have probably just thought of the money and acclaim, convincing themselves that it was simply a job that had to be done. And he was trying to fit in here, she could see that, despite his determination to go ahead with the holiday rentals.

She let out a heavy sigh. As far as she was concerned, now that she'd gotten some advice on how to fight them, his plans were a non-starter. Hopefully there was a good chance that they would be refused.

Her fingers went to her lips as she remembered the warmth of his mouth on hers, the softness. The kiss had confused her, tested her resolve. Her pulse thrummed in her throat; it had been so hard to pull away from him. She couldn't afford to let that happen again. She had to stay focused on objecting to his plans.

Standing up, she walked determinedly out of the pub and into the street, where normal people were going about their normal lives, just as they did day after day after day. She had better things to do than think about Will Devlin. He had no part in her life. The sheep needed checking, Floss had to be worked today and there were all the other animals to see to, too…oh, yes, and she had a petition to start on.

One thing was for sure: if there was any way to stop him from getting planning permission, then she was determined to find it.

CHAPTER FOURTEEN

"HEY, MAX," CALLED WILL as he untied Max and let him into the backseat before climbing into his vehicle. The big cream-colored dog tried to jump into the passenger seat, whining and attempting to lick his face. "Not so tough now, are you, Mr. Insecurity?"

Will laughed, pushing him back. "I haven't been gone long, and the nice lady did stop to talk to you when I left you in the car earlier, didn't she? Now settle down and I'll take you for a walk when we get home."

The fact that Chrissie had shown some affection for the dog was promising. It was him she was mad at, not Max, so perhaps she could be persuaded if he went about it the right way.

As he followed the narrow lane that led up the fell, he couldn't help thinking about how different she had looked today in that rust-colored jacket with her glorious hair cascading over her shoulders. Of course, he didn't usually go for independent shepherdesses who spent most of their time helping sheep give birth, tending to newborn lambs and training dogs. Then again, he'd never actually met a shepherdess before. Six months ago he would have laughed at the idea of falling for a woman like Chrissie, but now... Now he wasn't so sure.

The women he tended to date were more high-heeled, smartly suited and career-minded women who would stop at nothing to get what they wanted... Then again, aside from the high heels and suits, perhaps those women had a lot more in common with Chrissie than he'd previously realized. She was tough and strong-minded, too. Ruthless, in a way, like him.

"Is that true, Max?" he asked out loud, reaching back to scratch the dog's ears. "Do you think I'm ruthless?"

Max just wagged his tail happily and Will felt an unfamiliar rush of emotion, suddenly getting the whole dog-owner thing. Dogs didn't ask questions, didn't judge you, no matter what you did, and were always there for you with smiles on their faces. "I'm going to convince her to train you somehow, boy," he promised. "After all, you are my best friend."

That thought made him chuckle as he imagined what Roy Wallis and all his high-powered colleagues would think if they could see him now. Well, he'd spent the past ten years trying to make the right impression—confident, powerful lawyer with no scruples and the world at his feet—but from now on, he was just going to be himself...whoever *himself* was.

Spring sunshine flooded into the car and he opened the driver's window, inhaling the sweet, clear air. This place was so real, so honest, and he knew it would help him figure out what he really wanted from life. Pulling over into a lay-by, he sat for a moment, looking back down the fell. Way, way, below him ordinary people were living ordinary lives, getting through their highs and lows in the best ways they could...and above him loomed the awesome sky, stretching toward eternity.

"Come on, boy," he said as Max bounced up and down excitedly on the backseat. "Let's take a walk."

Will walked for almost half an hour with Max straining on his long leash. And then he stopped and sat on a rock to ease his aching muscles. The fells still loomed above him, more colorful now that spring was bringing new life to the world, and beautiful in a stark, magnificent, almost scary way. He was aware that up here the weather could change in an instant, bringing dangerous conditions, mist and rain and storms that could make you lose your way in minutes. Surely not today, though. Today was full of the promise of spring with fresh new life all around.

"Come on, Max," he said. "We'll go as far as that huge rock and then we'll head back down to the car." The dog gazed up at him, clearly pleased to be spoken to in the affectionate tone Will had adopted of late.

The rock was farther away than it seemed, and the way was steeper. He was exhausted by the time they reached it. Even Max was ready for a break, and he collapsed, panting, onto the tufty grass, his pink tongue lolling from his mouth. Will lay back, staring into the glory of the vast open sky, surprised to see how much it had darkened and how many menacing gray clouds were gathering above him. Alarm rippled down his spine and he sat up.

Max pricked his ears in Will's direction.

"I think it's about time we got back, boy," Will said.

It was harder than he expected to walk down the rough slope. Harder, almost, than going up, since his legs were working overtime to keep him balanced. Beside him Max trotted easily, stopping occasionally to sniff at an enticing scent…until, suddenly, he leaped against his leash, almost yanking Will off his feet.

Will looked around to see what could have excited him. It had become eerily quiet, and dark gray clouds had rolled in, threatening rain. "Do you know, boy," Will said uneasily, "I think you're right that we need to go a bit faster. I can't see any sheep so I think I'll let you off." He crouched down to undo the dog's leash. "Promise me you won't run off, though." When Max planted his wet tongue on Will's cheek, he laughed. "Okay, so I guess that's a yes. Now, come on, we need to hurry."

Will shuddered, pulling his light jacket

more closely around him. It had seemed quite warm for the time of year when he had set out to walk Max, and he'd grown even warmer with the exertion. But now the sun had disappeared and a wind had whipped up from nowhere. He tried to pick up his pace but the loose gray scree moved beneath his feet, making him step carefully.

He took a deep breath, trying not to let the mist rolling down the fell worry him too much. How hard could it be to just walk straight back down to his car? At least Max was staying close, spooked by the conditions. All he had to do was get to the road. If he kept going down, then he had to hit it eventually.

When the mist caught up to them, turning Max into a ghostly form and curling around Will in a wet, white cloak that soaked into his bones, he stopped and searched for a landmark. There was nothing...nothing but the opaque, swirling mist. The beginnings of panic cut through his composure, and he tried to stay calm. He'd lost his bearings, but he could still keep walking downhill.

Ten minutes passed by, ten minutes of struggling over rocks and undergrowth that hadn't been there when he walked up the fell in the early afternoon sunshine. How could he have gotten so off track? The cold was getting to him now, making him shiver, and he trod uncertainly as the terrain got even worse.

They came to what appeared to be the edge of a rocky outcrop and Will came to an abrupt halt, peering over the edge. He couldn't see the ground below because of the mist, and his heart beat hard at the base of his throat. Panic was an unfamiliar feeling to Will, as were loneliness and fear, and now he had a full measure of all three. If the mist had been the slightest bit thicker, he could have stepped right off...

He gulped, reaching out to Max for comfort. If he took a fall or stepped into a crevice, he could lie there all night—assuming he survived. There was no one to come looking for him, and by tomorrow it could be too late. Fumbling for his cell phone, he tapped the screen with numb fingers. An automated female voice intoned, "You have no signal."

Will crouched beside Max, clinging to his warmth and solidity. "Which way then, boy? Which way?"

The big dog wagged his tail, and as if he understood, he set off along the top of the ridge with Will close behind. Eventually, when the rocks gave way to scree and grass, Will was able to start descending again, totally disorientated but determined to stay calm.

Max, on the other hand, seemed to have lost his previous unease. His nose was low to the ground and he trotted along happily, seemingly unaware of Will's distress. Suddenly, he let out an excited whine and ran ahead, disappearing into the mist. Will called for him to come back, yelling his name into the opaque silence.

What had he been thinking, coming out here? Not just today, but at all. The city seemed so friendly and safe by comparison as he headed on alone. He checked his watch and saw that the afternoon was gone. He had to find his way back to the car, or at least the road, before darkness fell... He just had to.

"Max!" he yelled again, his voice hoarse with the effort. All he heard was a distant, excited bark.

AFTER SPENDING SOME time with Floss and checking the sheep, all Chrissie wanted was to sit down in front of the fire with a nice cup of tea.

A ewe had given birth to twin lambs, one big and strong and the other tiny and weak. Drained from getting them into the barn and making sure that the little one had suckled, but satisfied with her efforts, Chrissie headed for the house. She was almost at the kitchen door when she heard a bark. She stopped in her tracks. Why would a dog be barking up on the fell on an evening like this? She couldn't ignore it.

Walking over to the field gate with Tess and Fly at her heels, she tried calling the dog. "Hey, boy…here, boy!"

Her cries were met by a heavy silence broken only by the moaning of the wind. Chrissie pulled her thick down jacket around her and turned back toward the house. Had she imagined it? Maybe she was mistaken and it was just a fox calling for its mate.

The barking came again as she opened the door. It was nearer now and definitely a dog. She grabbed her flashlight and went back out into the darkness with a rush of apprehension. She couldn't just leave it there.

Chrissie strode across the low meadow

where the lambing sheep grazed and went through the gate, leaving its smooth, green safety for the open fell's wild untended slopes. But getting lost wasn't an option. She knew the fell's every nook and cranny. Even in the mist, she could find her way home.

The fog was so thick that she could barely see in front of her, but she kept on calling for the dog, following the sound of its yelps. It sounded desperate, she thought, and she hoped it wasn't stuck somewhere or injured.

Finally the animal emerged from the gloom, leaping up at her in delight. She grabbed hold of its collar.

"Max!" she cried, recognizing him at once even though he was covered in mud. Max whined in delight, spinning in crazy circles, while Tess and Fly cowered behind her, wary of his exuberance. Was there no way she could get away from her annoying neighbor? she wondered. Now she'd have to contact him when she would rather keep well away.

"All right, boy," she said with a sigh, pulling a piece of baler twin from her pocket and tying it onto Max's collar. "You're coming with me."

Tired, afraid and happy to be rescued, Max followed obediently.

She was almost back at the meadow when it occurred to her that Will could be out there, too. Despite his faults, he really did love the daft, silly dog. What if he was out searching? What if he'd gotten lost? And if he was, she'd bet he wasn't prepared at all for the conditions. She brought up his name on her phone and called him, relieved when she heard a ring. It was hard to get a signal on the fell, but fortunately she appeared to be in one of the patches that had reception. Standing still for fear of losing the signal, she mentally begged him to pick up.

WILL WAS TRYING desperately to keep it together and wondering how a lovely spring walk could have turned into such a nightmare. He was cold, bitterly cold, and shivering from head to toe. He'd lost Max, he'd lost his bearings and night was closing in through the thick wall of fog that surrounded him.

When the mist had first rolled down, engulfing him, he'd thought it would be easy to keep on going downward. Eventually, he'd reach the road. Or so he'd thought. But fear had made him make mistakes and he'd been blundering around the rough terrain for hours with no idea if he was making any progress. He was still trying to go down, yes, but sections of steep slope and sharp drop-offs kept sending him back up.

Maybe this was it. Maybe he was going to die here…all alone. He pushed the thought aside, but deep down he knew it was a possibility. Even if the fog cleared, the night was still very much steeped in winter. Exposure was a terrifying thought, and his light jacket was already doing a poor job keeping the cold and damp at bay.

"Max!" he called half-heartedly, knowing the dog was gone. What if he never saw him again?

And then his phone rang. He struggled to answer it with fingers that refused to do his bidding, managing to pick up just as it stopped its stupid melody. He cursed at it. He'd given up on the thing after trying it again and again when Max ran off. There wasn't even one bar of a signal anywhere. Even now, seconds after a call had gotten through, the signal was gone.

Desolation settled over him like a cold, wet blanket as he stumbled down the slope. He tripped over a rock and went sprawling into damp brown bracken…and then his phone rang again.

This time he was able to answer it. "Hello? Hello?" he cried. "I need help!"

"Where are you, and are you okay?" a calm female voice replied. *Chrissie?*

"Chrissie!" he yelled. "I'm lost."

"It's going to be okay," she said. "Just stand still and tell me where you are."

"I don't know. I took Max for a walk on the fell and—"

"I'm going to try and find you," she told him. "I have Max here, so you can't be too far off. Your signal will probably go again, but don't panic. Stay where you are and keep on shouting."

CHAPTER FIFTEEN

"I THINK MAYBE it's your master who needs training, not you," Chrissie said to Max.

The labradoodle whined, and she placed her hand on his head, ruffling his sodden coat. "Well, we'd better try and find him, I guess."

She called the two collies over and they bounded to her side. "Seek," she said. "Where is it?"

They ran on ahead, familiar with the command when looking for sheep but somehow aware that this was something different. "Will!" she yelled into the cold, murky night. "Will!"

The mist was slowly lifting but darkness had swept in, replacing the thick whiteness with something just as intense. Chrissie swung her flashlight around, seeking landmarks. Her familiarity with and knowledge of the fell meant next to nothing if she couldn't see where she was.

"No point two of us being lost," she said to Max, who was pulling on his piece of string. Her beam lit up a pile of rocks and a small crooked tree, telling her exactly where she was, and she started to climb, retrieving her whistle from her pocket.

WILL HEARD THE SHORT, piercing blasts from somewhere below him. Forgetting Chrissie's instructions to stay put, he followed the sound, hurrying over the hostile ground that seemed determined to trip him up.

How could somewhere so beautiful turn so swiftly into a place to fear? Yet even as he stumbled toward the sound of Chrissie's whistle, he knew that it was his lack of respect for his surroundings that had gotten him into this position. It felt as if the fell itself was laughing at him. She would be laughing at him, too, he realized with embarrassment. If she ever found him, of course.

"Chrissie!" he shouted into the wind. "Chrissie!" His voice blew away as if he'd never even spoken at all.

It was Fly who finally found him. She

burst out of the darkness like an avenging angel, barking like a banshee. Will dropped to the ground, shivering all over, his own voice just a whisper in his ears as he called Chrissie's name over and over…and then she was there.

"Don't you know any better than to wander around here without the right gear?" she yelled, but her eyes in the glow of the flashlight were kind. "Come on," she said more softly. "Let's get you down to the farm. You'll feel a lot better with a warm drink inside you."

Half an hour later, sitting in front of the stove with a blanket around him and a mug of hot chocolate between his hands, Will's shivers finally subsided.

"Right," said Chrissie. "Now, I want you to tell me whatever it was you thought you were doing, wandering around on the fell in adverse conditions totally inadequately dressed."

"I feel like an idiot," Will admitted.

"You are," she told him, but there was a smile behind her eyes. "You do realize that if Max hadn't come and found me, you could have been up there all night?"

"*Would* have been there all night," Will corrected her. "I was completely lost."

"You have to respect these fells, Will."

He liked the new softness in her voice, and for a moment he held her eyes with his. "I know. And for what it's worth...thanks."

"It's the exposure that gets you." Reaching out, she covered his cold hand with hers. The warmth of her slender suntanned fingers seemed to seep right into his soul. "See? Your hands are like ice."

"My whole body still feels like ice," he told her. "I just can't understand how it happened. I was driving home from a meeting..." He paused, not wanting to bring up the unpleasantness between them about the holiday cottages. "The view was out of this world. I'll never forget it—it just drew me in, made me want to walk in the clear air and drink in its vastness and beauty..."

"Why, Will Devlin," she said, sitting back and smiling. "You are waxing almost lyrical. Where has the hard-nosed lawyer gone?"

"Sorry." He smiled back. "The exposure must have addled my brain. Anyway, we walked for a while and then it got cloudy and a mist kind of rolled down from nowhere. It wasn't just the fact that I couldn't see—that didn't bother me at first because I thought that if I kept walking down, I'd get back eventually. It was the cold that worried me..."

"As it should have, since you're underdressed, as usual," she chimed in. "The fog disorients you, you see. And before you know it, you're walking around in circles. Once darkness falls, it gets colder, you're tired... You do realize you could have died?"

"I'm beginning to," he said, taking a sip of the sweet, warm chocolate.

Chrissie leaned forward, her strong features animated. "That's what I love most about the fell, I think—its ferocity. It's beautiful and yet dangerous, a compelling mix."

Will reached out take her hand in his and she left it there. "Thank you," he said. "For saving my life."

She pulled her hand back sharply. "It's not me you should thank...it's Max."

Hearing his name, the muddy dog jumped up and placed both front paws on Will's knee, giving his master's cheek a lick with his long pink tongue.

"So now that you know he does have some sense after all…will you train him for me?"

CHRISSIE WANTED TO say yes, but hesitated, and it was that impulse to hesitate that swayed her. Will Devlin was just like the fell, she realized. He, too, had different faces, sometimes calm and serene, sometimes fierce. That night with the sheep he had been so helpful and no one would question that he was handsome, but simmering just beneath the surface was the fierce and often ruthless lawyer.

She sensed that he would do anything to get what he wanted, and he could turn on the charm like a tap. He was gazing at her now with soft gray eyes, but she knew they were capable of turning instantly into steel.

"I'm sorry," she said, standing up. "I really don't have the time to take him on right now. I'll run you home if you like. I can help you get your car in the morning, or maybe you can collect it on the way if you feel up to it." Noting the way his jaw clenched, she knew she'd made the right decision. How could she agree to train Max when she was intending to fight against Will's plans? That would be dishonest.

"I won't give up," he told her.

"And I won't stop saying no," she replied. "Come on, then. I have the sheep to check when I get back."

"Do you want me to stay and give you a hand?"

Her response was immediate. "No. What you need is to stay warm and have an early night."

They drove back to Craig Side in an almost companionable silence, deep in their own thoughts. What was it about Will Devlin that had this effect on her? He was charismatic, of course, and handsome, but it was more than that.

She sneaked a glance in his direction, and when he caught her eye and smiled, her heart seemed to roll over. It didn't matter what *it* was; it was just there. She wanted to be close to Will Devlin...*needed* that closeness. But she had to be strong enough to resist those feelings. She couldn't let attraction cloud her judgment, her determination to stop his plans. There was too much at stake.

Suddenly, he laughed, and she saw once

again the endearing side he'd shown the first time she met him, when Max had chased her sheep and he'd made a total idiot of himself. A smile penetrated her reserve.

"You are a strange man," she told him. "Did you know that?"

He nodded. "I suppose. I guess I just haven't figured out where I fit in life yet. Whereas you…"

"I what?"

"You know exactly where your place is."

Chrissie reflected on his remark. Did she know where her place was? Of course she did—her place was here. There was no doubt in her mind about that. But did she want to be alone in this place forever, or did she believe deep down that one day she would share it with her family? She had never taken Aunt Hilda's pointed comments seriously, but was there actually some truth in her advice? Well, if she did eventually have a family, it wouldn't be with someone like Will. It would be with a likeminded farmer who had the same goals as she did; someone who truly loved this life of hers.

They didn't speak much for the rest of their

drive, and Chrissie dropped Will off with strict instructions to get a good night's rest.

As she headed up the hill toward home, she passed Will's Range Rover again, tucked up tight against the fence. What a fool he was, she thought. A change in the weather had been forecast since yesterday, so what had he been thinking, walking off up the fell like that wearing only a thin jacket? He needed training as much as his dog, and that wasn't a task she intended to take on, either.

Chrissie pulled into the yard at High Bracken and parked outside the house, running to get her coat and calling for the dogs. Taking Will home had delayed her late-night check on the sheep, and knowing her luck, there would problems. It always seemed to work like that, problems happening at the worst times.

Outside it was bitterly cold and raining, the kind of heavy drizzle that soaked you through in an instant. As she approached the little red tractor that had served her well for years, she found herself smiling at the memory of Will Devlin, hotshot criminal lawyer, appearing through the darkness following Tess. Would the man never learn? The fells weren't for the fainthearted, and that's why tourists shouldn't be encouraged here.

And there, she realized, was a good point for her objections to the planning council. Health and safety was all-important nowadays—even up here all alone on her hill farm she knew that—so encouraging inexperienced, unsuspecting people to put their lives at risk in this place might be the kind of thing to get a planning application denied. Add that to the list she'd already made, including damage to property, not to mention the environment, and she was pretty sure she had a solid case against Will's holiday rental scheme.

The dogs hopped into the trailer and she started the tractor, which shuddered into life. She followed the headlights' beam to the gate to the meadow. When she jumped out to open it, the rain hit her full in the face and she pulled up her hood, realizing that in her haste she'd forgotten the broad-brimmed hat she usually wore. Will's fault again.

Driving slowly round the field, she peered into the gloom, searching for sheep that might need her assistance. To her relief, all the ewes seemed happily settled for the night, some tucked under the drystone walls to shelter from the rain and some grazing in the darkness while their lambs suckled or slept. Two big single lambs had been born since she was last in the field, but they looked healthy and had obviously suckled so she decided to leave them in the field with their mothers and check them again first thing in the morning.

Everything seemed so normal and calm, she almost missed the last sheep. Her headlights swept over it as she headed for home. She was right in the corner, all alone, lying down close to the wall. The light disturbed her, and she raised her head so that her eyes shone like two yellow torches in the darkness.

As the ewe tried to get up, Chrissie ran to her side, holding her firm, crooning softly under her breath as she did a hurried examination. Two tiny black hooves were protruding, but the small sheep appeared to have given up trying. With an expertise born of twenty years' experience, Chrissie felt for the lamb's head, desperately hoping it wasn't back. When, to her relief, she could feel the nose resting on its forelegs, she started to pull.

"Come on, girl," she murmured. "Help me, here."

The ewe lay there quietly, accepting her fate, but Chrissie refused to give in. She had to get the lamb out soon or it might be too late. It came suddenly, with a swishing noise, and lay limp and helpless, close to death, its heartbeat so faint that Chrissie could hardly feel it.

"Come on, little one," she pleaded, roughly rubbing its chest with both hands around the rib cage. The ewe struggled to her feet, bleating deep and urgently as she called for her baby, her tone becoming gentler as her black nose made contact with the damp, tightly curled coat of her lamb.

Working together in the darkness with a half-wild sheep to save a newborn's life was a familiar task for Chrissie, yet still, after all this time, when the lamb let out a tiny bleat, tears welled in her eyes.

With a flood of relief, she reached for the thick wool around the ewe's neck. Using her knee in expert fashion, Chrissie flipped the sheep onto its back and held it against her legs with one arm while picking up the lamb in the other. Thick yellow milk, rich with vital colostrum, oozed from the sheep's udder and Chrissie opened the lamb's tiny mouth with her finger, slipping in the warm, fat teat.

"This is life or death, little one," she murmured, willing it to swallow. The syrupy liquid trickled across her hand as the lamb lay still and silent, and she tried again, rubbing its neck to try and stimulate its swallowing again and again and again. She was about to give up when she felt the faintest movement. If she could just get enough milk into its little stomach then the newborn might have a chance.

The drizzling rain had become heavier, soaking Chrissie's hair and running down her face. Ignoring it, she concentrated on the lamb, and when it finally started to suckle a wide smile spread across her face. "That's it, little one," she said, releasing the sheep but keeping the lamb under its mother's nose. "Let's go get you warmed up."

Not needing a command, Tess and Fly positioned themselves close to the ground, alert to the ewe's every move as Chrissie gently persuaded her to follow her baby into the trailer. She closed the ramp and gave a low whistle. "Come on, girls," she called. "Let's get them home."

Knowing the routine, the collies jumped up into the tractor and settled themselves beside the seat, waving their plumed tails in excitement.

Back in the yard, Chrissie backed up to the big barn door, cut the engine and guided the sheep into one of the pens. After being out in the elements, she basked in the barn's warmth, and the aroma of sweet meadow hay filled her nostrils. Chrissie let out a sigh. She never tired of seeing a newborn happily settled with its mother, and this one seemed okay now, already up on wobbly legs and searching for a teat. The ewe nudged it close, nibbling and licking its rump, and Chrissie gave her an armful of hay.

"You'll be okay," she said. Now she could turn her attention to the barn's other inhabitants. The adopted lamb had been relieved of its lambskin jacket the day before and was totally bonded now with its new mum. Tomorrow she would return the pair to the meadow. She peered into their pen, pleased to find the lamb lying down next to its mother, stomach obviously filled to capacity.

There was nothing more satisfying, she thought, than seeing the weakest thrive; it was worth all the cold and wet and physical work. Some animals didn't make it, of course, and she had never become hardened to that. It felt like a personal failure when one of her charges died. Tonight, though, all was well. For once, she could go to bed without a worry.

Yet for some reason, as she made herself coffee and a sandwich and tried to relax in front of the TV before bed, Chrissie's mind kept on going back to Will. She wanted to avoid him, but somehow he always seemed to be there, interfering with her life. He had looked so helpless and lost when he came out of the gloom into the beam of her flashlight, but she knew that wasn't the real Will Devlin. She'd seen the other side of him when they'd clashed over the planning permission.

She sipped her coffee, appreciating the moment of calm in her normally busy life, but to her annoyance she couldn't seem to get him out of her head. On impulse, she decided to do a search for him on the internet.

She wasn't proud of snooping, but he was her nearest neighbor; surely she should have the right to know what kind of man he was.

When she typed in *Will Devlin criminal lawyer*, she found him right away. Tall, handsome and very smartly dressed, he stared out at her from the screen with eyes of steel and an arrogant tilt to his head. If she hadn't known it was him, she would have hardly recognized him.

The man in this photo was nothing like the Will Devlin she had met. This man was obviously in control, a man with confidence and assurance whose reputation for handling difficult and high-profile cases was known around the world. The kind of man she would normally move heaven and earth to avoid.

Intrigued, Chrissie scrolled down to an article in one of the top newspapers. There was a photograph of Will leaving court, his head held high and his jaw firmly set. The headline read, Criminal Lawyer or Just Plain Criminal?

Was that the case that had made him decide to walk out on his career? Either way, it didn't affect her, she told herself. Chrissie liked to try and take people at face value, and as far as she was concerned he was just her dysfunctional, albeit attractive, neighbor who always seemed to get things wrong, from the way he dressed to the way he behaved. The exception was when he'd helped her with the sheep that night... And the kiss, had he gotten that wrong? Her head said a determined *yes*, but her heart... Her heart hadn't decided yet.

He was a fish out of water, floundering around in an alien environment. The image made her smile. She might even like him if it wasn't for their clash over the land—and those moments when he showed his lawyer side. If he thought he was going to get away with bringing tourists to Craig Side then he had another think coming. Tomorrow she would start working on the petition properly. She was confident in her objections; she just had to put them down on paper. In fact, she didn't have to think hard about them at all. The negative impact tourists would have here was obvious. She remembered the ewe she'd helped earlier. What if a pack of tourists had come traipsing by, stressing out the already struggling creature by stopping to gawk at the proceedings like they were some kind of sideshow?

Or what if a hiker left the gate to the low pasture open and the lambing sheep got out? It could take weeks to herd them up again, assuming they all survived...

And then of course there were the dogs. Visitors always seemed to bring their dogs with them on holiday, and in her experience, the majority of them had no control over their pets. She'd seen it all before. Just last year one of her ewes had been half-eaten by a family's dog. She'd found the sheep motionless beside a wall, in total shock, its hindquarters chewed like a lump of raw meat. The dog had stood there, staring at her, some kind of German shepherd cross whose instincts had burst through all the layers of domesticity. That dog was probably still lying on a rug in front of someone's fire. The beloved family pet disguising the wolf.

The abhorrence she'd felt that day rankled inside her. She needed to think this through properly and make sure she got it right. She owed it to that poor ewe, if nothing else. She knew the Lake District needed tourists, and she was well aware that they would never go away completely, but at least she could fight to stop development up here on these fells. This was her home, not a resort.

CHAPTER SIXTEEN

CHRISSIE WOKE AT five thirty the next morning with a fog in her brain. Forcing her eyes open, she sat on the side of the bed with her head in her hands. "Get it together, Chrissie," she told herself. "Sheep are waiting." It was mornings like this that really made her question her choice of career.

A cup of hot coffee made her feel a lot better, and when she opened the back door to find that the rain had stopped, she even managed a smile. Floss ran past her and Chrissie called her back into the house; the little dog was coming on well, but she wasn't yet ready to work with the sheep.

"Won't be long, girl," she said, patting Floss's ruff of white hair and pushing her back into the kitchen.

The clear, sharp air quickly blew away Chrissie's cobwebs as she set off with Fly and Tess at her heels and a song back in her heart. Truth was, she loved this time of the morning, walking across the yard through the velvety darkness, so familiar with every inch of her surroundings that she didn't even need a flashlight.

The dogs went crazy, sniffing for rats, especially when a couple ran right in front of them, almost over Chrissie's toes. With a sharp whistle, she called them back. Immediately obedient, they followed her to the barn, waiting in excitement as she opened the big door and let out the aromas of feed and hay and sheep.

Inside, a low, yellow light gleamed through the darkness so that she could just make out the penned sheep and lambs clambering up from sleep. The big ewe in the farthest pen let out a rumbling bleat and Chrissie smiled to herself. This sheep had only been in the barn three or four days and Chrissie'd had a devil of a job getting her in here, but now it seemed the nervous ewe already knew the routine. That was the amazing thing about these sheep—they were wild and tough, but they knew how to adapt in order to survive, and even more importantly, for their young to survive.

"Here you are, girl," Chrissie said, throwing an armful of soft, sweet meadow hay into the pen. The ewe stared at her nervously, yellow eyes wide, and then she started nibbling on the hay while her lambs began eagerly feeding on their mother's rich milk, tails wagging and tiny rear ends bobbing up and down.

For a moment Chrissie stayed to watch them, satisfied with their progress. Tomorrow, she decided, she would let them back out into the meadow.

Checking on each pen's occupants, Chrissie gave out more hay and made sure the water containers were full before pulling the tractor keys from the pocket of her voluminous jacket and rattling them. Tess and Fly came racing over, and with a last quick look around Chrissie closed the barn doors and headed for the vehicle.

"Come on, then," she said to Tess and Fly, urging them to jump into the cab. "Time to do it all over again."

Except, she realized as she climbed into the driver's seat, she wasn't about to do it all over again. Although the routine might be the same, each morning presented new challenges; births, deaths and other problems filled each and every day at lambing time, and she wouldn't have it any different.

This morning, however, the problems were fewer, which told Chrissie that the lambing was almost over. The meadows were filled with healthy lambs and sheep, and soon it would be time for the single lambs to go back to the fell with their mothers, while the less hardy twins spent a little more time down in the shelter of home.

She felt a deep sense of satisfaction as she returned the tractor and went into the kitchen, kicking off her boots on the porch. Floss ran to her, whining softly, and Chrissie smiled, telling her to sit. When the little dog instantly did as she was bid, Chrissie pulled a treat from her pocket. Her methods of training might not comply with those of some of the other shepherds in the area, but her success rates were good and her dogs always wanted to please.

As she put on the kettle, she found herself wondering what it would be like to train the unruly Max, who had none of the collie's sharp intelligence but a very loving heart.

It didn't matter, she told herself. She wasn't about to find out anytime soon.

Since she had finished her tasks a little earlier than usual, after breakfast Chrissie allowed herself the luxury of sitting down with another cup of tea and yesterday's paper. Every morning, the postman brought a daily paper, but she didn't know why she bothered when it seemed that the news made her either sad or mad.

"Well," she said dropping the paper into the magazine rack. "What a waste of time."

Used to their mistress's ramblings Tess and Fly lay motionless in front of the stove, but little Floss jumped up and came across to sit in front of her, tail wagging and head tilted to one side. Chrissie smiled. "Don't take any notice of me ranting on, girl. It would just be nice to read something really happy for once."

She'd be sad, thought Chrissie, when Floss went back home. She'd become really attached to the pup, who would have a great future if her owner decided to do sheepdog trials with her. She'd suggest it to him, Chrissie decided, standing and stretching her arms above her head. Both the older dogs were up at once, knowing the routine.

"And today," said Chrissie, looking at Floss. "You get to come with us onto the fell. On a long leash, of course, but at least it's a start."

The mail van pulled into the yard just as she stepped out the door. With a cheery "Mornin'," the postman handed her a stack of envelopes, and she flicked through it. Three bills and a bank statement, she noted with a sigh, heading back into the house with her stomach churning. If Roy Eddery had sent her a big bill for the tractor then, basically, she was finished.

Putting off the dreaded moment, she opened the other bills first. The amounts seemed to glare out at her from the page: £500 for feed, £275 for fuel…and then the dreaded tractor bill. Her hand shook as she pulled it from its envelope. The amount was a staggering £1,502.45. She threw it onto the table in disgust, reaching for the bank statement. She'd had to get the tractor fixed, even though Roy had warned her that it would be expensive. The farm couldn't function without a tractor, especially at lambing time.

She'd been trying not to think about her

financial problems for the last few weeks;
life was stressful enough at this time of year.
But this bill had brought it all back with a
bang. She was used to going it alone, but
suddenly she felt lonely, her independence
in tatters. If only her parents were still alive.
Her mum had always been so good with the
farm finances, whereas she and her dad had
been more interested in caring for the stock.
This wasn't the first time she'd found herself
wishing she'd spent more time listening to
her mother, and it definitely wouldn't be the
last. Perhaps her aunt was right; perhaps she
did need someone in her life…a partner, like
her parents had been to each other.

Well, she had to try and find the money
somehow, and soon, for Roy's garage was
struggling just as much as her farm. In fact,
she thought, scanning the column of figures
on the bank statement, according to most of
the people she spoke to, it seemed as if all the
businesses around here were struggling to
survive. Her overdraft limit was sixty thousand, and at the moment she was way too
close to that line. She could just about manage the other bills, but the tractor payment
would take her way over.

Trying to retrieve her usual sense of calm, Chrissie sat down. A problem was not a problem, her dad had always told her; it was merely a challenge to be overcome. She always liked to think like that, but this time...

Placing her head in her hands, she fought off tears, searching for a way out. None appeared.

She would have no decent income until the lambs were ready for sale, and selling off grown sheep to pay the bills would be suicide for High Bracken because she would never be able to afford to restock. Fewer sheep meant fewer lambs the next year.

The future loomed bleakly ahead of her. She wouldn't be the first farmer up here to face this situation...nor the last. But she wouldn't give up the fight. Not yet. This land, her work and her life here on the fells, was too important to her. She had to find a way through this...somehow.

WILL WOKE EARLY and let Max out into the garden, making sure that the gate was firmly closed so there was no chance of his escaping.

He was just sitting down with his coffee when the phone rang. He picked it up impatiently. Today he had planned to call in at High Bracken with a bottle of wine for Chrissie to say thank you and maybe have another go at her about training Max. In a way, the dog had saved his life, and Will really felt that he owed Max the opportunity to prove himself. No matter what anyone said, he didn't believe Max was dumb; he was just full of life and love and exuberance, and surely those couldn't be bad traits.

"Hello?" he said in a sharper tone than he intended.

"Hey," replied Roger. "I'm on your side, remember."

"Sorry." Will liked Roger—he was upfront, straight talking…and kind of ordinary. He liked that, too. Will had met enough professionals who thought they were something special; up here on the fells, so close to nature, people didn't have egos like that. They just got on with their jobs—whatever they were.

Had he been like that once? he asked himself. Arrogant and full of self-importance? He hoped not, but he wouldn't bank on it. Power and glory had definitely gone to his head. "Bad night, I'm afraid."

"Ah…" Roger's answer, or lack of it, spoke volumes.

"And before you start any rumors," Will snapped, "I hadn't been drinking. If you must know, I got lost in the mist when I was walking Max on the fells yesterday… Chrissie Marsh found me and brought me home."

"Oh…well, then I'm glad you're okay," Roger said. He sounded sincere. "It was cold last night and exposure can be a dangerous thing."

"Look…" For once in his life, Will was at a loss for words. "I apologize for my short temper, but it was a bit of a traumatic experience. I'm trying to persuade Chrissie to give Max some training and I'm heading on up there soon, so if you want to see me—"

"It's just these plans. If you could stop in as you're going past we can maybe get them in to the planning council in time for this month's meeting. There will be objections, so the sooner the better…before they can get too much ammunition to fire at us."

"I'll be there in half an hour. So…you really think there will be objections?"

"No doubt about it. The local farmers always object when tourists are involved."

"Well, then they need educating," Will said. "The Lake District needs tourism if it is to survive."

For a moment, the line went quiet. "It's Chrissie who needs educating more than most," Roger told him. "She must be struggling—all the hill farms are—and she needs to find a way to make tourism work for her."

"I know how she feels about tourists, but surely she wouldn't actually put in a formal objection," Will insisted. "She's a bright, intelligent woman who must understand that things have to change." He formulated his next words carefully before speaking. "Anyway, we… Well, let's just say I've gotten to know her a lot better lately. She'll come round to my way of thinking eventually."

"I wouldn't be too sure of that," Roger said. "I've known Chrissie Marsh a long time, and she can be very stubborn when she wants to be. She won't change her mind easily."

Roger's comment dug deeper than Will would have liked, but Chrissie would have told him she was objecting. Surely she wouldn't go behind his back. She wouldn't do that to him.

Before Will could leave for Roger's place, Jim Wentworth caught him and insisted that he go and see how the work on the roof was progressing.

"Any more news on the planning?" Jim asked as they stared up at the rafters in the traditional old stone barn.

Will smiled. "I knew this was a ruse," he said. "The barn is fine. You just wanted to nag about the planning."

Jim looked him straight in the eye, and when he spoke his tone was serious. "The weather is improving now, and I'm nearly finished here. I have people ringing up every day with work for me, so if you're not ready for me to start on the accommodations soon, I'm afraid you'll have to get someone else."

"We're both in luck, then," Will said. "Because I'm on my way up to Roger's shortly to see if we can have the plans ready for next month's meeting."

"And you'll let me know how it goes?"

"I'll ring you later," Will promised.

Despite his assurances to Jim, Will's meeting with the architect proved to be anything but decisive. He was way too uncertain about what he wanted to be satisfied with Roger's ideas, and a new and as-yet unformulated idea was circling around in his head.

"Alright," Roger said eventually with an exasperated sigh. "Let's just go for outline planning for now, to turn the farm buildings into holiday accommodation. Then we can work on getting the details ready for next month's meeting."

"We might get refused anyway," said Will. "If as many people as you think are going to object."

"Get Chrissie Marsh onside," suggested Roger. "That's your best bet."

Will grinned. "I'm working on that."

ROGER'S ADVICE WAS still on Will's mind as he drove up the steep, narrow lane to High Bracken and parked in the yard. The whole place was bathed in spring sunshine and for the first time he realized just how pretty the farm was, and how steeped in time. Unlike most of the other farms dotted around on the fells, High Bracken hardly seemed to have been altered for at least a hundred years. Craig Side was old-fashioned, but at least the yard had been concreted; here the ground between the Lakeland stone buildings was still covered by cobblestones.

For a moment Will just stood there, taking in his surroundings. Brown chickens scratched in the dirt, clucking busily, and a big colorful rooster watched over them, full of his own importance. *Like I used to be*, thought Will with a smile. It occurred to him how narcissistic he'd always been in the city, never really stopping to look around and pay attention to anything other than himself.

"Can I help you?"

Chrissie's sharp voice came from over by the barn and he turned to her. She stood tall with her head thrown back, alert for trouble and on the defensive. He remembered kissing her, the feel of her lips beneath his and their fleeting softness. Every instinct urged him to do it again, to just walk across and take her into his arms. What would she do? Probably turn on him like a wildcat. Or melt in his arms, he thought, struggling to resist the impulse.

"Hi," he called. "I…I wondered if we could have a chat."

"I need to finish up in here first," she said shortly, retreating into the barn. Will followed, his heart racing and an unfamiliar churning in his gut.

He didn't see her immediately as he stepped through the big doors into the relative gloom of the barn. He had never really breathed in the aroma of sweet meadow hay before he came to this place, and he paused, savoring the smell.

"Someone should bottle that," he said, and Chrissie's low chuckle came from the farthest corner of the barn.

"What would you call it, High Bracken Hay...or maybe just Sweet Meadow Grass?"

"I would call it Nature's Elixir," Will announced, heading toward her. "Possibly with taint of sheep," he added, as the strong smell of the animals filled his nose.

"Let's get it out there, then," Chrissie said, standing. She'd been feeding the "pet" lamb. "I could do with the money. Here."

She placed the lamb's bottle in his hands. "Sooner I get done then the sooner I will be able to listen to what you have to say. If you just get this little one to finish its milk while I feed the sheep in the meadow then I might even have time for a coffee."

With that she strode away, leaving Will with the tiny lamb, which was gazing eagerly up at him.

"Right, then," he said, bending down to pick it up. It wriggled violently, so he put it down again, pointing the teat in its direction.

"Just cradle it with one arm while you get it going, remember," called Chrissie. "Like last time." Will glanced across to see her outlined in the doorway against the sunshine beyond the barn. Never had he met a woman like her, so comfortable and confident in her own space. That confidence and unselfconsciousness gave her a glow that no beauty product could ever match. She was radiant. He smiled at her and she smiled back.

"You're doing good," she told him before turning away, and something warmed inside him. Praise from Chrissie was praise indeed.

With fresh determination, he went about his task of feeding the lamb. His own confidence was soaring.

"Come on, little one," he urged as the tiny creature started to suckle. The tractor roared into life and he could hear Chrissie calling for the dogs. It felt as if he had stepped into another world.

By the time he heard the tractor coming back, the bottle was empty and with a feeling of satisfaction he put the lamb gently back down just as Chrissie came marching into the barn with the dogs at her heels.

"Oh, good!" she cried. "It's off to a new home later today, and a full belly will help it cope with the trauma of meeting its new mum."

Will's idyllic bubble burst in an instant as he realized anew how tough life could be here. "But why can't you just keep it until it's grown up?" he asked, feeling protective of the little creature that had been so dependent on him just moments ago.

Chrissie shrugged. "It needs to be back where it is supposed to be if at all possible. Sometimes I've been left with a lamb that never finds another mother—and don't get me wrong, they do okay on the bottle. They never really know who they are, though, that's the trouble. I had one a few years ago, named Hilda—after my aunt—who thought she was a dog and followed Tess and Fly everywhere."

"So what happened to her? Please don't say you sent her for slaughter."

Chrissie sighed. "I should have, of course,

but I managed to integrate her back into the flock… Not without difficulty, mind. She kept turning up at the back door trying to get into the house."

"And is she still a part of the flock?"

She was silent for a minute and then she dropped her gaze to the ground. "She died last year…difficult lambing." Chrissie met his eyes again. "Come on. I'll make you that coffee and you can tell me what you are really here for."

Chrissie still seemed troubled as she poured coffee into two mugs, which made Will wonder if something other than the death of the sheep last year was bothering her. She was quiet and withdrawn, as if her mind was elsewhere.

"Are you okay?" he asked.

Her answer came too quickly. "Yes, of course I am."

He tried again. "What is it…? Money? Romance?"

"It's nothing," she insisted. "Well, at least nothing that a few quid can't sort out."

Just as he had when he was a lawyer, Will saw his opportunity and moved in. "Well *there*," he said, "I just may be able to help you."

CHRISSIE LOOKED UP at him, startled. His features were both masculine and yet finely sculpted, she noted…and his lips…

She shut out the memory of their kiss.

"Two thousand pounds to train Max," he said. "That's what I'll pay you."

A spot of color rose in each of her cheeks. "But that's crazy," she said. "Anyway, I already told you, I'm way too busy."

Will reached out and took both her hands in his, holding them tightly. "Max quite probably saved my life. If he hadn't come to find you, then who knows what might have happened. I owe him, and I don't want him shot by some farmer. Please, Chrissie. The money is nothing to me."

Chrissie couldn't speak. So many thoughts were circling in her mind. Two thousand pounds would be life-changing right now, give her some peace of mind to concentrate on what she was good at… But at what cost to her pride, her dignity?

"You obviously *need* the money," he went on. She bristled at that, but let him continue. "It would be purely a business arrangement, of benefit to us both. No strings."

"But what about your plans for holiday

cottages? We're on different sides of the fence over that issue. Going into business with you would undermine my credibility with the members of the community who support my beliefs."

"But Chrissie…" Will held her gaze, tightening his grip on her hands, willing her to say yes. "Surely your friends and supporters wouldn't begrudge you doing what you have to, to survive. They'll probably pat you on the back and say, 'well done for taking his money.'"

A slow smile spread across Chrissie's face. Two thousand pounds would more than hold her over until she could start selling the lambs…but was it really worth it? Then again, did she have a choice? "And when would you intend to pay?"

"Is that a yes?"

She shook her head determinedly. "Just a question."

Still keeping a firm hold on her hands, he didn't let his gaze waver. She glanced away, her eyes wandering yet again to his lips. They formed words so eloquently, but were the words he spoke true and honest? Will's whole career had been based on clever words. What if Max proved to be untrainable—would Will still pay up?

"We'd need a contract," she said slowly, and his eyes shone.

"Here is my contract," he began. "A verbal one. I pay up in full here and now, and you try and train my dog."

Chrissie frowned, trying to pull her hands away but he wouldn't let go. An amused smile lightened his features. "What do you mean 'try'?'" she asked crossly.

"Ah, so we do have a deal?"

"No strings?"

"No strings," he promised. "If Max turns out to be too stupid to train, then no hard feelings."

"He isn't stupid," she insisted, jumping to the dog's defense.

"See," said Will. "You like him already."

"Of course I like him. I've always *liked* him. It's not his fault that his master doesn't know a thing about dogs…or anything else about the country, if we're being honest."

"Okay, then…" Will leaned toward her, so close that she could feel his breath against her skin. His aftershave was clean and crisp, and his breath held a hint of mint. "Another five hundred to train me, too."

This time she did manage to pull her hands away. "What!"

"Let me sit in on some of the training sessions so that I can learn, too, and I'll give you another five hundred pounds."

Every instinct told her to say no. Being in Will Devlin's company more than was strictly necessary was way too dangerous. The way she felt when she was around him frightened her; her own reactions to him frightened her. She stared at him, heat flooding her face.

"You would be helping the countryside, as well," he pleaded. "If you educate me, too, then all my ideas might change."

Was he talking about the planning permission? Perhaps it did make a kind of sense. She could definitely educate him about the countryside. And when she'd finished then maybe he'd finally see what she saw and drop his grand, disastrous ideas.

"Okay, then," she said firmly, feeling as if she was selling her soul. "But make it seven-fifty."

"You drive a hard bargain!" he cried. Then

he took her hand and shook it firmly, drawing her toward him. She wanted to pull away but he was already too close. She could feel his heat. And when his other hand came around her back, pulling her even closer, she surrendered.

Her lips met his and lingered there, and for an endless moment all Chrissie's reservations melted away. Her whole body softened against him and she felt her lips part, unresisting, moving so naturally against the sweetness of his. And then suddenly the dogs barked, racing across the kitchen in a frenzy, and she pulled away. What was she doing?

"That," she said, marching to the door, "was not a part of the deal." Outside, all was quiet and still. Tess, Fly and Floss stared up at her, their faces bright. "Crazy dogs, there's no one there." But she was relieved at their interference—they'd brought her back to her senses. She was behaving like a naive teenager, and it wasn't going to help her cause if Will thought she was unable to resist him.

When she turned back to him, he raised both his hands. "I'm sorry. It was a sudden impulse. You just looked so—"

"Forget it." Chrissie cut him off.

When his eyes met hers, Chrissie felt a rush of regret at taking up his offer. She would have to make an extra effort to keep things professional. She couldn't forget what Will wanted to do to her fells. He was determined to make a living out of holiday rentals, and she was determined to change his mind about it. He was paying her handsomely to do a job, and that was how she had to think of it…no getting too close, and no more impulsive kisses. No matter how much she might long for them.

And she would still fight his planning permission application if she had to. She just had to keep her feet on the ground and make him see how wrong he was.

CHAPTER SEVENTEEN

AFTER WILL LEFT, Chrissie sat at the kitchen table, staring at the check he had insisted on giving her for £2,750. She felt as if she had sold her soul, and in a way, she guessed she had.

No matter, she decided; at least now she could pay for the tractor repairs and have a nice lump left over to see her through until the lambs were sold. All she had to do was train one big, daft labradoodle…oh, yes, and train its big, daft owner, too. That would be the bigger problem, she suspected. Thankfully, she had a week's grace, for she'd told him she couldn't start until Floss went back to her owner and lambing time was about done.

To Chrissie's delight, over the next few days it felt as if the fells had decided to embrace spring and had worked out a deal with the weather. The snowdrops were dying, but daffodils sprang up to replace them in big yellow patches. Even the air smelled different, fresh and aromatic, so many scents mingling into one huge bouquet. If you could bottle it, she thought, you would be a millionaire.

As she walked toward the house after her morning chores, she dallied with the idea, remembering with a smile Will's suggestion to make the scent of hay a perfume. Then she laughed it all off. Bottle fresh air! Now that would really be a scam.

The phone was ringing as she walked into the cozy warmth of the kitchen with Tess, Fly and Floss at her heels. All three collapsed in front of the stove while she hurried to answer it. To her surprise, Tom Farrah's pleasant, confident voice filled her ears.

"Chrissie," he boomed. "How are you?"

"I'm fine…and you?" She tried to keep the apprehension out of her voice. Did he have news about Will's plans?

"Fine, too, thanks. Now, I can't get involved, but I did promise to let you know if a planning application for Craig Side came in…and it has. It is only for outline planning at this stage, and it will probably be heard next month, although as it is only the second today they have asked if there is any possibility of it being brought forward. We meet on the last Friday of the month, you see, so it will be over three weeks before this month's decisions are made."

Chrissie's heart sped up. She hadn't even begun trying to change Will's mind and already it seemed it was too late for that. She hadn't expected his application to go in so soon. A heavy lump formed in her chest. "So what exactly does that mean?" she asked.

"Well, he's applying for outline planning to turn Craig Side farm into tourist accommodation. If he wins, then that's it. There will be stipulations, though, of course, when he submits the detailed plans…"

"So obviously you think it's a foregone conclusion that he'll win?"

Tom didn't respond right away, and a trickle of anger strengthened Chrissie's resolve. Will hadn't won yet; that was the main thing.

"Yes, unless there is some serious opposition," he said. "I promised to keep you informed, but that is as far as I can go. Once we have looked at an application and any objections there are against it, my colleagues and I will make a decision purely based on the facts put before us. I can say no more than that."

"Well, thanks for that, Tom." Chrissie's tone was heavy and flat as she realized that now she had to face facts. She had agreed to train both Will and his dog, but if he thought their involvement would make her back off with her objections to his planning application, he was *so* wrong. It occurred to her that the handsome payment had been for just that very reason, to make her think twice…like a bribe. The idea did not sit well.

"I'll speak to you soon," she said, dropping the phone into its cradle. The rest of the morning would have to be spent in finalizing her objections and writing them out.

Half an hour later, Chrissie still sat in front of her blank computer screen. She had notes, plenty of them, but putting those notes into writing was a very different matter. Standing abruptly, she pushed back her chair and went into the kitchen to get a coffee. Coffee helped fix a whole heap of problems, but definitely not this one, she realized, as she ran things over and over in her mind, unsure how to start.

Surely health and safety came first? Or was it the environment? More tourists meant damage to the tracks and drystone walls that had covered the fells for centuries, tracks that the sheep here relied on. Uniquely hefted to the land, they knew their boundaries; too many tourists could change all that and alter their age-old instincts forever.

Going back to her computer with new enthusiasm, she sat down and started to type, her ideas now flowing thick and fast. Of course, she didn't want to sound too anti-tourism or they might think she was a crank. She would touch on the environmental and cultural impacts, then bring it back to health and safety, saying that while she was well aware of the importance of tourism in the Lake District, for the safety of the tourists who came here it was imperative that any accommodation provided for them should be situated lower down the fell. Most outsiders simply did not understand how dangerous these slopes could quite suddenly become, and accidents—even deadly ones—were a possibility.

She finished her last line with a satisfied smile.

Surely, when giving permission for tourist accommodation in what can often be a hostile and dangerous environment, the planning authority has a duty of care to their visitors and a responsibility to keep them as safe as possible.

She printed the document with a sigh of relief. There, it was done, and now all she had to do was send it off and wait for the outcome. She would have to tell Will, of course, when she found the right moment. He'd entered the application in the first place, she reminded herself, even after he'd agreed to put it aside. She'd try and casually throw it into the conversation, she decided, when they started the training next week. It wouldn't be a pleasant conversation, but she had to have it. The future of her home was at stake here, and that was way more important than any budding attraction between her and Will.

FINALLY, IT WAS Floss's last day at High Bracken, and Max's first—not much of a swap. Chrissie had never been so sad to see one of her trainees leave, or so apprehensive about a new one coming in.

She was putting Floss through her paces in the training paddock to make sure she was totally ready to go back to her owner. Chrissie asked her to sit and wait, and as usual, the dog's obedience amazed her, and when she gave her the command "Away...away out," the little black-and-tan collie ran counterclockwise around the Runner ducks. Gently and carefully, she herded the flock toward where Chrissie was waiting by the pen with the gate open.

"Lie down," she called, and Floss dropped to the floor, never taking her eyes off her charges until Chrissie gave the command, "Come by," to send her clockwise. When the ducks finally waddled in, perfectly calm, and Chrissie closed the gate on them, Floss began running round in crazy circles, knowing that her job was done.

"So, is that what you are going to teach Max first?" called Will from where he had been standing near the duck shed. She must not have heard him pull in.

Chrissie laughed. "I wanted you to see just

how much you can teach a dog in a short time. Floss hasn't been here long and she's just had initial training, but hopefully she'll be coming back when the lambs are grown, to train on the fell with the sheep and the other dogs. Her owner just wanted the basics established, and then he can do quite a bit on his own. What we need to do with Max is to try and teach him to be more obedient…and obviously not to chase sheep."

"That could be difficult," groaned Will. "All he has to do is see a sheep now and he gets overexcited."

"So that," announced Chrissie, "will be our first lesson. I do have a way to deter dogs from chasing after sheep—it's a bit basic, but it works. I'll set it up for tomorrow."

Will came closer as she let the ducks out of the pen into the meadow again and called Floss to heel.

"So will he stay here with you now?" he asked.

Chrissie shook her head. "Normally he would, but if you remember, you are paying me to train you, too, so as you're going to be very involved. He might as well stay with you—for now, at least. I'll give you training homework to do with him."

Will fell into step beside her as she headed for the gate. "Are you sure that I'll be able to do it, though?" he asked uncertainly.

Surprised by his lack of confidence, she smiled. "I thought that nothing fazed you hotshot lawyers."

"Well nothing in a court of law," he said. "This is a bit out of my comfort zone."

"That's because it's all about common sense, not words. Common sense, trust, an understanding of the way dogs think and a degree of discipline. Some of the sheep farmers around here only know discipline, but they will never get the best results if they rule by fear."

Will nodded. "Well, you're right that words are my forte, but I really do want to learn all the other stuff."

"Like what to wear," said Chrissie, hiding a smile as she pointedly looked him up and down.

He grimaced. "You didn't like my country look or my city clothes, so I thought I'd just do casual."

"Running shoes are hardly suitable for

mud and wet grass, though, are they?" she remarked. "The country boots you had on that day were fine—it was just the tweed jacket and moleskin trousers that were a bit too country gent for a working day. City suits, of course, have no place here. You just need Hunter wellingtons or your country boots, a pair of jeans and a warm, waterproof coat. A wide-brimmed hat is often a good idea, too, as long as it doesn't keep blowing off. Comfortable and warm—that's what it's all about."

Will laughed and Chrissie noticed how much softer and more approachable he seemed when he smiled. He really was two different people: the hard, career-minded lawyer and the man who was way out of his depth, floundering around in the country but desperately trying to get things right. Perhaps he was even three men, she decided, if you counted the goofy guy who always seemed to get it wrong but really made her laugh. Trouble was, she hadn't yet worked out which of the three was the real Will Devlin.

"Floss's owner will be here to collect her soon," she said. "But if you come back with

Max tomorrow—say nine thirty, to give me time to get my jobs done first—then we'll make a proper start on the basics."

He seemed disappointed as he moved away, but then he turned back. "So will you be putting Floss through her paces for him?" he asked.

Chrissie shook her head. "He came over a couple of days ago and saw her working then."

"Is he a farmer?"

"He does have a sheepdog that I am training to work the sheep, so…"

"Unlike me, you mean?"

Chrissie shrugged. "If the cap fits…"

"Perhaps I could stay until he's gone and we could make a start today," he suggested, ignoring her slight jab.

He really is looking forward to getting started on this, Chrissie thought with surprise. "I suppose that's fine," she told him. "But I have some jobs to do first." She liked the fact that he was so keen. It seemed genuine, which was a big step toward fitting in here. And if he felt like he was starting to belong, then maybe he'd be more likely to understand where she was coming from about the tourists. Maybe he could even come to share her passion for this way of life.

For the next forty-five minutes, with Will's help, Chrissie tidied up in the barn, taking down some of the makeshift pens she'd erected for lambing time that she no longer needed. They neatly stacked the hay bales and cleared out the dirty bedding with a wheelbarrow and shovel. Will had elected himself as chief barrow handler, and Chrissie smiled as she watched him stagger off across the yard to the muck pile with yet another huge load. He returned with a broad smile on his face, a healthy glow to his normally pale cheeks and Max bounding around him in circles.

"Who needs the gym?" he said.

Chrissie laughed. "There would be no need for people to go to the gym if they just did a proper hard day's work. Come on, that'll do for today. In fact, it's some of my work for tomorrow sorted, too, thanks to you."

"You know, I never thought anyone would ever get me to shift muck," said Will, leaning his fork against the wall.

"I never got you to," Chrissie reminded him. "You decided to do it all by yourself."

"So I did," he agreed, catching her eye. "And I have to say, I quite enjoyed it."

For a moment he held her blue eyes in his and the breath caught in her throat as she realized that his steely grays were now more softly sparkling silver. When the sound of an engine caught their attention, rumbling and chuffing up the lane, she felt a rush of relief. She didn't want this camaraderie with Will. The planning meeting loomed over them, and he didn't even know that she intended to stop his plans from going through. She needed to keep their relationship on professional footing. As it was, their training sessions hadn't even started yet and she was already losing her head.

The car shuddered to a halt right in front of them.

"Well, is she ready for home?" asked the elderly farmer who clambered out and hobbled toward them.

"Ready and waiting," Chrissie said, letting out a low whistle. All the dogs came running, including Max, who bounded around like a clumsy pup but with ten times the strength.

"Sorry," Will said, grabbing for Max's collar as the dog hurtled into the man's knees, almost knocking him off his feet.

Chrissie gave the command for Tess and Fly to lie down and called for Floss. "Time to go home, young lady." Then she turned back to Will. "I'll just be a minute."

WILL WATCHED THEM walk across the yard with the pretty little black-and-tan collie trotting behind them: the elderly farmer, stooped from years of hard, honest labor and the tall woman with her head held high, both knowing exactly who they were and where they were in their lives. They had a real place in the world, whereas he... Where was his place? He used to think it was in the courtroom, but now...now he had to admit to himself that he was lost.

To his amazement, after Chrissie disappeared into the house Tess and Fly remained totally still, heads on paws and bright eyes watching for their mistress's return.

Will reached down to scratch Max's broad head. "Will you be like that soon, boy?" The labradoodle looked up at him, smiling and wagging his tail. Will laughed. "I guess that's a no, then. Well, I for one am excited to learn this dog training stuff."

As the rusty blue car struggled out of the yard with blue smoke pouring from its exhaust, Chrissie strode purposefully over to where Will stood with Max.

"Well, I really am sorry to see that little dog go," she said. "She's been one of the easiest dogs I've ever had to train."

Will grimaced, peering at Max. "Unlike this one, then," he said. "He's probably going to be the worst."

Chrissie shook her head, brushing a tendril of long blond hair behind her ear. "If you think like that then it will never work," she insisted. "We have to look at Max fairly and be totally objective about his behavior in order to decide why he acts the way he does. After that, we can work out how best to make him learn."

"No magic tricks, then."

She shook her head determinedly. "No magic tricks. Just a lot of common sense and determination."

"So, what's the plan?"

Chrissie sighed. "It's easy to work with collies—some are sharper than others, more aggressive perhaps, or more nervous. But they have certain instincts I know how to build on. I'm not as familiar with labradoodles, obviously, but the principles are the same. The first thing I do when I get a new recruit is to get to know its nature so that I can decide which approach to use. With Max...well, let's just say that I already have a good idea about his nature."

Will leaned forward, all ears. "And that is?"

"Well..." she began, "we have to take into account what he is. Labradors are bred to be working dogs. They tend to be very trainable and are usually loving, easygoing and generally happy, with strong instincts to retrieve and naturally soft mouths. Poodles, however, have a reputation for being highly strung, excitable and nervous. So a mixture of the two can go toward either end of the spectrum."

"And which way has Max gone, do you think?"

Chrissie smiled, warming to her task. "No, which way do *you* think he has gone?"

Will shrugged. "I guess he swings more toward the Labrador. A client of mine used to have a chocolate Lab, as I remember. She was a bit dopey and daft."

"There you are, then," agreed Chrissie. "So Max is daft and dopey rather than nervous?"

"He isn't nervous about anything." Will smiled. "Or *of* anything."

"So, would you say he lacks respect?"

"Absolutely. He thinks the sheep are just playthings."

"And there lies your problem," Chrissie told him. "He doesn't even respect you."

Max looked from one to the other as if he was aware they were talking about him, and they both laughed.

"So how do we go about teaching him respect?" Will asked.

"Well, as I mentioned, some farmers around here like to rule by fear, and while you do have to be firm, sometimes they can take it too far. The first thing I'd like to do with him is to teach him to respect the sheep, and maybe that will change his attitude to us a little. We will be there to protect him, you see."

"Protect him from what?" asked Will with a puzzled frown.

"From the sheep." Chrissie smiled secretively. "No more questions—let's just see if it works."

"You've tried it before, right?"

She shook her head. "Not exactly. At least, not on purpose, although I know people who have and I've seen it happen often enough in a normal working situation. Come on— nothing ventured, nothing gained. All training works like this to a degree. We read the situation, decide what approach to take and move on from there, learning all the time."

Before they reached the Runner ducks' paddock, Chrissie spent some time teaching Max basic commands. "I want to try and get his attention without the distraction of the ducks or anything," she told Will. He wondered what the "anything" was but decided not to ask. No doubt he'd find out soon enough.

Chrissie's plan worked to a degree. That is, it worked when Max could be bothered to listen.

"To him, life is just a game," she explained. "And he is still quite young, isn't he?"

"Almost eighteen months," Will offered.

Giving a firm command to sit, Chrissie backed away slowly, holding up her palm. "You need to use body language," she said. "Animals understand that—horses as much as dogs, actually. I had a pony right through my teenage years, and I used to love playing around with horse-whispering techniques. Everything to do with animals is a learning curve, and you have to stay open-minded."

"So why did you stop? Riding, I mean."

Chrissie shrugged. "Oh, I don't know. I outgrew my pony, Sunny, and always intended to get another, but..." Her expression grew wistful. "After my parents died, I just seemed to be so busy all the time. I was—and still am—determined to keep this farm going for them, but it's tough sometimes, on my own."

Will placed a hand on her arm. "I heard about your parents, and I'm so sorry. You must still miss them very much."

"Every day." Chrissie sighed, and her eyes filled with tears. "Anyway..." She seemed to be making an effort to pull herself together. Not one of those tears fell. "I couldn't afford to buy a horse even if I did have the time."

"You could use the training money I gave you," Will suggested, and she shook her head, smiling at him. Somehow, in that moment, he felt closer to her than when he'd kissed her.

"I don't think there will be much left once I've settled the bills."

Max still sat obediently and she leaned forward, patting her knees. "Here, boy," she called, and he ran toward her eagerly. "You see?" she cried. "He's enjoying being given something to concentrate on."

Observing the animation in Chrissie's face, Will was flooded with an unfamiliar emotion. She was just so...so sure of who she was. Losing her parents must have been devastating, but she'd been strong. She'd never wavered and never let them down. He hadn't met anyone like her before, a woman who was motivated by the love she had for her life here, by her dedication to the creatures in her care. Her independence was admirable, yet her solitude also made him kind of sad. She had so much to give, so much love; he could see that in the way she treated her animals. So why was she alone? Perhaps she just hadn't met someone she wanted to share her life with. Or maybe she didn't want to share it at all.

"How come you are on your own?" he asked, regretting the question the moment the words left his lips. It was way too personal.

She stiffened. "How come you are?"

He grinned. "Touché. I guess I deserved that."

"You need to do this kind of training with him constantly," she said, ignoring his question and changing the subject. "Come here, sit, stay and lie down—basic commands are the whole way forward. Just spend time with him, and have some small treats in your pocket initially if it makes it easier to get his attention. Be firm and strict but never lose your temper—that is negative. Praise him when he gets it right and never let him off until he's done what you've asked. He will learn to *want* to please you if you persevere. That's why I don't think you should leave him with me, as Floss's owner did. It's important to build up your relationship with him. Right now he sees you as just a friend, not a master."

"And what about the sheep-chasing?"

asked Will, already enthusiastic about the prospect of training Max. "What is it you've set up to solve that?"

Chrissie smiled. "All right, I'll show you. But first I want you to tell Max to sit. Then attach the long leash and repeat the command every now and then until he does what you want without thinking about it."

As CHRISSIE WATCHED Will's attempts to control the big, boisterous dog, a warm glow spread inside her. His awkward but determined efforts were surprisingly touching.

"So, tell me again," she said. "Exactly why did you buy a dog like him?"

He glanced up at her before turning his attention back Max, who had decided to roll over instead of sitting. "I don't really know," he said, shaking his head and smiling at the dog's antics. "I've never had much to do with dogs, but when I set my mind on moving to the country and bought Craig Side it just seemed like a good idea. I saw him advertised online and he was so cute, I called the seller and bought him."

"What?" Chrissie couldn't believe what

she was hearing. "You mean you never even went to see him?"

"No...the man delivered him for me and I gave him the cash."

Will looked sheepish, but Chrissie found his embarrassment and vulnerability endearing. "I don't think I have ever met anyone who knows as little about animals and the countryside as you," she told him, amused. "So, whatever made you buy yourself a farm, especially one as isolated as Craig Side?"

Gathering up Max's leash, Will shrugged. "You're going to think I'm even more stupid now. I stayed in Little Dale once with my parents, when I was just a kid. When I walked out of the courtroom and out of my career that day, I remembered loving it here. It seemed so far away from everything I was used to. So I just got in my car, drove here and booked into a guesthouse. I saw Craig Side advertised in an estate agent's window and loved its isolation. I put in an offer as soon as I'd been to look at it, and here I am."

"I don't think I know anyone as difficult to understand as you are," Chrissie said.

Will was immediately on the defensive. "What do you mean?"

Chrissie hesitated, unsure if she should admit to Googling him. "I found you on the internet," she eventually admitted. "Not to be nosy, I promise, but you could have been a serial killer or something for all I knew—I just wanted to feel safe."

Will's face darkened. "And?"

"And I found out that you had a huge and very successful career in law—I mean, you'd told me you were a lawyer, obviously, but I didn't realize quite how big your reputation was. There was a headline, too…"

His jaw tightened. "Don't tell me…Criminal Lawyer or Just Plain Criminal?"

She nodded, her cheeks heating up. "Something like that."

"Listen…" He let go of Max's leash and took hold of both her hands, forcing her to meet his gaze. "I've already told you. I'm not proud of what I was. It's true that I was successful, very successful, but it was for all the wrong reasons. Maybe all I've done is run away, but whatever happens, I will never go back to where I was."

Chrissie let her hands sit in his as she studied him with curiosity. "It's just such a huge step to take from where you were as a city slicker lawyer to this isolated existence surrounded by sheep and dogs..."

"And good neighbors," he cut in with a small smile. "Well, one good neighbor, at least."

"I just wonder if all this will be enough, though," she went on, ignoring his attempt at humor. "You are so far out of your comfort zone..."

Will's eyes glittered and he stared intently at her hands, kneading her knuckles with his fingers. "I stepped out of my comfort zone on that day in the courtroom," he said. "I looked at my client's face, the man I was defending. His smug expression held so much arrogance, so much deceit and cruelty that it made me sick. It seemed that a veil had been lifted from my eyes and I was ashamed... ashamed of all my previous successes... ashamed of the man I had become. If that's what it meant to be in my comfort zone, I don't ever want to be in it again."

Chrissie stayed very still, acutely aware of his vulnerability. "Then learn from your mistakes," she urged him, closing her fingers around his. "Become a better man."

He smiled. "That," he said, "is exactly

what I am trying to do...with your help, of course."

"But do you think that's really the answer? Hiding yourself way up here with dogs and sheep?"

His eyes were intense and piercing, and she couldn't pull hers away. "And with you," he murmured. "Life here feels honest, Chrissie, honest and true and real. I want to go with it, to find myself again. That's enough for me right now...especially with you to help me."

"And now you're making me feel guilty for taking your money," she cried. "You've paid me way too generously."

Will shrugged. "Don't worry about it. It's well worth it to me."

"Well then, just pay me for training Max. I was way out of order making an extra charge for you to be involved, anyway."

He shook his head. "I told you, it's just money...although..." He raised his eyebrows, lightening the mood. "It seems to me that you're not doing your job very well so far."

Chrissie bristled, all traces of guilt fading. "What do you mean?"

"I mean that you aren't doing your job very well because your charge is currently hightailing it off up the fell."

With a horrified cry, Chrissie turned to see Max racing off across the meadow. "Max," she yelled, hurrying after him and calling him back with as much calm and determination as she could manage. Despite her best efforts, her voice rose with frustration when he ignored her.

"Firm but always calm, remember," said Will, attempting to keep up with her. "And never lose your temper."

Chrissie shot him an angry glare, their moment of closeness relegated to the back of her mind. "I am not losing my temper… I'm just displaying my authority."

"Ah," Will teased. "So that's what they call it now."

CHAPTER EIGHTEEN

DESPITE, OR PERHAPS because of Max's disobedience, Chrissie was determined to go ahead with her sheep respect and awareness program. It had taken a full half hour to catch up with him, and he had shown no regret at all for his actions.

Biting her lip to control her temper, Chrissie had reprimanded Max in a firm tone that bordered delicately on anger. Will had struggled not to smile as he watched her wrestle with her self-control, but she'd managed it. In fact, he thought Max seemed contrite by the time she'd finished scolding him. Then she'd spent another twenty minutes doing her disciplining exercises: sit down, stay and come here. She'd kept a firm hold of the leash, jerking on it if Max did not do as he was told immediately, and giving him a treat when he did.

"You see," she said to Will eventually, her face bright with triumph. "Calm but firm."

"Only just," he said, smiling. "You were on the edge there for a minute, but I have to hand it to you—you didn't lose your temper. So is that it for today?"

"No," she said, loose strands of hair blowing around her face. "We're still doing the sheep awareness and respect exercise. He deserves it after his disobedience."

"Lead on, then," urged Will. "I'm intrigued to see what you plan to do."

They headed in silence to the Runner duck paddock. Chrissie insisted that Max walk quietly beside her and refused to allow him to either pull or stop and sniff.

"Right," she said to Will when they reached the paddock gate. "Just hold him here for a minute while I lock the ducks in."

"Won't we need them?"

"For teaching a dog to respect sheep?" she asked.

When he finally led Max in through the gate, Will was surprised to see a sheep and single lamb over in the corner. The ewe looked nervous, and when she saw the dog she started stamping her forefeet on the ground and nuzzling her offspring.

Shutting the gate and double-checking that it was properly fastened, Chrissie took hold of Max's collar and unclipped his leash.

"Sit down," she told him, and he obeyed... until he saw the sheep and its lamb. He began to whine loudly, shiver in excitement and wag his tail madly. "Stay," said Chrissie, but his discipline completely unraveled and he took off toward the sheep.

"Are you crazy?" cried Will. "Why have you let him go?"

Chrissie placed a restraining hand on his arm. "Just watch," she insisted.

As the dog approached, the ewe turned to face him, standing next to her lamb against the wall. Max barked, expecting her to run, and when she stood her ground, stamping her feet, he paused, unsure. The ewe seized the moment. Lowering her black-and-white head and curling horns with all the fury of a bull in a fight, she charged.

Max hesitated for a moment too long and her head made contact with his rib cage, pushing him into the drystone wall. He let out a yowl of pain followed by puppy-like yelps of fear. Will stood there, aghast. What was she thinking? Was she trying to get his poor dog killed?

"Call him," urged Chrissie. "Be his savior."

Not knowing what else to do, Will leaned forward, patting his knees in encouragement. "Here, boy," he yelled. The not-so-brave-now, almost comical labradoodle heard his master and raced toward him in terror. "Good boy!" Will exclaimed, grabbing his collar and making a fuss of him. "Did the naughty sheep chase you?"

Max hid behind him and Chrissie followed, running her hands expertly over the dog's rib cage.

"No harm done," she announced, and Will let out the breath he was holding. Her methods were extreme, to say the least. "Just a bit of bruising and a big knock to his ego."

Will patted Max exuberantly and clipped the leash onto the dog's collar, looking across to where the ewe was now suckling her lamb with one eye firmly fixed on the big cream-colored dog.

"Motherly love, eh?" Will said. "I would never have believed it could be so strong."

Chrissie nodded. "These fell sheep may seem nervous, but they're very tough and brave when they need to be. She would die to save her lamb. Now walk him round the paddock and see how he reacts."

Will set off with Max right behind him, clinging close. When they got near the sheep he stopped, backing up so far he almost pulled his collar off. Will reached down to reassure him, but Chrissie called to him to stop.

"Don't stroke him—he needs to keep his fear of sheep. It's not as if he's ever going to be a sheepdog. Hopefully he'll give them a wide berth now. Do you want to test it out?"

Will faltered. He had been quite freaked out by the ewe's aggression. That such a nervous creature could actually attack a dog had been shocking, and to realize that even in nature creatures could act out of character was kind of disturbing, especially when he had firmly believed animals to be beyond the often cruel and violent behavior of humans.

His discomfort must have shown, for Chrissie's expression was sympathetic. "The ewe was just defending her lamb," she told him. "Watch."

She walked briskly toward the wide-eyed sheep and its lamb, taking big, confident strides. As she drew closer, the ewe stamped her front feet just once before racing off with a series of stiff jumps, her tiny offspring at her heels.

"She knows she can't beat me, you see," Chrissie explained. "But to her, the dog is like a wolf. Old instincts kick in when she's cornered, and as I said, she would happily die defending her lamb. I don't think you'll have any more trouble with Max chasing sheep now, and he should respect you more, too, because you were there to save him."

"But I wasn't," Will said.

Chrissie shrugged. "He doesn't know that. Most animals don't think things through, they just react. Unlike people, any aggression they show is usually to win a mate, get food or protect their babies. Survival is the name of the game. Anyway, if you don't believe me, let's test it out."

"Are you sure about this?" Will grumbled, following Chrissie toward the home meadow.

"I just want to show you, and Max, while it's fresh in all our minds." she said. "It won't take long, and then we'll go get that coffee I promised you."

The flock of sheep moved as one rippling entity across the fresh green pasture. To Will's amazement, Max hung back, sticking close to his human companions and eyeing the sheep nervously. When a ewe with twin lambs stamped her feet at the sight of him, he whined in fear, pushing up against Will for protection.

"I guess that's enough," said Chrissie. "Lesson learned. It seems that our desperate measures paid off."

"It's a miracle," Will agreed.

The afternoon was drawing to a close by the time they arrived back at the house. Will glanced at the sky, noting the gray clouds that hung menacingly on the horizon. It would be getting dark soon.

Chrissie seemed to have noticed the changing light, too. "Right. We have just enough time for that coffee before I go check the sheep and finish up in the yard."

"It's endless, isn't it?" Will remarked. "Don't you ever get fed up?"

Chrissie shrugged. "It's life. Animals don't

have days off, and I can't afford to pay staff. Anyway, what else would I do?"

There was an air of quiet in Chrissie's homey kitchen as she and Will sat in companionable silence, sipping contentedly on their coffees. It occurred to Will that he had never felt so at home with anyone before. Who did he know in the city that he could spend time with, without feeling the pressure to make meaningless conversation?

Chrissie's head was bowed and her blond hair, loose now, tumbled over her shoulders. When she looked up at him and smiled, his heart turned over.

He didn't want to kiss her. He wanted so much more. He wanted to see her face, her smile, every day. Sit beside her in the evenings as the sun went down and hold her forever, through good times and bad. The strength of his own feelings took him totally by surprise. This was crazy, like a spell. What was this woman doing to him?

"It shocked you, didn't it?" she said, startling him. Had she read his mind? "The ewe's aggression, I mean. I saw it in your face. Now you've seen, even experienced, how hostile and violent this place can be.

It's not for the fainthearted, but it is true to itself."

The glow inside him faded as he realized what she was getting at.

"You're talking about my plan to bring tourists here, aren't you," he said with a rush of irritation. "Is this your way of trying to put me off the idea? A ruse to get me to retract my application?"

"I do want to educate you about life here," she admitted. "And you know how I feel about your holiday cabins. Today, though, has been about training Max, not dwelling on your plans. You have paid me well to do a job, and I'll do the best I can with it. Your holiday rentals are something else entirely."

"Fair enough," Will said. "And thank you for today—it has certainly been a learning curve. How you made that exercise with Max and the sheep work, I don't know."

"Well, I was a bit worried about that," Chrissie admitted with a slow smile.

"You were worried!"

"It worked though, didn't it?"

Will nodded. "It was pretty impressive, actually…and it certainly taught me about animal behavior."

"Will…" She reached across to take hold of his arm. "I'm determined to be professional about this. I don't want either of us to mention tourists or your planning permission again. We know where we both stand on that subject, but it has nothing to do with the agreement we have about training Max… and for what it's worth, well, I get why you're here now."

He placed his hand over hers. It was warm and strong, he noted…a working hand. He liked that. When she tried to pull away, he tightened his grip. He held her gaze, daring her to look away, but she returned it steadily.

"Okay," he agreed. "Totally professional it is. Now, do you want some help or should I head home?"

"I can manage… You just go and see your architect or something."

He cupped the back of her head, drawing her face toward his. "Totally professional you said…so why the sarcasm?"

She had the grace to blush. "Sorry. I was out of order. It won't happen again."

"What time do you want us tomorrow?" he asked, releasing her. "Or do you want us at all?"

"We have an agreement, and I already told you I wouldn't be breaking it, so of course I want you. Two o'clock any good?"

Will grinned. "Anytime is okay for me. See you at two, then."

AS SOON AS Will and Max left, Chrissie hurried outside, determined to fill her head and hands with work.

Oh, how she wished that she'd never gone along with Will Devlin's proposition. There was something about him that really got to her, a kind of understanding between them that frightened her with its intensity, especially when they knew full well that inevitably they were going to clash over his plans. They were wrong for each other, their goals too far apart. When he realized that she intended to jeopardize his plans, he would hate her. She couldn't face that, not since she knew what he'd gone through and how vulnerable he could be. Those plans were his future, yet how could she accept them when they threatened everything she cared about? The best thing he could do was to go back to his lawyer job in the city and forget all about Little Dale. Tomorrow afternoon loomed high on her horizon; she had to do this, so she might as well make the best of it.

WILL FOUND HIMSELF humming as he poured soup into a pan and brewed a pot of tea. How long had it been, he mused, since he'd eaten at one of the upmarket restaurants that had once been his norm? Nowadays soup or beans seemed to have become his staple diet.

While he waited for the soup to heat up, his mind went back to Chrissie and the afternoon they'd spent together. The way she had taken control of the whole situation with Max and the sheep had deeply impressed him. Her understanding of how each animal was going to react was, to him, almost an act of magic. She was magic, he decided, tall and strong and sure, needing no one to help her through the tough life she had chosen. What a lawyer she would have made.

His phone interrupted his reflection.

"Well, when are you coming back to us?" Roy Wallis's voice burst into his ear, deep, well-spoken and always expecting to get his own way. Even Roy's wife, Margaret, was unaware of just how ruthless he could be,

Will suspected, though he recognized that he had been equally ruthless not so long ago.

Will sighed. He could do without this right now. "We've been through this, Roy. I am not coming back to work."

"But what about my suggestion? You could build a new portfolio of clients, to make up for all the bad guys you helped get off."

"I was doing my job the best way I could, but I lost the heart for it. All of it. So if you don't mind..."

"I saw Miranda yesterday." Roy paused, presumably to give his news full impact. "She was asking after you, since you never answer your calls. So what do I tell her?"

"Why would you tell her anything? She was my girlfriend, fleetingly, but that was ages ago. I've moved on."

"She wondered if you'd like to meet up with her when you came back to the city, for old time's sake...have dinner, maybe."

Will contemplated hanging up on him. "Look, Roy, if you don't mind, I'm in the middle of something, so—"

"There's a case coming up that you may be interested in. Please, before you hang up, just hear me out. It's the kind of case that you would have once really sunk your teeth into—corruption, murder and everything that goes with it. The thing is, you defended Tom Crawford last year, if you remember."

"How could I ever forget?" growled Will.

"No one but you could have got him off… and the headlines after Criminal Lawyer or Just Plain Criminal were priceless."

"And your point is?" Will's throat tightened as all the reasons for him turning his back on his career flooded his mind.

"The guy who took the blame has appealed and we have new evidence that might get him off. Can't you see, Will?" pleaded Roy. "This is your chance…your chance to make amends…to at least make sure that justice is finally done. Rightly or wrongly Tom Crawford walked free—thanks to you, remember—but at least now you can help the man who was wrongly accused of his crime. That should help appease your conscience, surely."

Will's voice was strained. "You mean it's your chance to try and persuade me back to work," he said. "Well, you'll have to get someone else to do it. I have enough on my plate."

"Like what?"

A smile found its way through Will's anger. He felt safe here, safe from the mess of his former life. Fell country might be dangerous, but that was nothing compared to the damage that life had done to him.

"I'm training my dog," he said, and the phone went dead. Had Roy hung up on him? He checked the screen and saw that the signal had been dropped. Will almost felt sorry not to be able to hear Roy's shocked reply.

Imagining the expression on his ex-boss's face lightened his spirit, but when his phone rang again and Roy's name flashed across it, he almost declined the call. However, he couldn't resist hearing his former boss's reaction to the dog training.

"Sorry," he said, "I lost you. Reception's not so good around here."

"Did you say you're training your dog?" asked Roy.

"Certainly did…although, to be honest, I need the training as much as he does. It's costing me a fortune."

"All the more reason to come back and do some work for Marcus Finch," Roy suggested.

Will's response was immediate. "I already told you how I feel about that."

"Well, at least come back for the dinner next month—you know, our annual bash at the Hilton. You've always enjoyed that, and I promise I won't even mention work."

About to give a determined no, Will held back as an idea came into his head. What if he invited Chrissie? Being with her might make them see just how settled he was in his new life and hopefully accept his decision to stay here. He cringed. Was he so short of self-confidence these days that he still needed to prove himself to the likes of Roy? No matter how ashamed he sometimes felt about the way he'd walked away from Marcus Finch, he knew that leaving had been the right thing to do.

"Do I get to bring someone?" he asked.

"Of course." Roy laughed. "Don't tell me…a farmer?"

"A sheep farmer, actually."

"It will certainly make a change from the string of would-be models and film stars that usually accompany you."

He clicked off the phone, asking himself what had possessed him to suggest taking

Chrissie to the Marcus Finch annual dinner, to which were invited prestigious clients, lawyers and their partners. After dinner, Roy always gave a speech about the successes of the previous year and then usually a famous singer would perform, with dancing later. To even think that Chrissie would agree to go was ridiculous; she wouldn't know what to wear, and he wouldn't be able to stand all his ex-associates looking down their noses at her. But why should they? Chrissie Marsh was a gorgeous, confident woman. If they did sneer at her, she could stand her ground. She was very much a part of his life now, and he realized that he would be proud to have her at his side.

And that realization scared him.

THE NEXT DAY, while he was driving to Bracken Hall with Max after calling in on Roger to discuss the plans, a new idea came into Will's head.

It was just the beginning of an idea, a different slant on his original plans that might be more acceptable to Chrissie and help the Lake District, too. But before he could dig deeper into its implications, he reached his destination. He logged the idea in the back of his mind and turned his attention to Max.

He wanted to show Chrissie that he really was taking his "homework" seriously and he had already spent a full hour that morning getting the dog to sit and lie down and stay. He was proud of his results; it was rewarding to be building a stronger bond with the dog he had bought so impulsively.

Will reflected on how he, who had always been a man to act deliberately, with great thought and planning, had for the very first time in his life made two huge, spontaneous decisions in a very short time: the decision to buy Craig Side and, shortly afterward, the decision to buy a dog.

Sometimes it felt as if someone else's brain had been transplanted into his head, except if that was the case, he wouldn't still have his childhood memories…or the guilt he felt whenever he thought of his parents. Too many phone calls in the past ten years, asking him when he was coming to see them… too many times when he didn't go.

After his dad had retired from his driving job in Penrith, they'd moved to Spain to live out their lives in the sunshine, and now he only spoke to them once a month or so.

A heavy sadness replaced his sense of well-being as he realized just how selfish he had been, how vain and arrogant with his high-flying job and upmarket friends. Here, where people's values were so very different, he was slowly coming to see what really mattered in life.

"What do you think, boy?" he asked, and Max placed his paws on the back of Will's seat, planting big, sloppy kisses on Will's nape.

CHAPTER NINETEEN

CHRISSIE WAS FEEDING the chickens when she heard a four-by-four coming up the lane. Recognizing the sound of Will's vehicle, she carefully closed the shed door and headed for the yard with a basket of smooth brown eggs over her arm and the dogs at her heels. She made an effort not to hurry. The fact that his arrival brought a flutter of anticipation irritated her.

Instead of the usual showers, April had brought glorious sunshine for once, and she shaded her eyes with her free arm to see Will climbing out of the driver's seat. Max raced across to greet her like an old friend, and she put down her egg basket so she could crouch down to make a fuss of him, glad of the opportunity to avoid talking to Will. What was wrong with her? No one had ever made her feel so awkward. Perhaps it was guilt over objecting to his plans while she was taking his money.

"Well!" he announced with a broad grin. "We've been doing our homework."

She stood up slowly, forcing herself to meet his gaze with a cool expression. "And is it going well?"

"Very well," he said. "I think."

He looked like the cat that got all the cream. "Well you certainly seem pleased with yourself," she remarked. "I'll just take these eggs into the house and then you can show me how well you've progressed."

"Everything you've taught me is beginning to make sense," he told her, his tone high with excitement as he fell into step beside her.

Well, maybe not the cat that got the cream, she thought, but maybe an overexuberant schoolboy. He certainly was a man of many faces, and this was the one she was most drawn to. He glanced sideways at her, smiling, and on impulse she took his hand. "I like this side of you, Will. Carefree and happy."

"Why?" he asked. "Am I usually too serious?"

"Sometimes..." Heat crept into her cheeks

and she let go of his hand, embarrassed by her spontaneity.

"This place has changed me, you know, Chrissie," he said, his voice quiet but so intense that it made Chrissie's heart race. Gone, she realized, was the laughing schoolboy. "*You* have changed me."

"For the better, I hope." She laughed, trying to lighten the moment. "I'll just put these eggs away and then you can show me exactly how much you and Max have progressed."

WILL WAITED OUTSIDE in the sunshine while Chrissie took the eggs into the house. He sat on a low wall with Max, Tess and Fly at his feet, feeling as if he was in charge of the world as he gazed out across the valley.

The spring sunshine had brought freshness and new life to the fells. The shades of vibrant green at their feet were slowly spreading upward to meet the stark grays and browns of the higher ground where winter still lurked, unwilling to let go quite yet. Spring was chasing it away though, he noted, for patches of golden daffodils were visible everywhere, little bursts of sunshine from the earth itself.

"Right, then," came Chrissie's voice from behind him. "Shall we have the demonstration?"

He jumped up enthusiastically. "You just sit down here," he said. "And I'll begin."

As Chrissie chose a comfortable place to sit, Tess and Fly trotted after her, and Max made to follow them.

"Stay," ordered Will. The dog ignored him, and Will didn't fail to notice Chrissie biting her lip to suppress a smile.

"Max," he repeated, trying not to sound desperate. "Stay!"

Max wavered between his master's command and running off to see his sheepdog friends. Heat flared in Will's face.

"Here, boy!" It was a plea now rather than an order.

Will held his breath. This was so important to him. Chrissie's opinion of him mattered. For a moment it felt as if the whole world had stopped, and then, making up his mind, Max turned and headed back to Will, sitting at his feet, keen eyes watching his every move. Will glanced at Chrissie, and when she smiled encouragingly he knew the red in his cheeks was deepening, but for a different reason now. Walking backward, he held up his hand, palm forward.

"Stay, boy. Stay…"

Max sat, quivering in anticipation of the treat in Will's pocket. Will felt a rush of pride. He'd really done it. He took a final step, then all of a sudden, Max bounded toward him. He held up his hand, desperately trying to remember everything Chrissie had taught him.

"Sit down, Max," he said. "Sit down." The dog continued to ignore him, bounding this way and that. Will stood still, ignoring him back, and when the treat did not appear Max stopped, whining softly.

"Sit down," Will repeated, and when Max obeyed, he was quick to praise, giving him the treat.

"Now do the stay again," called Chrissie. "Repetition, remember, and no backing down."

Will did the stay procedure again, not backing quite so far away this time. When Max waited, coming to Will's call like a pro, he glanced at Chrissie and pumped his fist in the air.

"Who would have thought that such a

big-time criminal lawyer could be so easily pleased by getting a dog to sit and stay," she called, laughing.

"He could have done it the first time," grumbled Will.

"Patience and perseverance," she told him. "That's the key. It's character building…for you, I mean. Now, let's go up to the meadow and see if yesterday's lesson with the sheep has stuck."

Will followed Chrissie around for the next twenty minutes or so, getting Max to sit and stay, again and again, as she checked on the sheep.

"Look how strong the single lambs are," she said proudly, stopping to survey the scene. "It's almost time to let them back up the fell. The twins will need a bit longer, of course."

"But they're so small," Will remarked, watching the lambs run in groups up the hill and back, tails wagging madly as they played the age-old game.

Chrissie nodded. "They are full of life, though—that's the key. I've been watching lambs play like that every year for my entire life. No one teaches them and they always use that same rock. Chase Me Charlie and King of the Castle, I call it."

"You're a very strange woman, Chrissie Marsh," Will said.

"I prefer 'different.'" She pushed back a strand of blond hair and tucked it neatly behind her ear in a way that was becoming achingly familiar to him.

For a moment he just watched her, standing against the glorious magnificence of the landscape, as much a part of this place as the fells themselves and equally glorious and magnificent as she stood tall and proud with her head raised high. She looked back at him, her blue eyes warm with sunshine.

"And do you know that you are a bit odd, too, Will Devlin? At least I know who I am. Come on, time to unclip the leash."

When Will hesitated, she moved forward and unclipped it for him. "Have confidence," she said. "You'll see."

It was well after five by the time they arrived back at the farmhouse after seeing to all the animals.

Chrissie beckoned him in as she kicked off her boots on the porch. "The least I can do is to make you a cuppa after all the help you've given me," she said.

When Will began painstakingly trying to pull off his wellies, she laughed.

"Let go of yourself, Will, and just kick them off into the corner."

Will did so with a sense of release, and laughing out loud together, they went into the warmth of the kitchen.

"You may as well have something to eat," Chrissie said as she brewed a pot of tea. "Unless you're going out to dinner or something... Isn't that what you posh lawyers do, eat out at fancy restaurants?"

"Used to do," he said. "And for your information, there are no fancy restaurants around here."

"Scrambled eggs, then?" Chrissie offered, handing him a mug. "I have to use up the eggs somehow."

Fleetingly, Will's idea from earlier came back into his head, and a new image joined it. Visitors—he preferred the word to *tourists*— collecting their own eggs for breakfast...

"Hello?" Chrissie said, waving her hand in front of his face.

A dull flush crept up Will's neck and he

looked away. "Sorry, I must be tired. Scrambled eggs sound great…if you're sure you don't mind."

"Not at all," she insisted. "Don't feel that you have to, though."

Will smiled. "I'm looking forward to it… It would only have been soup or beans at home, anyway. That's all I seem to live on nowadays."

Chrissie began cooking, and when they tucked into the simple meal, Will reflected on how nice it was, having a meal made for him for a change. This was almost the complete opposite of his life in the city, but he held no longing for the way things used to be.

"Do you miss your city life sometimes?" asked Chrissie, as if reading his mind.

He looked at her in surprise, putting down his knife and fork. "No," he said. "Not really. I like it here—it feels right. And, as you know, I became totally disillusioned by my career."

"So you'd never go back?"

"Funnily enough, Roy Wallis, big boss at Marcus Finch where I used to work, has been trying to get me back, but to work with a different clientele. He says it will bring some closure."

"And do you think it would?"

Will shrugged. "I have what I want here. Peace of mind, a connection with the world around me…and honesty. Soon, I hope, I'll be making a living, too. I know you hate the idea of tourism, but I'll be able to keep an eye on anyone who—"

"We made a deal about not mentioning tourists, remember," Chrissie said sharply, biting her lip. "What if you took on just enough cases to support yourself, so you didn't have to have tourists?"

"Now who's mentioning tourists?" he teased her, raising his eyebrows. "I have thought about it, though…just to please you, if nothing else. I know how much you hate the idea. But I really don't want to go back to law, even just to work occasionally." He scratched the back of his head. "By the way, I've been invited to our annual bash in a couple of weeks…why don't you come with me?

Chrissie looked startled. "Me? You're asking me?"

He shrugged. "Why not? You'd enjoy it."

"No…no, I don't think it would be my kind of thing."

An amused expression spread across Will's face. "That's what I thought you'd say. You can't always wear jeans, though, you know, Chrissie. Anyway, the offer stands if you change your mind. I don't particularly want to go by myself and I'm sure you'd enjoy it, but if you'd rather not, I understand."

Chrissie's cheeks reddened. "I suppose you think I'm worried about meeting your important associates," she said. "That a sheep farmer like me would feel out of her depth. Well, you're wrong."

"Prove it, then," said Will, his silvery eyes glittering.

"Fine. You're on."

"It's not for a couple of weeks so if you change your mind…" he said, knowing the chance to back out would make her all the more determined to go. He loved the way her proud, headstrong expression lit up her face.

She drew herself up to her full height, a haughty tilt to her chin. "Just because I choose to live here, living a life I love, does not mean that I am incapable of mingling with people of…well, *your* kind of people. I have been away from here, you know, and I've been to fancy parties. People really don't impress me with their wealth, importance or auras of success. We are all the same underneath the visual crap. We all have hopes and fears and worries. In fact…"

The flicker of a smile crossed her lips, lending softness to the taut contours of her face. "It was my mum who taught me that. I'd been invited to a charity ball by someone…"

"A man?" asked Will.

She nodded. "More of a boy, really—I was just out of school, and his dad's company was hosting it. Anyway, I was very nervous about it and my mum…my mum always knew how I was feeling."

Her eyes filled up with a sadness that touched Will's heart; he had never seen her vulnerability before.

"She took both my hands in hers and stared straight into my eyes," she went on. "'Chrissie,' she said. 'Always remember that you are just as good as anyone else you might meet in life. We are all born naked with nothing, each and every one of us. We all have our doubts and our fears, no matter who or what we are, and our times of self-doubt and vulnerability. We all want love in our lives, but we so often get dealt heartache or tragedy, and most of us offer ourselves up to the world in the way we think we should be seen…or the way we want people to perceive us. Always be true to yourself, Chrissie, for you need never be in awe of anyone.'"

Chrissie was silent for a moment, and then a mischievous smile replaced her sadness. "And another thing she told me. 'Always remember that we all go to the toilet…even the Queen. So when someone is making you feel less than what you really are…just imagine that and smile at your self-doubt.'"

Will squirmed. "So is that what you did when you met me?"

"Why? Do you think you're that daunting?"

"Well…" he began awkwardly.

She met his eyes, smiling. "Several times actually," she admitted.

He pulled a face. "Whoa…that's way too much information."

"It's okay," she said. "I don't need to now."

"Why is that?"

"I've seen beyond the hotshot lawyer you perceive yourself to be. I've seen you vulnerable and afraid and way out of your depth. I've seen *you*, Will, and you don't scare me anymore."

This time it was she who leaned across to place her lips on his, with a soft, sweet tenderness that took him totally by surprise. And before he could even react she'd drawn back, clearing the plates away as if nothing had happened.

"So, tomorrow," she said, "we'll work on Max's recall… It really isn't solid enough yet."

"But…" Will reached out to her.

"But nothing." She busied herself at the sink to hide her emotion. "Just take it for what it was. I like you, Will, and I wanted to show it, but we have different priorities. We can't forget that. I'll see you tomorrow—don't forget to keep practicing."

CHAPTER TWENTY

WILL DROVE HOME in a daze, his head full of
Chrissie. Her kissing him so tenderly had
knocked him for six. He was used to being
the instigator, used to taking women by surprise, not the other way around. It was the
first time in his life that he had been kissed
with such pure emotion; it had come straight
from Chrissie's heart…or that's how it had
felt, at least.

The more he got to know Chrissie Marsh,
though, the more puzzled she made him.
There were so many different facets to her
nature. Would she really go to the dinner
with him, or was she just winding him up?
And if she did, would she wear something
totally unsuitable?

He wanted to retract that thought as soon
as it came into his head. He felt as shallow as
she expected his colleagues to be. But maybe
the things her mother had told her, about her

own self-perception and her views on others, had made her oblivious to how she came across or what she wore. He remembered how out of place he'd looked when he'd tried to climb the fell in his suit and couldn't bear the idea of everyone looking down on her if she turned up in the wrong outfit…even if she didn't care.

And of course she wouldn't care, he realized, smiling to himself, for she would be too busy imagining them all on the toilet. He found himself wishing he'd met Chrissie's mother. She must have been a remarkable woman.

AFTER WILL LEFT, Chrissie busied herself by doing a last check on the sheep, even though the lambing was almost over. Soon they'd all be back on the fell, and the home meadows would be left for the spring grass to grow in time to make hay for the winter.

There were always jobs to be done on the farm: shearing the fleeces, worming, trimming hooves, sorting the sheep and looking for strays… And then the lambs had to be weaned before the sales. Chrissie hated the sales. Hardened shepherdess that she was, she felt sad when the lambs she'd nurtured were sold.

Buying sheep to add to the stock was another matter. Browsing the catalogue beforehand for the best bloodlines, checking out the animals in their pens and bidding against other farmers were days to remember, filled with anticipation and camaraderie as she tried to buy the best sheep she could afford.

For now, though, there were other things to think about, like taking the sheep and lambs back to the fell, arranging for the clipping… And the event that Will had invited her to was on the horizon. Her bold talk of not caring about what people thought felt like a sham now… Perhaps she should tell Will that she couldn't go.

Her mother's face slid into her mind. No, of course she would go, and she'd show Will Devlin just how proud of her he could be. Why, he was probably worrying right this moment that she might turn up at his bash dressed like a country bumpkin. Well, she would show him.

She'd kissed him because she wanted to, and she didn't regret it. But it couldn't happen again. There were too many obstacles between them for any kind of relationship to work. His planning application was the big one right now, but his background was so different from hers. He might not be ready to admit it, but she could tell there was some part of him that missed the law. One day he would probably get bored of the country and want to go back to his other life. Where would that leave them?

Sadness welled up inside her. Of all the men in all the world why did Will Devlin have to be the one to make her feel this way?

FOR THE NEXT few days, Chrissie was busy making sure that every sheep and lamb was fit and strong enough to take its chances on the vast slopes that backed onto High Bracken. The forecast was good for Friday, so that was the day she had chosen to herd them back up the fell. She'd told Will he could come, too, with Max—but on a long line, just in case.

They'd turned up every day that week with smiles on their faces, and Chrissie had come to look forward to seeing them both. Usually Will drove over, but yesterday he had walked to High Bracken across the fell with

Max loose behind him. He'd been so pleased with himself, his face alight as he told her how obedient Max had been. It was funny how fond she'd become of the big, useless labradoodle. But he wasn't useless, was he? He was a friend.

And what about Will—was he a friend? She'd buried her feelings for him deep in her heart, and they were going to stay there, she promised herself. Neither of them had mentioned her kissing him, but the memory of it was sealed on her lips every time she laid eyes on him. And they didn't bring up the lawyers' dinner, either, or his planning application. Both events were huge in her mind, as she assumed they were in his, but they skirted around them, afraid to face both their feelings and their differences. Just living for now.

Watching Will and Max approach across the fell on Thursday, she decided she was sick of pretending. It felt so false. He threw a stick and the big cream-colored dog leaped and bounded after it, so full of life and energy. Perhaps it was time she was honest, that she tell him about her carefully logged objections to his plans.

There was no good moment to bring it up during the training session, however. Max seemed to thrive now on trying to please, as if he'd suddenly grown up. So while the lessons had become more routine, Chrissie had also made them more intensive to get the most out of the boisterous labradoodle.

"Come on," suggested Will halfway through their usual session. "We've done enough training for one day. Let me take you out for lunch. You've cooked often enough for me these last couple of weeks."

"Just using up the eggs," she told him with a smile, considering whether this might be her opportunity to tell him that she was objecting to his plans. Good food and a glass of wine might help him take it better…because she knew that he wouldn't take it well.

Although they had both agreed not to mention tourists or planning, certain comments he'd made told her that he thought she'd come around to it. Well, he might think that paying for the training was paying her off, too, but he was wrong.

They ate at a lovely old country pub, sitting outside in a secluded garden with the dogs at their feet. The sun was warm for late April, and Chrissie sipped her glass of sauvignon blanc feeling totally relaxed and happy. It was strange, she thought, how she and Will could just sit in silence, enjoying their food and the sunshine and the wine, like an old married couple who knew each other so well they needed no words.

He glanced at her and when she caught his eyes, a slow flush spread across her cheeks.

"You're thinking about that kiss, aren't you?" he teased.

"Maybe," she admitted.

"Well, here's another," he murmured, and when his lips closed over hers, something inside her blossomed. All that mattered was this moment. She didn't hold back. It just felt so right, so good, so real.

They left hand in hand, their shoulders almost touching. As he opened the car door for her, he spun her around, placing his palms on the sun-warmed metal, pinning her against the big vehicle. She could feel his heat and her heart raced madly. But when he lowered his lips to hers, she forced herself to pull away, guilt washing away her desire.

"No, Will, this isn't right."

He stood back, relaxing his hold, a puzzled expression on his face. "You know that's not true. Why...why isn't it right?"

"It's just... I don't think we should let ourselves get involved so quickly," she told him. "And we agreed that our relationship had to be professional, remember?"

"Then I absolve you from our professional agreement and declare Max's training a success," he said, reaching out for her again.

She gave in, melting against him as his lips found hers, warmth coursing through her body. Was this love? she wondered. Was she in love with Will Devlin?

Her blood turned cold. What was she thinking? She couldn't let this go any further until she'd been straight about her objections, and she couldn't bring that up now. He knew she didn't agree with his plans, but he had no idea she'd sent a list of strong objections to the council...not to mention the petition she'd gotten dozens of local farmers to sign.

Pulling away from him, she called to the dogs. "Sorry, Will," she mumbled. "I can't do this."

His face was cold and hard as they climbed into his four-by-four. Was that just because he hadn't got his own way? Maybe she'd been too naive; maybe she'd misread his signals. Her feelings were real, but maybe all he wanted was a lighthearted dalliance…a bit of fun to ease the boredom of living in the country.

"I'll take you home," he said, not meeting her eyes.

He drove too fast, staring intently at the road as he swung around corner after corner. Chrissie wanted to tell him to slow down, but he seemed so unapproachable that she stayed silent. Should she just come out and tell him why she'd pushed him away? She thought about how she would phrase it. *I've put in some pretty strong objections to your plans, I'm afraid. Nothing personal, but that idea you had about making a living from your holiday rentals might just be about to come crashing down around you.*

Put so bluntly, it sounded bad. Then again, perhaps she was being too sensitive to his reaction when she'd turned him down. Will must have had loads of girlfriends in the city; being rejected by a country girl probably barely even dented his pride. She didn't intend to be just another notch on his belt, so perhaps it was for the best. She was slowly and reluctantly falling in love with him, and she had no time in her life for love. Especially not when the man in question was a city lawyer with a dodgy past who intended to build her worst nightmare right next door. No matter how she felt, she had to stop him. She cared for Will deeply, but that didn't mean she would let him put her animals, her livelihood and the entire landscape in jeopardy.

When they pulled into the yard at High Bracken, she began getting out before he'd fully stopped the car. "Thanks for the meal," she said.

He nodded curtly, his tone dismissive. "My pleasure."

As he drove away without a backward glance, his tires sliding on the gravel, a heavy weight settled on Chrissie's chest.

Her chance at love was slipping away, and there was nothing she could do about it… Nothing she *would* do about it. Unless he retracted his plans.

CHRISSIE WOKE EARLY after a long and restless night. Today, the sheep and lambs were

going back up the fell. Will was supposed to
come, along with Max, but now she didn't
know if he would appear or not. Her heart
wished he would drive into the yard this very
moment, but her head told her a very different story. Still, her ears strained to hear the
sound of his vehicle.

When he hadn't arrived by nine, she figured he wasn't going to show. Calling to Tess
and Fly, she picked up her crook and strode
off toward the home meadows. She opened
the gates onto the fell and sent both dogs in
different directions, calling "come way out"
to one and "come by" to the other.

The collies knew the routine, and they
worked together efficiently until all the sheep
were travelling as one, a flock of white rippling over the rough terrain, climbing ever
higher toward the vast blue sky. Overhead,
a buzzard circled, looking for small prey
pushed out of their hiding spots by the mass
of cloven hooves.

The morning went well, and by lunchtime
all the sheep were where Chrissie wanted
them to be, happily grazing back in their
own wild territory while their lambs suckled contentedly. Now it was time for the next

generation to learn the ways of the flock and become hefted—or bonded—to their area of the fell with its invisible boundaries.

She saw Will on the fell's lower slopes as she headed home. He walked determinedly and Max raced ahead, sniffing the exciting and enticing smells all around. She raised her hand to catch his attention, but immediately drew it back. It was weird to feel like she couldn't call out to Will.

Perhaps she should have come clean yesterday, about her feelings and her objections to his plans. What did it matter now, though? He'd chosen to stay away today. Okay, so she'd rejected him without much explanation, but surely there was more to it than hurt pride...wasn't there? Was she reading him all wrong? Perhaps she had done more than dent his ego; perhaps, like her, he felt the dawning of something real and meaningful between them. What if she ran down to join him, threw caution to the wind? She could admit everything—the attempts she'd made to sabotage his plans, yes, but also the way she truly felt about him.

But then he disappeared from view and the moment for action was gone. It was for the best, she decided. She needed to have a cool head when she spoke to him. When it came to Will, acting impulsively had only gotten her into trouble.

After Will's invitation to the big dinner, Chrissie had earmarked the afternoon to go and find a dress. Obviously she wouldn't be going now, though, so what was the point? A rush of disappointment took her by surprise and she realized just how much she'd been looking forward to it. She'd wanted to impress him by revealing her feminine side in a glamorous dress that made her stand out from everyone else. That wasn't going to happen now.

Except...

Will hadn't yet withdrawn his invitation. She'd wanted to prove herself to him and she still could if she was courageous enough. The ball was tomorrow. She'd just call him and ask what time he was picking her up.

Excitement fluttered inside her. "You shall go to the ball, Chrissie Marsh," she said out loud. "All you need is a dress and a handsome prince."

She winced at herself as she dialed his

number. Will might be handsome, but he was certainly no prince.

"Hi," she said when he answered. "I just thought I'd better check on what time you're picking me up tomorrow."

She could tell by his hesitation that he'd either forgotten all about it or just presumed she wasn't going. "What... You mean you still want to go?"

"You invited me, didn't you? I said yes, so why wouldn't I be going?"

"I just thought—"

She cut him off. "Well, you thought wrong. Just because I didn't want to get too involved too quickly doesn't mean I'm going to stand you up. A date is a date, and anyway I've bought a dress."

"Well, then..." He sounded unsure. "A date it is. Five thirty okay? We need to allow plenty of time to get there."

"I'll be ready and waiting," she said, smiling.

It was after three by the time Chrissie had parked the car and begun scouring the shops—not long to find a dress in a small market town, she thought, heading for Illusions, the classiest shop in Little Dale.

"Going somewhere special?" asked the smartly dressed and beautifully made-up assistant as Chrissie browsed.

She nodded. "An important dinner. There will be dancing, too, I think. I need a dress. Something long…and unique."

The girl looked her up and down. "I may have just the thing," she said, gliding to a rack at the far end of the shop. The dress she returned with made Chrissie gasp as it shimmered under the lights. "It's like living, moving opal," she cried. "Almost iridescent!"

"You are so right," agreed the assistant. "It is like opal, because the colors are constantly changing in the light. And on you it will take on a silvery-blue sheen and bring out the blue of your eyes. Try it on… You'll see."

When Chrissie slid the dress over her hips in the changing room, she gasped again; it was perfect, showing off her slender waist and long thighs. The plunging neckline revealed just enough cleavage.

"Jewelry?" asked the assistant when she emerged.

Chrissie shook her head, "No, thanks. I have just the thing already. Some high-heeled, strappy sandals would be nice, though."

It was late when Chrissie finally arrived home. Dumping her bags onto the kitchen table, she pulled on her work clothes, called for the dogs and ran out into the yard. Her two shorthorn cows were lowing restlessly, unused to the change in routine, and she tied them up in their stalls and gave them a feed before drawing the milk from their warm, soft udders.

"I'll be earlier tomorrow," she told them, excitement rising inside her. The flutter of anticipation brought a smile to her face. She'd need to have all her chores done by four thirty, she realized, if she wanted plenty of time to get ready.

"IT'S CERTAINLY AMBITIOUS," Roger Simmons said, rubbing the side of his face. Will had just aired his new idea for the buildings.

"Forward thinking, too," Roger continued. "I would hazard a guess that it could turn out to be a big step forward in getting the local farmers to accept visitors around here. I wouldn't mention it publically yet, though. Let's just get the outline planning accepted, and in the meantime I'll draft out some plans. You do know that there have been objections?"

Will nodded. "I knew that there might be. It'll be the local farmers, I suppose."

Roger nodded. "Chrissie Marsh, perhaps."

"No, not Chrissie. She would have told me."

The architect raised his eyebrows. "Are you sure about that?"

"I've been working with her, training my dog. We've had our disagreements, but no matter what she might think of me personally I don't believe she would be underhanded like that."

"Fair enough," Roger said. "She's a woman of principle, though, Chrissie. She'd never drop a belief for anything. I hope you're right, because if she is leading some kind of campaign against your application, then we might be in trouble."

"Well, I'm taking her to my old law firm's annual ball at the Manchester Hilton tomorrow," said Will. "I can ask her then."

Roger's friendly face shone with surprise. "A date?"

"Well, not so much a date as…" Suddenly

he was smiling, too. "A challenge, I guess you'd call it."

"I'll look forward to hearing how it goes. And leave your idea with me. I'll have some rough sketches for you in a couple of days. I like it, though... It's innovative and new and definitely something that could bring Chrissie Marsh around."

"I know she hates tourists, but I think you're wrong about her objecting," Will said. "She would have told me. I'm excited to show her my new idea, but I want it to be a surprise... I'm hoping it will be something we can work on together."

Roger raised his eyebrows. "Let's hope it works out, then," he said.

CHAPTER TWENTY-ONE

CHRISSIE WOKE UP to sunshine on Saturday morning. Something fluttered inside her, a kind of nervous anticipation. Vague memories crept in as she blinked away the clouds of sleep. What was it about today? And then she turned over and saw the dress hanging from the wardrobe door, a shimmering mass of pearly opal. Her heart shut tight; she couldn't do this...

Her mother's voice filled her ears. *Oh, yes, you can.*

"I can, I can, I can," she repeated.

Slipping reluctantly from the warm comfort of her bed, Chrissie crossed the room and picked up a small box from the dressing table. She held it reverently as she flipped it open to reveal a simple, beautiful opal necklace and drop earrings, her mother's pride and joy. It felt somehow as if the dress had been made especially for her, to match her mother's gift, lending her the confidence she needed to carry her through tonight.

She knew full well that Will would be worried about what she'd look like, worried that he'd be embarrassed by her. Well, she'd show him. Her blue eyes glittered as she held the necklace against her throat, and her nerves evaporated.

"You'll be beside me, Mum, won't you," she whispered, and through the open window she heard the wind sigh.

The day passed quickly, so much to do, so much to think about. Just before lunch she drove into town to get some feed, and she was carrying bags of pellets and sheep feed out to her battered old Land Rover when she heard Will's voice behind her, farther inside the store. She froze, annoyed with herself for being so affected by his presence.

"Which dog food is best?" she heard him ask Clifford, the store manager.

"It's really up to the individual," Clifford replied. "I can tell you about each one and—"

"Well, which one does Chrissie Marsh use?" Will cut in. "I presume she buys her dog food here."

Chrissie put down the bag she was carrying and turned around, spotting the two men perusing bags of dog food. "I use the working dog complete," she called, amused by the momentary embarrassment on Will's face.

"Then that's what I'll get," he announced. "You still okay for tonight?" he said more quietly.

She held his gaze. "Oh, yes," she said. "I can't wait."

WILL ARRIVED EARLY, and Chrissie heard him knock as she was dusting gold powder across her cheekbones to enhance her tan. With a touch of dark shadow to widen her eyes, a sweep of black mascara and a dab of shimmering pink lipstick, she was done.

"Let yourself in," she called from the window. "I won't be a minute."

With bated breath, she slipped on the dress. It slid it over her shoulders and cascaded in a shimmering mass to her feet. She twisted around to do the zipper, pulling and tugging but still not quite reaching the top. What now?

Will's voice floated up from downstairs; he was talking to the dogs. Asking him to help zip up her dress felt way too personal, but it seemed she had no other choice. Strapping on the extravagant shoes she'd bought with the dress, she shook out her long fair hair. It fell over her shoulders in loose gold-streaked waves. She smoothed her hands over her waist nervously. What if it was all too much?

Too late to worry about that, she thought, grabbing her purse and heading for the stairs.

HEARING THE SOUND of stiletto heels on the wooden staircase, Will went into the hallway and peered upward, intrigued. The vision of Chrissie in a perfectly fitted, shimmering dress with a discreet slit that revealed a glimpse of her smooth, gleaming thigh blew him away.

"Will I do?" she asked, nervously fingering the material. "I feel like a princess."

"We're going to a lawyer's dinner," he said. "Not the red carpet at a film premiere. You didn't need a designer dress, but..."

"But what?" He reached out to take her hand and she smiled.

"But it was worth it because you do look like a princess."

He tried to draw her toward him, but she twisted away, breaking the moment.

"Could you help me with this?" she asked, lifting her hair from the nape of her neck. He saw that the dress wasn't done up all the way.

He took hold of the zipper and pulled it neatly up to the top. "There," he said, and on a sudden impulse he planted a gentle kiss on the back of her slender neck.

She shot forward, wide-eyed with astonishment, and he smiled. "Sorry. I couldn't resist."

"No harm done," she said lightly. "But just remember—totally professional."

"Like you were when you kissed me back the other day?" he reminded her, and she had the grace to blush.

"I'm sorry about that," she said, her voice husky. "I just…"

"Forget it," he insisted, breaking the awkward moment. "And remember what your mother said. I do hope you realize that that's going to make me smile every time I introduce you to one of my colleagues or clients."

Chrissie laughed, crouching down to stroke the two sheepdogs. She cupped their faces one at a time to plant a kiss on each nose. "Be good, girls. I'll be back later."

"Much later," said Will, surprised by an unexpected rush of emotion. Chrissie looked like a princess in her obviously expensive dress, but she still put her beloved dogs first. It was an image that would stay in his mind forever. Unlike many of the other women he'd met in his life, she was totally genuine, someone to trust. For the first time, he realized he had found someone he wanted to spend the rest of his life with. He just wished she felt the same way. Sometimes he was sure she did…and then she would draw back and push him away. He hoped that tonight she might finally let go and admit that she loved him, too.

THEY ARRIVED AT the hotel early. Will wanted to drop Chrissie at the front doors so that he could park the car, but gazing at the grand entrance, she declined.

"I know I said I would be totally unfazed by your fancy friends and acquaintances, and that is true. Fancy hotels, however, are something else. I'd rather walk in on your arm if you don't mind."

"Mind!" he said. "I'd be proud to have you on my arm, Chrissie Marsh."

By the time they'd parked and walked back to the front doors, other guests were beginning to arrive. Chrissie took a breath and stood tall, taking long, slow, deliberate strides. Will glanced sideways at her, amused, and she tightened her fingers on his arm.

"Too much?" she whispered.

"You could never be too much," he told her. Her eyes burned into his and his heart swelled.

He held his breath as Chrissie squeezed his arm tighter, reaching up to whisper something in his ear, but Roy Wallis approached and the moment was broken.

He patted Will heartily on the back. "Good to see you," he said, his eyes fixing on Chrissie. "I'm glad you could come. I thought you said you were bringing some shepherd friend of yours, though."

"Shepherdess," Will corrected him, wondering what Chrissie was thinking.

She caught his eye and her cheeky grin made him turn away to hide his amusement.

Not that Roy would have noticed; he was far too busy staring at Chrissie.

"It's a joke, isn't it," he cried, as if he'd figured out some big secret. "I know—you're an actress and you are playing a shepherdess in a film or something."

Chrissie drew herself up tall, shaking back her remarkable hair so that it rippled down her back. "I am a sheep farmer from the Lake District," she said proudly. "And Will is my neighbor."

"Well, I can see now why he's not too keen on coming back to work," somebody else put in. Will turned to see Gilbert Waters, another former colleague. He was sporting a bright red bow tie and cummerbund instead of the usual black.

Will sighed. "Chrissie meet Gilbert, criminal defense lawyer extraordinaire."

"And outrageously over the top, as usual," Roy remarked dryly.

"Well, it was lovely to meet you two charming gentlemen," said Chrissie. "No doubt we will see you later? Will and I are just on our way to the bar."

Both Roy and Gilbert seemed a little put

out but were gracious enough to smile. "Of course," said Roy. "We'll catch you later."

"And I need to mingle." Wally gave an exaggerated bow. "But you'll save me a dance?"

"We aren't staying late," Will growled before she could answer. He did not want anyone dancing with Chrissie. The thought of dancing with her himself set his pulse racing.

Wherever they went, there seemed to be someone who wanted to talk to them…or rather, Will realized, flirt with Chrissie. Timothy Mackie, a bruiser of a man who appeared to be busting out of his dress suit, made a huge fuss over seeing Will again but soon turned his attentions to her.

Will made their excuses, leaning closer to Chrissie as they stepped away. "Now, there's one you might take your mother's advice about," he murmured. When she started to ask him why, he just raised his eyebrows. "Believe me—you really don't want to know."

When it was time for dinner, Will found their table while Chrissie slipped off to the ladies' room. They were seated between Laura James, another lawyer from Marcus

Finch, and Roy himself. Seizing his opportunity, Roy insisted that Will tell the truth about his date. "And don't insult me with your story about her being a farmer," he said. "She has to be either a model or an actress."

"Be careful," Laura whispered in his ear. "Roy and Margaret are getting a divorce, so he's on the prowl. You know what a sucker he is for a pretty face."

Jealousy hit him like a punch in the stomach, and Will had to bite his lip to avoid making a strong retort. "Back off, Roy," he said, forcing a laugh but unable to keep the ice out of his tone. "Chrissie is with me."

NOTICING THE TENSION between Roy and Will as she crossed the dining room, Chrissie paused just close enough to overhear the heated exchange. Could Will really be jealous? And what did it mean?

Will looked so handsome in his black dress suit and tie. He glanced over at her, and as their eyes met it felt as if they were alone in the room.

She slid into her chair beside him, and when he reached for her hand and their fingers entwined, the unfamiliar flutter inside her grew stronger, and she longed to feel his lips on hers again. She tightened her fingers around his. Being this close to him felt so right.

To her relief, Roy Wallis announced that he was going to the bar, and Will's other former colleague, Laura, turned away to talk to the man on her left. Will leaned in, his lips close to Chrissie's ear. The whole room seemed to fall silent as his breath warmed her skin.

"I think I could almost be falling in love with you, Chrissie Marsh."

"Almost?" she whispered.

Before he could respond, Roy returned, a broad smile on his face. He slapped Will enthusiastically on the back. "Apologies," he cried. "Didn't realize that you two were an item. Now I can see why you're insisting on hiding away in the country."

And so the night wore on. The room got louder and louder as the drinks flowed, but Chrissie felt removed from the whole proceedings. Did Will feel the same? she wondered, catching his gaze.

"Let's get out of here," he mouthed, and she nodded eagerly, grabbing her purse as music sprang from the ballroom. With no warning, he took both her hands, twirling her toward the doors, and then they were lost amid the other dancers, alone in their own little world.

When the musicians took up a slower tempo, he wrapped his arms around her and she leaned her head against his shoulder, allowing the music to seep into her soul. His hands were warm and gentle. She lifted her face to his, and his lips brushed hers in a kiss so soft and sweet that it made her heart pound.

When the song ended, he broke their embrace and headed toward the exit.

"Come on," he said, and she followed him willingly out into the cool, dark silence of the night.

He pressed her back against the wall, but she didn't notice the roughness of the stone. All she could feel was him, his heat, his lips, invading her senses. When, finally, he drew away he looked deep into her eyes, gently stroking her hair back from her face.

"I was wrong earlier," he murmured. "I *am* falling in love with you."

She laid her cheek against his silky jacket,

breathing in the scent of him. Elation flooded over her, laced with guilt. Wasn't love supposed to be based on trust? Would he still be falling in love with her if he knew that she'd been less than honest with him? Oh, how she wished she'd been straight from the start. Then she wouldn't have to watch his expression change when she finally came clean…as she was determined to do. She didn't want there to be any lies between them. Chrissie was quiet and thoughtful on the way home. She lay back in her seat, high heels removed, watching Will's hands on the wheel. He drove with confidence, his eyes firmly fixed on the road ahead.

"Did you mean it?" she asked. "You know… what you said."

He glanced at her. "I wouldn't have said it if I didn't mean it. I'm in love with you, Chrissie."

A heavy silence fell between them as she took in what he'd said.

"And you?" he asked, staring at the road ahead. "How do you feel?"

She hesitated, knowing that now, in this moment of closeness, she should come clean and tell him about the objections she'd sent in to the planning council. But the words wouldn't come. There was time yet she told herself, wanting to cling to the moment. "Honestly?" she said.

"Honestly."

"I wouldn't have let you kiss me if I didn't have strong feelings for you, but love is huge."

"Then let's just see where it goes," he suggested. "Strong feelings will do for now. I will be kissing you again, though, you do realize that?"

Leaning across, she pecked him on the cheek. "Thank you, Will Devlin, for a wonderful evening."

"And maybe the start of a whole new life?" he prompted.

"Maybe," she said.

Was this love? Was this really what love felt like? Then why was she objecting so fiercely to his plans? If she really loved him, wouldn't she at least try and understand his ambitions? Wouldn't she have been honest and told him what she'd done? She would never compromise her principles, but surely if you really loved someone you would tell them everything, talk things through...no secrets.

She'd go tomorrow, she decided. She'd go to Craig Side and tell him that she loved her land, her job, the sheep and the Lake District with the same passion she felt for him. Tell him why she'd placed her objections and explain that it had nothing to do with her feelings for him. Surely, if he loved her, he'd understand.

CHAPTER TWENTY-TWO

CHRISSIE TOSSED AND turned all night, stressed and sleepless. She should have been honest with Will about her intention to get his planning permission refused. To go behind his back and lodge a list of objections without telling him had been callous, and she regretted it now.

Should she retract the petition to prove how sorry she was? The answer came at once. *No.* That wouldn't be truthful, either. She had to come clean and explain how she felt. Only then could they move on.

She didn't want to think about what might happen if he didn't understand what she'd done and why. She didn't want to rock their budding new relationship. She wanted to feel that shiver as his lips closed over hers. Because this really *was* love, she realized. She was crazy in love with Will Devlin, for better or for worse.

Eventually Chrissie slept, but she struggled through her chores the next morning, feeding the animals and milking the cows with the heavy weight of worry in her heart. She didn't want to lose Will now; he'd told her he might be falling in love with her and she knew that she loved him back. She had to tell him the truth today, make him understand.

The phone rang just as she finished her coffee. Her heart leapt, but then she saw Tom Farrah's name on the screen and it fell immediately.

He cut right to the chase. "Hi, Chrissie, I've just heard that they've brought the planning meeting forward. It's today."

"But they can't." She was on her feet, already reaching for her jacket. "How can that be?"

"Seemingly, there was some confusion with dates. Anyway, the architect has pointed out that since they made their application within the appropriate time frame, it was only right to bring it forward to this month instead of next. I've been away for a couple of days and missed my messages. Our meeting is at eleven this morning."

"And has Will been informed?"

"I did ask that, and Ellen, one of the girls in the council office, said a letter was sent out a couple of days ago and he came in as soon as they opened today to peruse all the available information."

Chrissie tried to keep calm, but panic churned inside her; perhaps there was still time, perhaps he didn't yet know that it was she who'd objected. "What kind of information do you have available?" she asked.

"Well, there are the outline plans, of course, and the reasons why they should be approved...and then there are the objections, as you obviously know."

Chrissie felt sick. Oh, why hadn't she told him? "And do you think he knows that the objections have come from me?"

"Considering you put your name on them, I would guess that it is quite likely," he said. "Anyway, it is your prerogative. Don't worry about it—it had to come out sooner or later."

"It would have been better later," she said with a heavy sigh. "Thanks anyway, though, for letting me know as soon as you could."

"Go and see him," he said, "It's the only way, you know. Be honest."

Chrissie's elderly Land Rover bumped and banged in the potholes as she sped down the narrow lane from High Bracken. Although Craig Side appeared quite close as the crow flies, it was a long and winding trip by road. She had several close calls as she threw caution to the wind and went a bit too fast.

Now that Will probably wouldn't want her anymore, he felt like the only person who mattered in her world. He *was* the only person. She'd taken his funny little ways for granted, the way he dressed all wrong and tried too hard, the way he was so much of a man when he needed to be. She'd always thought of him as a man of many faces, but just recently she'd found the real Will Devlin, the one who had let her into his heart.

Oh, why hadn't she been honest with him from the start? And how could he love her now when everything he had believed about her must seem like a lie. She was well aware that a large part of his feelings for her were born of admiration; he'd spent so much of his life with people he didn't trust, people who would stab you in the back in an instant just to get their own way.

He'd believed that she was different...that

she was as honest and true as the earth beneath their feet. So how could he love her when she'd kept such an important secret from him? It wasn't what she'd done. She'd been honest and vocal about her opinions of his holiday rentals, at least, and in a way, Will respected them. Chrissie knew it was the underhanded way she'd kissed him last night, allowed him to open up to her while keeping secrets that could affect his plans, that would do him in.

She saw his Range Rover as soon as she drove into Craig Side. It looked lost and lonely, she thought, abandoned in the very center of the yard, the driver's door wide open. Her heart was banging so hard in her chest that she could hear it in her ears, and tears welled in her eyes. Was that how he felt? Abandoned?

The farmhouse door was open, so she walked right in, moving silently through the kitchen and into the hall. He was sitting in a chair at the window that looked out onto the awe-inspiring hills, staring up at the vast ocean of the sky.

"So it was all just a sham, then," he said without turning, his voice dull and flat. "A ruse to try and get me to change my mind about the planning. Well, your scheme didn't work, did it, and neither will your objections, so all that effort has been for nothing."

He whipped around to glare at her, and she saw the agony in his eyes. "How could you kiss me like that when it was all such a lie? I truly believed you were the one woman I could really trust in this world, the only one who was totally honest and true to herself and others. The one I could give my heart to…maybe even my life."

Tears poured down Chrissie's face as she stood in front of him. "But I am. I am still all those things. I meant to tell you, but the time just never seemed right. I love you, Will, I know that now, and I don't care about the stupid planning council. Bring as many tourists as you like, just please believe me. I wanted to tell you. I tried to so many times, but…"

He stared right through her with a lawyer's cold gaze. "Just go," he said. "It's too late for us."

Ignoring him, she went on. "I wanted to tell you about the objections, but when I first started training Max, we both agreed to put that all aside so we could get along. You knew how I felt about your plans—I've never pretended otherwise, and when I sent in the letter, I felt no obligation to tell you about it. And then we got closer and I started to feel guilty. I wanted to tell you last night, but… I didn't want to spoil everything. I thought I had plenty of time, Will. How was I supposed to know they'd bring the meeting forward?"

Will stood, glaring down at her, and she felt herself wilt. "Thank God they did. I paid you way over the odds for that training… I thought that at least you might be loyal."

"Loyal!"

Chrissie's blue eyes flashed icy cold with anger. "You give me all that drivel about trust, and yet you obviously thought that you'd bought me."

"No…" He raised his hand in objection, but she kept going.

"Well, I'm glad I found out what you were really like before it was too late. I thought you'd changed, Will, I really did, but it seems that you're still the arrogant, unscrupulous lawyer you used to be…just like the people you tried to get away from."

"So we've both finally found out the truth about each other, then," he said, his mouth a grim line. "Don't bother looking for me here again if you get my plans stopped, Chrissie, because I won't be here. With no future income to rely on, I may as well take up Roy's offer and go back to Marcus Finch."

She faltered. "But you hate that life."

Will shrugged, his eyes as cold as ice. "You may have left me no other option."

On the drive home, Chrissie clung to her anger to fight off her heartache. How could he have said that about the money...how dared he? She'd give it back right away, she decided...borrow it from the bank if necessary. And yet she knew he hadn't meant it like that; it was she who was in the wrong. She'd been so selfish with her idealism that she'd ignored the truth: in trying to stop Will's plans, she would be destroying his dreams for the future. Yes, tourists could be a threat to the land, but deep down her opposition had been all about what *she* wanted, and now she had to confront her guilt and face the fact that she'd lost him forever.

For rest of the day she kept herself busy, fighting off tears and the image of Will's desolate face. He had never kept any secrets from her; she had known where she stood with him right from the start. He'd said once that he loved the honesty in her way of life, and she'd shown him just how dishonest she could be. Now she'd gotten what she deserved, and she'd just have to learn to live with it.

WATCHING CHRISSIE DRIVE AWAY, Will felt defeated. He'd opened his heart to her, let himself be vulnerable, and she'd used him, sneaking in her objections behind his back when her efforts to try and educate him out of his intention to go ahead with the holiday rentals failed.

He pictured her striding out across the fell, her father's crook firm in her hand. Had she really tried to trick him? Was she even capable of it? And why had he said that about the money when it wasn't even true? In that moment, he knew, he'd meant to hurt her. Perhaps he was still the man he used to be; the ruthless lawyer who would say anything to get what he wanted. Perhaps he could never escape from his past.

When his phone blared out into the silence, breaking his train of thought, he was relieved to hear it. "Hello, Roger," he said. His heart thumped hard when he was met with a moment's heavy silence.

"Look, Will... I really am sorry..." Roger's voice sounded strained. "But I'm afraid the planning application has been turned down. Just too many objections."

The line went silent. Will felt empty, hollow inside, as if there was nothing left to live for. All his dreams were shattered and the future stretched out before him like a black void. His thoughts went relentlessly to Chrissie. What would she be thinking, how would she feel? Happy, he supposed. She'd be safe again in the life she loved. Maybe there had never been any room in her world for him, anyway. "Why don't you come by?" Roger continued with a show of enthusiasm. "It's not over yet, you know. I've done some initial sketches for your new idea, and I'm really optimistic about the whole concept—a new take on tourism that might just change the locals' way of thinking. All we need is a new strategy to put to the planners then I'm sure they'll go for it."

"Forget it," said Will. "I've decided to go

back to law. I'm putting Craig Side on the market."

"But—"

"Just leave it please, Roger. I've made up my mind. Send me your bill, and thanks for all the work you've done up to now."

WHEN CHRISSIE HEARD from Tom Farrah that Will's application had been denied, she felt numb. She wanted to be happy, but all she could think of was how devastated Will would be…and all because of her self-righteousness. If she'd talked to him, as she should have done, discussed things and been honest from the start, then maybe she wouldn't have lost him…and she knew that she had. With her usual tunnel vision, she had seen only what was right for her, not listening to anyone else's point of view…

Her thoughts went round and round inside her head as she tried to take in the situation. She had won, but she'd lost Will, so her victory felt meaningless.

Maybe it was for the best, she told herself eventually. Maybe they were never meant to be. Will had tried to buy her off, after all; he'd admitted that. Perhaps the city was where he was really supposed to be. Even as she tried to convince herself of that, deep down she knew it wasn't true... The way he'd held her and the feel of his lips closing over hers was just too real and raw.

She had to see him. Now, before he left Little Dale for good.

Chrissie drove to Craig Side as fast as she safely could. Her heart sank when she arrived, as she noticed that Will's Range Rover was gone. Surely he couldn't have left town without speaking to her again. But why wouldn't he? She had broken his trust, betrayed him and turned out to be a whole lot less than the woman he had believed her to be. He didn't owe her anything. She'd been selfish and uncaring about someone else's dreams, and the worst part was...that someone was a man she had grown to love.

"If you're looking for Will Devlin, I'm afraid you've missed him," called a tall gray-haired man. He was gathering some stuff from the barn.

She headed toward him, her heart pounding. "Jim Wentworth, isn't it?" she asked.

He nodded. "That's right. And you are Chrissie Marsh. I did some work for your dad a while back… You were just a little nipper."

She gave him a strained smile. "Did he say when he'd be back?"

Tom threw a big hammer into his truck, seeming to revel in the clunking sound before looking back at her. "He isn't coming back," he said. "He told us to stop all work on the barn right now and send out his bill. Sorry."

"It's not your fault," Chrissie assured him. "Did he say where he was going?"

"He just told me it hadn't worked out here, so the whole place was going on the market and he was taking on a new job. Real shame, if you ask me."

Obviously annoyed, Tom continued throwing items into his truck while Chrissie headed back to her Land Rover, her eyes blurry with carefully withheld tears. She had won, but at what cost? The front door loomed ahead of her, firmly closed, like the future she had recently begun to envisage. She tried it one last time, just in case.

"Oh, by the way," called Tom. She glanced back at him hopefully. "I almost forgot. Will asked me to make you a delivery on my way home, but as you're here I may as well do it now."

"What delivery?"

"Just a sec…" He walked across to the barn, disappearing inside to return a couple of minutes later with a dog in tow.

"Max!" cried Chrissie, racing over to give the big labradoodle a hug. His tail wagged so madly that his whole body wriggled, and his face was one huge smile. "I thought I heard a dog whining," she said, extracting herself from his exuberant embrace. "But I figured it must be yours. You can't really mean that Max is the delivery for me. Why would Will do that?"

Tom shrugged. "Beats me. I just do as I'm told. He asked me to deliver the dog to you since there was no place for it in the city, and anyway…"

"Anyway what?"

"He just said, 'Anyway, she owes me.'"

A wave of emotion hit her hard. "I guess that's true," she eventually managed. So was that it? Her payback for ruining Will's plans was to have to care for Max? For how long? Well, she loved the dog so it was hardly payback, and she'd find a way to make sure he earned his keep.

Then another thought struck her. If Max was with her, surely she and Will would have to meet up again sometime. She couldn't imagine he'd abandon his dog forever, for he loved Max, too. A prickle of excitement and hope made its way into her heart.

CHAPTER TWENTY-THREE

IT HAD BEEN well over a month since Will left the Lakeland hills to take up his life in the city again, but to Chrissie it felt just like yesterday. She walked the wild fells in a daze, shadows clouding her vision. Nothing seemed the same anymore, nothing was enough. The little things that had once filled her every waking moment no longer seemed quite as fulfilling.

Only throwing herself so hard into her work that she fell exhausted into bed each night could make her temporarily forget Will Devlin, the way he'd looked at her, the way he'd held her…the way he had told her that he loved her. For a while she had hoped he might call to ask after Max and that maybe he had only left the dog with her as an excuse to stay in touch, but she'd been wrong. He had left Max with her because it was the right thing to do, no more and no less, and she had to come to terms with that idea.

Spring was giving way to the beginnings of summer with bumblebees buzzing in the sunshine and shearing time looming. Chrissie tried to apply herself to her usual summer jobs, but she couldn't get away from the feeling that there was something missing in her life.

When Aunt Hilda came to stay for the weekend, she noticed it at once and ferreted the truth out of her niece before heading home. To her it had been a no-brainer. "Just go to Manchester and tell him how you feel," she'd insisted.

"But I don't know how he'll feel," Chrissie told her. At that, her aunt had just shaken her head and told her not to talk nonsense.

Chrissie was thinking about that conversation over a hurried breakfast when a knock came at the kitchen door. Pushing the remains of her toast into the bin and tipping her tea down the sink, she went to see who was there.

To her surprise Roger Simmons stood smiling on the doorstep, a roll of paper tucked under his arm. "Oh…hi, Roger," she said with a puzzled frown, grabbing Max's collar to stop him leaping up in welcome. "Sorry, he's a bit exuberant."

"Oh, no problem..." Roger seemed distracted. He was dithering; she could see it in his eyes. "I'm not sure if I should have come. I mean, I don't want to intrude but..."

She held the door open, letting Max go. "You're not intruding. Please, come in and tell me...well, whatever it is."

Once settled on a chair at the kitchen table Roger seemed to get his focus back. "I've been meaning to come and see you for a while," he said. "But I kept thinking that I should let the dust settle first."

"Dust?" Chrissie asked vacantly. "What do you mean?"

"It's just that..." Roger leaned toward her. "I think you should know the whole truth."

"What truth?"

He hesitated. "Will left because his plans were rejected, or that is what he led us to believe, but I think there was more to it than that. I mean, it's none of my business, really, but..."

"Go on," urged Chrissie.

"Well, I believe his decision to go back to the city had as much to do with you as it did with his plans being refused. It's only fair that you know the whole truth."

Chrissie waited, digging her fingernails into her palms.

He rolled out the paper on her kitchen table. It was a set of architectural plans. "This is what Will had me working on before he left. It was his vision for the future. When he found out that his outline planning had been refused, or more to the point, when he found out that it was down to your objections, he was upset and angry. He told me to ditch the whole idea and to just send a bill for what I'd done so far, but I decided to finish off the drawings anyway. And it works, Chrissie, it really does. It's inspired."

Chrissie pored over the plans. A group of authentic-looking cottages were set around the yard at Craig Side, and just beyond them the big barn and some outbuildings seemed to have been opened out into one larger area.

"Why," she cried in surprise, "it's almost like some kind of schoolroom...and what is this paddock area beyond it?"

"Sheepdog training and handling," supplied Roger. "Will's vision was to educate the visitors and cater only to those who had come to the Lakes for the right reasons, people who wanted to learn about the age-old traditions here and help them survive."

Tears choked Chrissie's throat. "Will did this?"

Roger shrugged. "He wanted to, but…"

"I ruined it," she finished for him.

"That's how it felt to him, I guess."

"But he's been gone for over a month, Roger, so why tell me now?"

He seemed to consider his words before speaking. "Because I saw the for sale sign yesterday," he said finally.

"Craig Side? Are you sure?"

"It's in the real estate agent's window, too…at a knocked-down price. Call him, Chrissie…or go and see him. Take these plans if you like. I know he was angry, but time is a great healer."

To hide her emotion, Chrissie spread out the sheets again. "Thanks. I'd like to look at them properly, anyway…not that they really have anything to do with me."

"If you don't mind me saying," Roger remarked. "I think they have everything to do with you."

For a long time after he'd left, Chrissie

studied the plans. Oh, why hadn't Will included her in this? Why hadn't he told her that he respected her beliefs and wanted to try and find a way to work with them?

The answer came at once: because she hadn't given him the chance. How was he to know that she had gone behind his back to overthrow his dream? Roger had told her to go and see him now, but what was the point? She'd lost his trust and, with it, his love. It was too late for them...but not too late to at least set the record straight and help Will achieve his dream, even if she was no longer a part of his life.

Reaching for her phone, she scrolled down to his number; all she had to do was get him back here and then she could persuade him not to give up.

WILL HEADED ACROSS the fell toward High Bracken, reliving the first time he'd walked this way, remembering Chrissie striding out behind the rippling white mass of fell sheep, her dogs under perfect control...until he and Max had burst onto the scene.

Oh, how angry she'd been that day. And she'd stayed angry at him for ages; he'd seen it in her eyes…even after she took his money. Something tightened inside him. He really had believed in her for a while…loved her, even. He still did, if he was honest with himself, but love needed trust to make it work.

Her message about him needing to come back and see Max urgently had arrived when he was in court. He'd tried to return her call later, after a very satisfying verdict was given, but got no reply. Just hearing her voice had brought back so many memories and emotions that his first instinct had been to ignore her…but she'd said it was about Max. What if he was ill? What if he needed expensive surgery and she couldn't afford it?

It had made him feel sad to see the for sale sign outside Craig Side. He'd arrived in Little Dale with such hope and left with a sense of helplessness and failure. He couldn't have stayed, though, not with Chrissie so close by, and his plans were nothing without her to share them with.

Anyway, she had shown him where her priorities lay. The tearful apology she'd made before he left was just her guilt talking, he knew that; he'd seen enough such protestations to last him a lifetime. He had no doubt she'd felt relief as soon as he left.

But none of that mattered, he told himself. He was here for Max, and as soon as the problem was sorted, he would be on his way back to the city. As he took in the glory of his surroundings, though, the idea rankled.

Will had decided to walk across the fell because he'd never seen it in the summer sunshine, and he realized it would probably be his last chance. His heart hurt at the thought. He'd set the price so low that there had already been a lot of interest in Craig Side, and it would quite probably have been sold by now if he hadn't kept on stalling. Somehow, though, he was finding it hard to actually let go…especially now that he'd come back. Even this brief visit was only going to make it worse.

All she had said in her message was that he needed to come back and see Max as soon as possible. It had sounded serious, and his worry had increased when he'd been unable to get hold of her. What if she couldn't take care of the dog any longer? He'd called Roger, but he didn't seem to know anything. So he'd decided to just turn up at High Bracken and see for himself.

CHRISSIE HAD BEEN waiting since yesterday, when she'd left the message, her ears tuned for the sound of Will's vehicle driving into the yard. She hadn't expected to hear his voice first. For what felt like a lifetime, her heart seemed to stop beating.

"Hello…hello… Chrissie, are you there?"

He was wearing his country clothes, the ones she'd finally talked him into: scuffed brown boots, jeans and a checked shirt in bright summer colors. She watched him from where she stood in the barn door. He was shading his eyes from the sun as he looked for her, his dark hair blowing in the breeze. When he turned and saw her standing there, time seemed to stop, and then she stepped forward, breaking the spell. "Will," she cried. "You came."

His smile was genuine; his hand on hers was firm and warm and strong. She wanted to hang on to it, to press his palm against her cheek, to kiss each of his fingers. Instead, she dropped his hand as if she'd been scalded, drawing hers close against her chest.

"What is it?" he asked. "I thought something bad had happened... Is Max okay?"

She nodded. "Yes, he's fine. I'm sorry. I had to see you about something...and I thought..."

"You thought that I wouldn't come back just for you."

"Something like that."

He gazed at her with such emotion in his eyes that she longed to reach out and stroke his cheek. She settled on taking his hand in hers. "Come on—let me show you."

THE PLANS WERE spread out on the kitchen table, and he glanced at them with a puzzled frown. When he looked up, Chrissie's face was animated.

"Roger brought these to show me," she said. "He explained how excited you were by the idea when you first approached him, and how he was inspired to finish the plans after you left. Don't be angry with him—he really does seem to believe in the whole concept. I just needed you to talk me through it, to understand your vision..."

For a moment, she held his gaze, her blue eyes soft. "I didn't set out to trick you, Will, and I honestly did mean to tell you the truth.

Maybe I have been too immoveable when it comes to tourists, but I really am prepared to listen now…"

He stared at the plans, running his hand across them. "I saw this as our future, Chrissie, something that would bridge the gap between us…and maybe bridge the gap between the old traditions and modern society. I never meant what I said about the money, you know. I paid you well to train Max, but it wasn't a bribe. I just wanted to strike out, to hurt you the way that you had hurt me. I let you into my heart, Chrissie, and when I found out that you'd gone behind my back it seemed that everything I'd believed about you was a lie."

She took a step toward him, but he held up his hand. "No…please, I need you to hear me out first, need to you understand all this. Look, Chrissie, I know you hate tourists and that you want to preserve the way of life here…and I agree with that. The problem is that the farmers in the Lake District are struggling, and without tourism to help boost the economy, things will only get worse.

"More farmers will be forced to give up and the sheep will slowly disappear from the fells altogether...or become totally wild. The drystone walls will just become piles of stones and the heritage you love so much will be gone forever. I believe that the only way forward is to change your way of thinking. Instead of objecting to tourism, why not embrace it and make it work for you? That is what these plans are all about. To educate the visitors about sheep and farming. Teach them to respect the way of life here.

"I wanted to open a kind of education center," he went on, pointing to the plans with a rush of excitement. "That's what this larger building is about. Craig Side could become a working farm where visitors can stay and learn about respecting the countryside and about sheep and lambing and all the other aspects of sheepherding. You...er...someone could even teach people how to work dogs themselves. We could keep the old traditions alive, Chrissie, through education."

When Will stopped to gauge her reaction, Chrissie just stared at him. "So, why did you drop your dream so easily?"

He took hold of both her hands. "Because my dream dropped me."

"Your dream is still here, Will, here in

these hills…here inside me. Your dream can be mine, too. I'm so sorry for all the mistakes I've made, but the truth is, Will, I love you more than anything."

He wrapped his arms around her, drawing her close. Chrissie breathed in his scent, allowing her head to fall softly against his shoulder.

"I want to build this dream with you," he murmured. "To build a future with you. I love you, Chrissie Marsh, and I was a fool to ever doubt you."

For a moment she drew back, staring into his eyes, drowning in their depths.

"Marry me, Chrissie."

Something quivered deep inside her, something as primeval as the land itself. "Oh, yes," she whispered.

When his lips finally closed over hers, firm and sweet and all-consuming, it felt as if they were one being, together forever in the life they both loved…here in the wild and timeless fells.

* * * * *

LARGER-PRINT BOOKS!

GET 2 FREE
LARGER-PRINT NOVELS
PLUS 2 FREE
MYSTERY GIFTS

Love Inspired®

Larger-print novels are now available...

LARGER-PRINT BOOKS!

GET 2 FREE
LARGER-PRINT NOVELS
PLUS 2 FREE
MYSTERY GIFTS

Love Inspired®
SUSPENSE
RIVETING INSPIRATIONAL ROMANCE

Larger-print novels are now available...

YES! Please send me 2 FREE LARGER-PRINT Love Inspired® Suspense novels and my 2 FREE mystery gifts (gifts are worth about $10). After receiving them, if I don't wish to receive any more books, I can return the shipping statement marked "cancel." If I don't cancel, I will receive 4 brand-new novels every month and be billed just $5.49 per book in the U.S. or $5.99 per book in Canada. That's a savings of at least 19% off the cover price. It's quite a bargain! Shipping and handling is just 50¢ per book in the U.S. and 75¢ per book in Canada.* I understand that accepting the 2 free books and gifts places me under no obligation to buy anything. I can always return a shipment and cancel at any time. Even if I never buy another book, the two free books and gifts are mine to keep forever.

110/310 IDN GH6P

Name	(PLEASE PRINT)	
Address		Apt. #
City	State/Prov.	Zip/Postal Code

Signature (if under 18, a parent or guardian must sign)

Mail to the **Reader Service:**
IN U.S.A.: P.O. Box 1867, Buffalo, NY 14240-1867
IN CANADA: P.O. Box 609, Fort Erie, Ontario L2A 5X3

**Are you a current subscriber to Love Inspired® Suspense books and want to receive the larger-print edition?
Call 1-800-873-8635 or visit www.ReaderService.com.**

* Terms and prices subject to change without notice. Prices do not include applicable taxes. Sales tax applicable in N.Y. Canadian residents will be charged applicable taxes. Offer not valid in Quebec. This offer is limited to one order per household. Not valid for current subscribers to Love Inspired Suspense larger-print books. All orders subject to credit approval. Credit or debit balances in a customer's account(s) may be offset by any other outstanding balance owed by or to the customer. Please allow 4 to 6 weeks for delivery. Offer available while quantities last.

Your Privacy—The Reader Service is committed to protecting your privacy. Our Privacy Policy is available online at www.ReaderService.com or upon request from the Reader Service.

We make a portion of our mailing list available to reputable third parties that offer products we believe may interest you. If you prefer that we not exchange your name with third parties, or if you wish to clarify or modify your communication preferences, please visit us at www.ReaderService.com/consumerchoice or write to us at Reader Service Preference Service, P.O. Box 9062, Buffalo, NY 14240-9062. Include your complete name and address.

LISLP15

WESTERN WP PROMISES

YES! Please send me **The Western Promises Collection** in Larger Print. This collection begins with 3 FREE books and 2 FREE gifts (gifts valued at approx. $14.00 retail) in the first shipment, along with the other first 4 books from the collection! If I do not cancel, I will receive 8 monthly shipments until I have the entire 51-book Western Promises collection. I will receive 2 or 3 FREE books in each shipment and I will pay just $4.99 US/ $5.89 CDN for each of the other four books in each shipment, plus $2.99 for shipping and handling per shipment. *If I decide to keep the entire collection, I'll have paid for only 32 books, because 19 books are FREE! I understand that accepting the 3 free books and gifts places me under no obligation to buy anything. I can always return a shipment and cancel at any time. My free books and gifts are mine to keep no matter what I decide.

272 HCN 3070 472 HCN 3070

Name	(PLEASE PRINT)
Address	Apt. #
City	State/Prov. Zip/Postal Code

Signature (if under 18, a parent or guardian must sign)

Mail to the **Reader Service**:

IN U.S.A.: P.O. Box 1867, Buffalo, NY 14240-1867
IN CANADA: P.O. Box 609, Fort Erie, Ontario L2A 5X3

* Terms and prices subject to change without notice. Prices do not include applicable taxes. Sales tax applicable in N.Y. Canadian residents will be charged applicable taxes. This offer is limited to one order per household. All orders subject to approval. Credit or debit balances in a customer's account(s) may be offset by any other outstanding balance owed by or to the customer. Please allow 4 to 6 weeks for delivery. Offer available while quantities last. Offer not available to Quebec residents.

WPBPA16R

LARGER-PRINT BOOKS!
GET 2 FREE LARGER-PRINT NOVELS PLUS
2 FREE GIFTS!

♦ HARLEQUIN®

super romance®

More Story...More Romance

YES! Please send me 2 FREE LARGER-PRINT Harlequin® Superromance® novels and my 2 FREE gifts (gifts are worth about $10). After receiving them, if I don't wish to receive any more books, I can return the shipping statement marked "cancel." If I don't cancel, I will receive 4 brand-new novels every month and be billed just $5.94 per book in the U.S. or $6.24 per book in Canada. That's a savings of at least 12% off the cover price! It's quite a bargain! Shipping and handling is just 50¢ per book in the U.S. or 75¢ per book in Canada.* I understand that accepting the 2 free books and gifts places me under no obligation to buy anything. I can always return a shipment and cancel at any time. Even if I never buy another book, the two free books and gifts are mine to keep forever.

132/332 HDN GHVC

Name	(PLEASE PRINT)	
Address		Apt. #
City	State/Prov.	Zip/Postal Code

Signature (if under 18, a parent or guardian must sign)

Mail to the **Reader Service:**
IN U.S.A.: P.O. Box 1867, Buffalo, NY 14240-1867
IN CANADA: P.O. Box 609, Fort Erie, Ontario L2A 5X3

Want to try two free books from another line?
Call 1-800-873-8635 today or visit www.ReaderService.com.

* Terms and prices subject to change without notice. Prices do not include applicable taxes. Sales tax applicable in N.Y. Canadian residents will be charged applicable taxes. Offer not valid in Quebec. This offer is limited to one order per household. Not valid for current subscribers to Harlequin Superromance Larger-Print books. All orders subject to credit approval. Credit or debit balances in a customer's account(s) may be offset by any other outstanding balance owed by or to the customer. Please allow 4 to 6 weeks for delivery. Offer available while quantities last.

Your Privacy—The Reader Service is committed to protecting your privacy. Our Privacy Policy is available online at www.ReaderService.com or upon request from the Reader Service.

We make a portion of our mailing list available to reputable third parties that offer products we believe may interest you. If you prefer that we not exchange your name with third parties, or if you wish to clarify or modify your communication preferences, please visit us at www.ReaderService.com/consumerschoice or write to us at Reader Service Preference Service, P.O. Box 9062, Buffalo, NY 14240-9062. Include your complete name and address.

HSRLP15

READERSERVICE.COM

Manage your account online!

- Review your order history
- Manage your payments
- Update your address

> *We've designed the*
> *Reader Service website*
> *just for you.*

Enjoy all the features!

- Discover new series available to you, and read excerpts from any series.
- Respond to mailings and special monthly offers.
- Connect with favorite authors at the blog.
- Browse the Bonus Bucks catalog and online-only exculsives.
- Share your feedback.

Visit us at:

ReaderService.com